"Hunter Blueeyes, I'd like to know more about you."

She met his gaze, but all she saw in the dark eyes that held hers was the enticing allure of the unknown.

"You already know all you need. Your father trusted me because he knew I'd have the skills, training and the contacts to help you."

Hunter was a mysterious man—full of secrets he wouldn't share. The question now was how much information should Lisa share with him?

Dear Reader,

Like the heroine in this story, I've lived with asthma all my life, and like the hero, my husband, David, has been by my side through thick and thin. I believe in the power of love. It surmounts anything; it fills the heart when there doesn't seem to be any reason to continue.

We now give you a tale of heroism, loyalty, honor and, of course, love. Life gives us many challenges, but with love, we can soar and accomplish anything.

From our hearts to yours, enjoy!

Aimée and David Thurlo

AIMÉE THURLO

COUNCIL OF FIRE

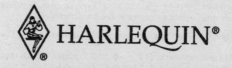

HARLEQUIN®

TORONTO • NEW YORK • LONDON
AMSTERDAM • PARIS • SYDNEY • HAMBURG
STOCKHOLM • ATHENS • TOKYO • MILAN • MADRID
PRAGUE • WARSAW • BUDAPEST • AUCKLAND

To Ruth I. Cruse and Diana Flanary-Bray—
two very special ladies who work hard to make other
people's lives just a little brighter.

ISBN-13: 978-0-373-88762-0
ISBN-10:   0-373-88762-0

COUNCIL OF FIRE

Copyright: © 2007 by Aimée and David Thurlo

All rights reserved. Except for use in any review, the reproduction or
utilization of this work in whole or in part in any form by any electronic,
mechanical or other means, now known or hereafter invented, including
xerography, photocopying and recording, or in any information storage
or retrieval system, is forbidden without the written permission of the
publisher, Harlequin Enterprises Limited, 225 Duncan Mill Road,
Don Mills, Ontario, Canada M3B 3K9.

This is a work of fiction. Names, characters, places and incidents are
either the product of the author's imagination or are used fictitiously,
and any resemblance to actual persons, living or dead, business
establishments, events or locales is entirely coincidental.

This edition published by arrangement with Harlequin Books S.A.

® and TM are trademarks of the publisher. Trademarks indicated with
® are registered in the United States Patent and Trademark Office, the
Canadian Trade Marks Office and in other countries.

www.eHarlequin.com

Printed in U.S.A.

ABOUT THE AUTHOR

Aimée Thurlo is a nationally known bestselling author. She's written forty-one novels and is published in at least twenty countries. She has been nominated for a Reviewer's Choice Award and a Career Achievement Award by *Romantic Times BOOKreviews*.

She also co-writes the Ella Clah mainstream mystery series, which debuted with a starred review in *Publishers Weekly* and has been optioned by CBS.

Aimée was born in Havana, Cuba, and lives with her husband of thirty years in Corrales, New Mexico. Her husband, David, was raised on the Navajo Indian Reservation.

CAST OF CHARACTERS

Lisa Garza—She was at a crossroads, torn between her family's honor and her love for a man with too many secrets.

Hunter Blueeyes—Recovering the legendary dagger for his tribe would be a test of his courage and strength, but parting with it would cost him his soul.

Hastiin Sáni—As leader of the Brotherhood of Warriors, the medicine man knew how important it was to keep secrets. He had one of his own that could cost the tribe its future.

Arthur Duncan—To most, he was just the old man who ran the trading post, but he held the key to Lisa's future.

Carlos Trujillo—He was the king of thieves around the Four Corners, and now he was gearing up to steal the ultimate treasure.

Happeth Kincaid—Had the tall, attractive redhead's relationship with Lisa's late father been personal—or lethal?

Bruce Atcitty—He claimed to be Lisa's friend, but for a police officer, he never seemed to be around when he was needed.

Paul Johnson—A Navajo who'd betrayed his own people, he found himself alone even among friends. But was there more to him than met the eye?

Prologue

They sat around the piñon-log fire deep within the cave of secrets, a tall, deep recess in the sandstone cliff high above the trees of the forest. The full moon was visible through the vertical slit, which was less than four feet wide at its base. The participants were guarded by a warrior keeping watch on the ladder that provided access to this holy place.

The Council of Fire had been in existence since the time of Kit Carson and the Long Walk. Established after the tribe had finally been allowed to return to its traditional land between the sacred mountains, these handpicked men remained in the shadows, protecting the tribe—never identified and rarely seen but always felt. Clandestine warriors bound by loyalty and traditions, they stood between the tribe and its enemies—an unbroken line of defense. They'd each been hand-selected and tested to the breaking point until only the best of the best remained. The Council of Fire existed so the Diné, the Navajo people, could go about their lives, honoring the past and looking forward to a secure future.

Hunter Blueeyes glanced at the others present. Some were friends he'd known for years, others he'd never seen outside this chamber. One place beside the fire—the one the Council's *bá'óltáí*, their teacher, had occupied at one time—remained vacant, a sign of respect for a missing comrade. With effort Hunter tore his gaze away. It was then he saw his brother, Ranger, enter the Council chamber and take his seat.

His fraternal twin, born minutes after him, didn't resemble Hunter, not in physical appearance, nor in character. Although bound by blood and as close as two brothers could be, their relationship had always been a highly competitive one. The fact that they were different, though equally matched, had made for interesting times.

The *hataalii*, the tribe's most revered medicine man, stood and looked at the warriors gathered there. He was known as *Hastiin sání* to most, a name that literally translated meant "older man."

"We are facing a very difficult challenge," he announced in a strong, clear voice. "*Hashkéts'ósí* is no longer in our possession."

Hashkéts'ósí was the war name given to a unique antiquity—an obsidian dagger that had come to the legendary warrior Largo as a result of an answered prayer. Kit Carson and the cavalry had been hot on his trail. Largo, exhausted and close to losing hope, had sung a song of power calling for the help of the Holy One, Monster Slayer.

Alone in a cave near Red Mesa, Largo discovered the dagger and used the weapon to stay alive. Eventually, after the treaties were signed, Largo had been able to rejoin the Diné back in their land between the sacred mountains.

Though theories abounded, no one knew how the dagger had come to be hidden there on Red Mesa, or where it had originated. But, since then, the artifact had been used in countless ceremonies. The dagger known as *Hashkéts'ósí*—"slender warrior"—was said to have medicine that could restore the spirit of those engaged in battle.

To non-Navajo collectors, the value of the large, uncut diamond on its hilt was paramount, but to the tribe, the dagger was a venerated antiquity.

Every warrior in the Brotherhood of Warriors had competed for the honor of being the one to go after *Hashkéts'ósí* and finish what would have to be done. Each of them had been assigned a task to complete—the retrieval of a closely guarded object, an assignment that had required a combination of endurance, strategy, harsh physical and mental conditions and superb infiltration and evasion skills. Since *Hastiin sání* had determined that a sole operative would have a better chance of accomplishing the undercover operation that lay ahead, only one man among them would be selected today—the best of the best.

"Two of you have shown complete mastery of all the skills this mission requires," *Hastiin sání* said, then looked at Hunter and at Ranger. "Though physically and emotionally exhausted, you both found a way to complete the assigned task within the time allowed."

Hunter waited as all the others except his brother stood, nodded to their leader, then left wordlessly. Only the *hataalii* knew how his brother and he had fared in comparison to each other, but Hunter knew Ranger and he were closely matched.

Now with only three of them present, the *hataalii* continued, looking at Hunter. "Your code name will be Fire because you've got the strength and ferocity of that element. You go through whatever stands in your way."

Hastiin sání paused, then looked at Ranger. "You'll be called Wind, because you carry secrets and can sweep past any obstacle. Like Wind, you're fearless and nothing contains you for long or stops you from achieving your goals."

The medicine man gave Hunter a nod. "You'll go." Then turning to Ranger, added, "You'll be his contact and second—if your brother fails."

"That won't happen," Hunter responded.

"I'll be standing by," Ranger said.

The old man smiled grimly, satisfied with their answers. "Make your arrangements here and now, brother warriors. Your mission starts today."

Hastiin sání moved into the adjoining, smaller chamber, giving them time alone.

"Sure you can handle this, bro?" Ranger said, a grin curving his lips.

"Yeah. I'm used to taking point. The best always lead," he answered, a playful challenge in his tone.

Ranger chuckled. "Always cocky. I'll let that pass for now, but stay sharp." Ranger raised his arm and met his brother's raised palm in a healthy, strong grip. "Watch your back."

"Always. And you, too." Hunter's grip remained unwavering as they both pushed against each other, each trying to topple the other. "Give?"

"Not during your lifetime," Ranger answered with a grin.

Hunter put his shoulder into it, but their palms remained locked in position, neither gaining the advantage.

Beads of perspiration had just started to form on their brows when *Hastiin sání* came back in and cleared his throat.

Ranger nodded imperceptibly to his brother, then they released their grip.

Moments later, Ranger climbed down the ladder and was gone. Hunter alone faced the *hataalii*.

"It was your personal ties to the case that made you my *second* choice at first," the old man said.

Hunter nodded slowly. "I suspected as much. Safeguarding that dagger was John Garza's responsibility, and the man saved my life once. He's one of only a handful of *bilagáanas* I would have ever trusted unconditionally," he said, using the Navajo term for white man.

"How strong is your faith in him—or who you believed him to be?"

"Not so much that it'll keep me from doing what needs to be done, uncle," Hunter said, using the term out of respect, not to denote kinship. "I know my assignment, *Hastiin sání,* and I'll do what has to be done."

Chapter One

It was a clear early autumn evening, and a full moon filtered through the ancient cottonwood trees lining the graveled driveway to Lisa Garza's home in Albuquerque's South Valley. For her, tonight was just the beginning—the first step on what promised to be a long, hard road to justice.

"You've been a million miles away all night," Bruce Atcitty said while parking.

Lisa looked at her Navajo friend. She'd met the young police officer two years ago when he'd agreed to moonlight for Rio Grande Security Services. An Albuquerque policeman's salary made it a challenge to meet all the expenses of raising a family.

"Tonight we identified the client's security threats and recommended fixes. But it's the last job on the schedule. Business has dried up. No one wants to hire a firm owned by a man most people have been told was a thief. To make matters worse, they're not totally sure I'm innocent either," Lisa said.

"I'm concerned about you and particularly the

decision you've made. Field ops is not your area of expertise. Intelligence gathering, threat analysis and countermeasures, those are your strengths. You don't even carry a weapon. As far as I know you've never even fired a gun."

"I hate guns. But I *can* take care of myself without one. The self-defense instructor for the police department was a friend of Dad's and taught me privately for years."

"Think long and hard about this, Lisa. Once you start down this road, there'll be no turning back. If you're right and your father didn't commit suicide, but was murdered, *you'll* be walking right into the line of fire. You start pointing fingers, and somebody might start pointing guns in your direction."

"It's a risk I've got to take. But I won't be alone. I've got Dad's contacts, people trained to carry weapons, who'll work alongside me. There's one man in particular Dad trusted and suggested I get in touch with if I ever needed an ally up in the Four Corners. That's where I'm headed tomorrow."

"Who's this guy?" he asked. ·

"He's Navajo, like you, but Dad said I should keep his name to myself," Lisa said, remembering the call she'd put in to Hunter Blueeyes. "Dad saved his life once, and he said that the man was a pro and would honor the debt. So I left a call for him a few days ago."

"Just be careful, Lisa. You're diving into the middle of something that has the potential to become lethal in a hurry, especially if there is a conspiracy involved."

"I'll take things as they come. But I do have a favor to ask. Will you keep an eye on my mother while I'm gone and find someone to watch out for Dad's assistant, Happeth Kincaid? I'll be stirring things up, so I need to know they'll be safe."

"Consider it done," he said, then, gesturing toward the porch with his lips, Navajo style, added, "The light must have burned out. Let me walk you inside."

"Thanks, but don't bother. It's probably a fuse again. I'll take care of it before Mom gets home from her quilting meeting."

She fumbled for her key as he drove off, then went inside, her hand over her shoulder bag. Unable to locate her father's diary after his death, she'd carried with her since his death his daily planner and the last note he'd written, in order to safeguard them.

In the note, which Lisa had found in her desk drawer a few days after his death, her father had explained that if anything ever happened to him, her search for answers should begin with their fishing trip.

She'd gone only on one fishing trip with her father. It had been on her ninth birthday, and she'd hated every second of it. But that clue had led her to page nine of his daily log, where he recorded his trips. There, she'd found a sketch of a trading post she was able to recognize. She'd be heading there tomorrow.

Lisa went inside the house, suspecting they'd blown another fuse, the third in two weeks by her count. The porch light-switch was on. She flipped it off then back on. Then she turned on the light in the hall. Nothing happened, so that ruled out the bulbs.

Slipping her purse off her shoulder and setting it on the wooden chair just inside her father's study, Lisa continued down the hall. A minute later, she opened the fuse box, tried the switches, but got nowhere. The wiring was ancient. It was time to call an electrician.

Lisa was heading back when she heard what sounded like the squeak of a hinge from somewhere down the hall. Remembering that the closet door in her father's study sometimes made that noise, she froze, listening.

With her back pressed to the wall, she crept toward her father's study, taking slow, soft steps to avoid giving away her location.

Lisa cursed herself silently for having left her purse containing her father's planner, not to mention her car keys, on the chair in the study. She'd been too complacent, but the fuse box acted up so often she hadn't given it a second thought.

The idea of allowing a stranger to remain in her home unchallenged made her bristle, but she bowed to logic. Although she was proficient in martial arts, she wasn't invincible. Weight and strength—and lung power—still had the advantage. Asthma was her Achilles' heel, though she'd learned to work around it. And if the intruder had a gun... She remembered what her father had taught her—to turn limitations into strengths. She knew the house and the layout. The intruder didn't.

Lisa listened, still trying to get a more precise fix on the intruder's location. All she had to do was slip her hand inside the study, get her purse from atop the chair, then sneak out the front door, less than twenty feet away. Her car was parked near the entrance.

A glance revealed moonlight coming from inside the study, which meant someone had opened the blinds or the French doors. That explained how the intruder had gotten inside. Then she heard the faint rustle of wood inside her father's study. Someone had brushed up against the blinds.

Confident that she knew the intruder's approximate location, she crouched and reached out for her bag.

Suddenly a hand clamped down hard on her wrist, holding her in a steel-like grip. Instinct and training overpowered her fear. Lisa hurled herself against her attacker instead of pulling away, throwing him off balance. They both fell farther into the room, and the shadowy figure let go.

Lisa rolled toward her father's desk and scrambled to her feet. In the moonlight she could see the man was a head taller than her, with the lean, leggy build of a runner. He was wearing a stocking cap that concealed his hair and facial features, but his pale eyes gleamed with deadly intent. He was fast, and back on the attack instantly. She barely managed to counter his punches and kicks, which came with fluidlike precision.

"Give me the journal your father kept while the dagger was in his possession and I'll let you live."

"How did you—"

"I know all about your father, and you, too, Lisa. Your martial arts training isn't good enough. You've got asthma. I'm bigger and stronger, and I'll wear you down. I can break you—piece by piece," he said, then almost as if to prove his words, he reached out, pulling a tall bookcase down on top of her.

Somehow she managed to avoid being crushed, but the weight of the heavy oak unit pinned her to the brick floor. Lisa rolled onto her stomach and tried to crawl out, but the man pushed the bookcase down with his foot, trapping her underneath. The pressure made it nearly impossible for her to take a full breath, but she managed to turn onto her side, easing the strain just a little.

He leaned down and studied her face in the moonlight. "You *knew* I was here, yet you didn't run away. What made you stay…" He looked around, his gaze stopping at the chair. "Ah, now I know. Your purse. Your inhaler…or something more?"

As he stepped away, footsteps sounded in the

hall. Seconds later, a tall, broad-shouldered man appeared in the doorway. As her assailant bolted for the French doors, the newcomer reached for something at his belt. With a flash of silver, the bag was stripped from her assailant's hand and pinned to the wall with a throwing knife.

Surprised by the sudden attack, the intruder spun around, but Lisa saw another weapon appear instantly in her rescuer's hand, a long-bladed fighting knife.

Her assailant ran out the French doors onto the patio and leaped the low wall, disappearing.

"Smart man." Lifting the bookcase off her, the second man offered her his hand and helped her to her feet.

His palm was rough, but his touch gentle. The newcomer, a Native American judging from his skin tone, was wearing a tight black T-shirt that accentuated his muscular shoulders and low-slung, dark blue jeans.

"Thanks for your help," Lisa said in an unsteady voice. Everything about him spoke of confidence and…maleness. But he had more than looks. This man had *presence*. Her heart beat just a little faster as she looked at him. "Who are you?"

"I'm your father's friend, Lisa, the man you've been trying to reach—Hunter Blueeyes."

Chapter Two

Lisa retrieved her bag from where it had been pinned to the wall by the blade. "That's a very useful skill," she said, handing the knife back to him. The way his eyes drifted over her, assessing silently, made her skin prickle. No woman with a pulse could have helped responding to that strong build and those piercing eyes.

"You asked for my help. I came," he said in a deep voice.

Hunter Blueeyes was obviously a man of few words, but his actions had already spoken volumes, not to mention his good sense of timing. Lisa explained what she needed, then added, "My father didn't steal your tribe's dagger. The purpose of the replica couldn't have been to fool the tribe. He would have known that wouldn't work. My guess is he had that replica made to throw off thieves hot on his trail, and he was trying to buy himself time to identify them."

He nodded but said nothing.

When his silence stretched out, she continued. "The loss of that ceremonial dagger has cast a shadow over my family. Some people don't put a lot of stock in family honor and integrity these days, but it matters to us…to me. And no matter what the police say, I'll never believe my father committed suicide."

Lisa remembered finding her father in his car, about half a mile from their home. He'd been behind the driver's seat, slumped over, dead of a bullet wound to his temple. His skull, the blood, his pistol on the floor of the car… She'd never forget it if she lived to be a hundred.

"I can't—*won't* let this go. I owe my father more than that." Her lungs tightened, the all-too-familiar beginning of an asthma attack, and she forced herself to draw in a deep breath and relax.

"I've looked into your situation," he said in a calm voice. "The evidence *is* consistent with suicide. It was his weapon, and his fingerprints were all over it. There was no sign of any kind of a struggle."

"My father would *never* have killed himself. It went against everything he was and believed in. His fingerprints were on his pistol, but what else would you expect? And they never ran a GSR to prove he'd actually fired the pistol," she said referring to a gunshot residue test. "I know what the scene looked like, but it was all staged. I intend to find out what really happened—to him, and the dagger."

"Give me the leads you've got and I'll handle it. As you've seen, I'm trained for this," he said.

It wasn't false confidence. "Walking away isn't my style," she said. Her breathing was still slightly labored so she reached for her inhaler, and took a deep puff.

Hunter's eyebrows shot up, but he said nothing. Then again, he didn't have to. She'd seen the look before. Growing up with asthma, she'd often been forced to the sidelines, the kid who could never quite keep up physically. These days, with new medications, she could do just about anything except run a marathon.

The same fighting spirit that had allowed her to endure back then, now gave her the strength to accomplish whatever she set her mind to do. "Someone's out there thinking he's gotten away with framing and killing my father—but he's going down."

"This assignment may require more than your body will allow," he said slowly.

Though diplomatically put, his words filled her with frustration. She'd heard different versions of the same thing a million times. It was the implication that she'd never be able to cut it, that nature hadn't made her quite as good as other people.

"My father has left a trail for *me* to follow, and I intend to do just that. And as for my asthma, I know what I need to do and when to keep it at bay—and it works. I can and will get the job done."

"I'm assuming you have clear leads you intend to follow," he said.

"I was close to my father," she said, careful not to divulge more than was necessary. "I understood the way he thought. That'll guide me." She watched him. His thumbs jammed into the front pocket of his jeans, he looked completely at ease. Yet there was nothing relaxed in the way his dark eyes stayed on her, probing, giving her the impression that he could see way too much.

"There's more you're not saying," Hunter said at last. "If you expect me to help, you're going to have to put all your cards on the table. I don't go into things partway."

Hunter certainly didn't beat around the bush. He went right after what he wanted—in this case, all the information she had. But one person already knew about her father's habit of writing things down, and that was one too many.

"There's a trading post I need to visit on the reservation. That'll be my first stop. What happens after that will depend on what I find out there." She saw the skepticism on his face and bristled. "We each have our own skills. I know what I'm doing. Believe it. I contacted you because my father recommended you. Once I'm on the Navajo Nation I'll need someone who knows their way around and can help me fight whoever or whatever comes after me."

"And in return for becoming your partner?"

"You square your debt to my father and, once

we're successful, you'll be able to take the dagger back to your people."

"Deal."

As the wail of a siren rose in the air, he took a step closer to the hall. "One of your neighbors must have heard or seen something disturbing and called the police. I'd like to avoid any official involvement. Can you handle things from here?"

Lisa nodded. "Go. I'll take care of this and leave you out of it completely."

"Proving your father didn't steal the dagger will bring you up against the person who did, and he won't want you to succeed. Watch your back. You're likely to find enemies at every turn." He moved toward the door quickly.

"Wait! Where should we meet tomorrow?"

"I'll find *you*."

He stepped out into the entryway and was gone before she could say anything more.

Lisa glanced around the room, noting that it actually felt different—calmer, and slightly more bleak—without Hunter.

Lisa shook her head. Though he was undeniably tempting, this was no time to get sidetracked by a pair of penetrating eyes, broad shoulders and strong hands. She had to stay on track and prepare for what lay ahead.

SHORTLY AFTER EIGHT THE following morning, Lisa drove into Albuquerque to her father's downtown office. This was the heart of Rio Grande Security Services, the company he'd founded after leaving the police department. He'd had a small space at the university as well, because he'd also organized security for the various exhibits at the anthropology museum.

Lisa parked in her father's reserved slot behind the building, and noticed Happeth Kincaid's old sedan farther down in the employee parking lot. Happeth had been her father's assistant for only a few months, but she and John Garza had shared a special relationship. Both had been devoted workaholics who'd clicked professionally from day one.

Lisa was almost at the elevator when Hunter appeared from around the corner—out of nowhere, as before. "You certainly know how to make an entrance," she said, feeling the impact of those dark hooded eyes, which seemed to cut right through her.

"I'm here to cover your back, not hold your hand," he said, then with a crooked smile, added, "But I can do both…and more."

If anyone else had said it, she would have dismissed the words instantly as nothing more than flirting, but instinct told her this was a man who liked to back up what he said. She swallowed, aware that her throat had suddenly gone dry. The nuance didn't escape him.

"So, it's open for negotiation," he added smoothly. It hadn't been a question and the boldness took her by surprise. "No, Mr. Blueeyes, it most certainly is not. Keep your mind on business."

"You *are* my business."

His voice was like a smooth drink that went down easily and left you tingling. With effort she focused on what she had to do next. "I'm on my way to pick up some of my father's paperwork. His assistant should already have it ready for me. Since you're here, why don't you come with me?"

He shook his head. "I can guard your back better from this vantage point. I'll stay down here."

"Have it your way," she said, turned and started to walk away.

"Anything that well built should never be in danger."

It had barely been a whisper, but she'd heard him. When she glanced back she saw his gaze focused on her lower half. "That, sir, is my backside, not my back."

As Lisa stepped into the elevator, she finally took a deep breath. Why couldn't her father have picked someone as appealing as, say, a day-old hamburger? Things would have been much simpler then.

A moment later, Lisa walked inside the glass entrance leading to the reception area of her father's suite, leather tote in hand.

Happeth greeted her with a tentative smile. "I put everything you asked for together after I got your message. Here are the maps and all the documentation pertaining to the dagger," she said, handing her a large manila envelope.

Happeth then walked into John's office, took the small laptop off the side extension, unplugged the power cord and battery charger, then brought them over and placed them on the desk beside Lisa. "Everything on the hard drive is encrypted. If you try to access his private files without the proper password, it'll erase everything. And I'm afraid I have no idea what his password was."

"I do," Lisa said, placing the recharging unit, then the computer into the tote. "Thanks."

"If you need anything else, just call. I'll keep the office open and continue to accept new clients Bruce and I can handle. I've been paid till the end of the month, and that's two weeks away."

Bracing herself for whatever might lay ahead, Lisa headed back to the car. Instinct told her Hunter was near, but she didn't see him again until later that day.

IT WAS MID-MORNING WHEN SHE arrived in the small northern New Mexico city of Farmington, east of the Navajo reservation. She was still in the city, driving a rented sedan, when she noticed a blue pickup approaching behind her. The driver flashed his lights, then as the truck pulled up parallel to her in the passing lane, she glanced over and recognized Hunter behind the wheel.

A few minutes later, parked by the side of the street, Lisa unlocked the passenger-side door, and Hunter slid into the seat next to her.

"An informant warned me that it was likely you'd pick up a tail the second you reached the Four Corners region. I haven't spotted anyone yet, but that doesn't mean you're not a target. Now that you're close to the Rez, we'll be sticking together, but first I wanted to make sure no one had you under surveillance."

"I didn't notice a tail," she said. "And I would have," she added flatly.

"Here, with less traffic, you can be watched from a distance," he said. "But no one's following us now. Are you going to Arthur Duncan's trading post?"

"How did you—"

"A good guess based on your direction of travel and what you'd said before," he answered. "Leave your sedan here. Someone will pick it up and take it back to the rental agency. From this point on we'll use my wheels. My truck's got more... versatility."

As they got underway she studied the interior of Hunter's blue truck and noted the gun rack in the back. In New Mexico, that was practically standard equipment on pickups. There was nothing else that even hinted at the possibility that this was anything but an off-the-line type of vehicle.

He glanced over at her. "The body's tougher than you think."

She blinked. "Mine or yours?"

He grinned. "I meant my truck's. I saw you looking around, but I like the way you think."

She suppressed a groan and hated the excited ripple that touched her spine. With effort she focused on business.

Noticing his frequent glances in the rearview mirror, she concentrated on helping search for any sign that they'd picked up a tail.

"There's one car back there that may be on us," she said after they'd traveled for several blocks. "I remember seeing it, or one remarkably like it with that smudge on the windshield, back at the airport," she said. "The tan four-door."

"I see it. Two cars back. Good call," he said. "Hang on." He turned the wheel sharply at the next corner and the sedan disappeared from view.

It didn't follow them. She was about to breathe a silent sigh of relief when she spotted it again as they came to a stop at a busy intersection. The sedan was now to their left. "We've got company," she said. "Again."

"I see him," Hunter said. "But this is a well traveled street…."

"Let's find out how serious he is," she said, reaching into her purse. "This is a mobile infrared transmitter. The same device emergency vehicles use. The lights are going to change, so get ready. We'll get the green—everyone else will get a red," she said, turning the device on and aiming it forward. "Now."

The second they got the green, Hunter floored it and the truck's engine responded instantly. He raced out of Farmington, avoiding main streets as much as possible.

"He's gone—if he was ever really after us," she said after a while.

"There'll be others," he answered, then glanced over at her. "But you're well equipped."

She looked over at him and arched her eyebrows.

He gave her a slow, wicked grin that left her toes tingling.

Fifty minutes later they arrived at Duncan's Trading Post, located a few hundred yards west of the main highway on a desolate looking patch of hard-packed clay. Arthur Duncan's place had been one of her father's first stops when he'd come to pick up the dagger, and his last, after delivering the replica.

While Hunter lingered outside a while longer to make sure no one had tailed them, Lisa opened the door to go inside, but Hunter suddenly tugged on her arm, pulling her back out.

"Wait. Give me a chance to check things out. Then I'll let you know if you should go in."

His tone and words made her bristle. "Cover my

back. I can take care of what's in front of me." Disengaging herself, she went inside.

Arthur spotted her immediately and came out from behind the counter. "Lisa, I was so sorry to hear about your father. He was a good friend." Looking around, he gestured for the young Navajo clerk to take his place at the counter. "Let's you and I go into the back. We can talk in private there."

Arthur led the way to a small office in the rear. Still annoyed, she followed him without ever glancing back to look for Hunter.

"Tell me what's on your mind," the man said, sitting down and offering her a chair.

"Arthur, my dad left instructions for me to come here. But I'm not really sure why. I know he stopped to see you before leaving the reservation on his last visit. When he was here, did he say or do anything that might help me find out what really happened to him and the missing dagger—the real one?"

"Your father had a lot of faith in you, but there's something he refused to take into account. It's another world out here. On the reservation things are never quite what they seem. A lot stays beneath the surface, undetected. It's the way of life in these parts." He paused for a moment. "Are you sure you want to get involved in this?"

"I already am."

With a nod, he went to the bookshelf and pulled out several books. Behind them was a small metal box. He opened it and handed her a small key. "Right before he came here last, your father opened a safety deposit box in your name at the First Security Bank in Farmington."

She blinked. "Do you think—" Hearing footsteps behind her, she turned and saw Hunter at the office door.

Arthur smiled. "*Yáat'ééh*," he greeted with the Navajo word for hello, then turned to her. "Lisa, this is…" Arthur noticed their expressions and stopped. "You two already know each other?"

Hunter nodded, then looked back at Lisa. "We have to go *now*. Do you have what you came for?"

She slipped the key inside her tote bag and stood. "Ready when you are."

Chapter Three

Lisa knew Hunter was still trying to make up his mind about her. Though he hadn't spoken, she could sense the questions racing through his mind. He was assessing her, wondering if she'd pull her own weight or not.

"There's something I need to clear up," she said. "You're my *helper*—muscle, protection, whatever you want to call it. And if you think we're in danger, all you have to do is give me a signal. I react quickly. But *I'm* calling the shots."

"Then you should know that, so far at least, you're following a very predictable trail."

"I had to visit my father's contact. It was unavoidable."

"There are lots of people who don't believe that your father sold the dagger. They think he hid it somewhere. Did you think he left it with Arthur Duncan?"

Lisa hesitated. She was good at reading people,

and right now her intuition was telling her to hold back. "What makes you ask that?"

"He was your father's friend—and the trading post was his last stop on his way out of the reservation."

"How did you know that?"

"Stories travel at lightning speed around here," he said, as they reached the stop sign.

She forced herself not to look away though his gaze seemed to go right through her, searching out her deepest secrets. It was uncomfortably intimate and challenging all at once.

"You came to *me,* remember?" he added. "I'm on your side. But to protect you adequately, I need to know your plans *in advance.*"

Lisa hesitated. Hunter had a point. "To be honest, I can't make plans very far ahead. It's the way my father structured the trail he wanted me to follow. Each new step depends on the previous one. Right now, all I know is that my next stop will be the First Security Bank in Farmington. There's a safety deposit box there I need to open. That's as far ahead as I can plan."

"Your father left the key with Duncan?"

She nodded. "But don't kid yourself. The search for the dagger isn't going to be that simple. If all it took to retrieve the dagger was a visit to the bank, he would have made the key a lot harder to find. There's much more to this mystery than that."

Lisa thought of her father. The clues that had led

her to Arthur Duncan had been fairly easy to decipher, but finding the answer had required information that only she or her mother had. There were other sketches in his daily planner, too, and unclear references she still hadn't been able to make out.

"So our next stop's the bank. If you happen to find the dagger in the box, then what?"

Lisa shrugged. "I'll return it to the tribe, of course, but my job won't be done. To me, tracking the dagger is only a means to an end. I have no interest in the artifact beyond its connection to the truth. In order to prove that the replica was meant only to mislead, not defraud, I need to follow Dad's trail wherever it may lead me."

"There's another theory you should consider. If you're right and your father hid the real dagger before handing back a replica, then you're even more of a target. Those after the dagger will expect you to be able to follow his trail better than anyone else—to think like he does—and eventually find it. Then they'll do whatever's necessary to take it from you."

"What's your point?"

"You should let me do the fieldwork while you lay low. I'll turn everything I uncover over to you each step of the way, and you can call the shots. I'll find the dagger and get you what you need to clear your father."

She shook her head. "You just proved my point.

To anyone but me, recovering the dagger will come first, establishing my father's innocence a distant second. That's not acceptable because, to me, the most important thing is proving what really happened. If you don't want to play it my way and you want out now, let me know. I'll find someone else." It had been a bluff. She had no idea who else she would be able to get who was as suited for the job as Hunter. When he didn't answer, she began to grow worried. Maybe she'd overplayed her hand.

"You should trust me more, Lisa," he said at last. "Your father did, or he wouldn't have advised you to come to me for help."

"I *do* trust you. I haven't asked you where you're taking me—and it's not back toward Farmington. That much I know."

"Before we head to the bank, we need a little more information."

"About?"

"The bank manager, Simon Moore. My sources have told me that your father dug into Simon Moore's background—under the radar."

"How on earth do you know that?"

"Your father and I had mutual contacts."

She realized from the silence that followed that he wasn't going to share anything more about his informants. She understood. Under the circumstances she would have done the same. "So that places Moore in our list of potential suspects—but not necessarily on an enemies list…." Lisa thought about it for a moment. "Unfortunately, caution takes time, and our greatest ally is speed. The quicker we wrap things up, the less prepared my father's enemies—my enemies now—will be."

"No, not *your* enemies—*ours*. I owe your father a debt and, as far as I'm concerned, it's binding," he said firmly. "No matter what you face, you'll have me beside you. We're in this together. It's a matter of honoring my word."

Honor. It was the reason she was in this to the end. Her family name meant something to her, and defending it was the right thing to do. "Integrity is sometimes all we have, and it's worth fighting for," she said softly. "I'm glad we see eye-to-eye on that."

THEY ARRIVED AT THE PARKING LOT beside the bank a little more than an hour later. Hunter was poised for whatever happened next, focused but not tense, senses sharp and attuned to danger. He loved his work—the uncertainty, the challenge, the constant testing of his skills.

His gaze took in the area around him, but he was aware of everything about Lisa at the same time. The woman was a problem and a distraction—a bad combination. She had courage and brains, all wrapped up in a dynamite, leggy package. Lisa was softness over steel, and the combination teased his imagination.

Knowing he had a job to do, Hunter shelved those thoughts into a corner of his mind for now, concentrating on the upcoming events. "Simon Moore will recognize me," Hunter said. "And he and I are *not* friends. I don't think it would be a good idea for us to walk in together. But I won't be far behind you. Remember that your father's interest in Moore was not coincidental, so tread carefully."

She nodded, then climbed out of the truck. "I'll keep my guard up."

He watched her walk toward the entrance, then step through the double doors. By the time he finished his mission, the Council would have the dagger and Lisa would have lived to tell the story. That wouldn't be enough, not for her, but it would have to do.

Lisa Garza had courage, but others were involved, thieves and killers she knew nothing about. To stay alive, she'd need someone like him who'd seen life's darkest corners and could always kick his way to the light.

THE BANK, LOCATED ONE BLOCK OFF Main Street, downtown, was busy at midday. Spotting a clipboard at an unoccupied front desk, she signed in, indicating she wanted to access her safe deposit box. Her father had probably listed her as a co-renter so he could have used it at will, too, and simply forged her name on the signature card.

Lisa glanced around. The lines to the teller hadn't moved. A long haired, elderly Indian man, judging by his walking stick, hunched-over back and gray hair, was busy at the center island, muttering to himself in Navajo and counting money as he moved it from one small stack to the other. Yet there was something familiar about him....

A clerk called out her name and Lisa stood. Once inside the vault, she was given access to a booth. Alone, she opened the safe deposit box and found her father's missing diary as well as a thick manila envelope.

She touched the diary, memories bringing tears to her eyes. Taking a breath, she wiped them away. She had a job to finish. The diary contained her father's thoughts and a record of his cases. The envelope was a mystery. Lisa looked inside and found what appeared to be a series of reports written by a man named Paul Johnson. The reports detailed the dagger's specifications, including photos, dimensions and sketches, plus similar information about other artifacts owned by Pueblo tribes. Who Johnson had written the specification reports for, or to, was unclear to her.

Her father's familiar scrawl also filled the margins of each sheet. In one place there was a note mentioning a high-tech PDA device Johnson had used frequently, and a comment that it seemed to work even where her father's cell phone couldn't get service.

To safeguard the originals, Lisa scanned everything into her father's laptop. The originals would remain where he'd left them—a backup.

After Lisa came back out into the lobby, a clerk came to meet her. "Our manager would like to speak to you before you go. He had to take a call, but he won't be long."

"I'll wait," Lisa answered, stepping to the side station where the old Navajo man in the flannel shirt was adding up some numbers.

"Don't look at me," he warned softly.

His voice gave him away. It was Hunter, in disguise.

"Simon Moore knows you're here. He's been pacing in his office, talking to someone on the phone, but all the time he's been watching the vault."

Before she could reply a tall, dark haired man with a salt-and-pepper mustache came toward her.

"Lisa Garza," he said smiling. "You don't know me, but I'm Simon Moore, the bank manager. I was a friend of your father's and wanted to offer you my condolences," he said in a rich, smooth tone. "If you have the time, why don't you come into my office and have a cup of my special coffee. It's the least I can do for the daughter of an old friend."

Lisa saw his gaze drop to her big tote bag and the laptop just visible at the top. Determined not to let him see her uneasiness, she smiled. "Coffee would be fine."

Once inside his wood paneled office, he poured some coffee from a carafe into two china cups.

"How'd you recognize me, Mr. Moore?" Lisa

asked. She wanted to put him on the defensive a little, or at least test his mental reflexes.

"Call me Simon. I believe your father showed me your photo while at a business conference in Albuquerque. He was very proud of his business partner, you know."

Lisa recognized the lie instantly, but managed a smile, not giving herself away. Her father had never carried personal photos in his wallet, a practice left over from his days as a cop.

"John and I didn't always see eye-to-eye, especially when it came to politics, but we had great respect for each other," he continued.

She'd never heard her father mention Simon Moore at all, and she knew he wasn't a former client. As she leaned back in her chair, Lisa could see out into the lobby. Hunter had selected a great disguise. No one would give an old Navajo man, especially one who talked to himself, a second look. If anything, he'd probably be avoided. But what really mattered was knowing Hunter took this assignment so seriously.

"Are you here trying to retrace your father's steps, hoping to locate that missing Navajo artifact?" Simon asked, calling her attention back to him.

The blunt question surprised her. "What makes you assume that?"

He shrugged casually. "Anyone who knew your father, knew you and he were partners in your security business. With your company's reputation on the line, I'd guess you're hoping to find that dagger and cancel out some of the bad press you've received. Everyone knows about the replica and how John was blamed when it got switched with the original."

Moore was polished, but something about his tone, or his presentation, made her skin crawl. It was like coming face-to-face with a beautiful but deadly reptile. "I'm going to set things right and, in the process, find out exactly what happened," she said.

He regarded her for a long moment. "Then I wish you luck."

"Thank you," she replied. "Since you brought up the subject, do you happen to know a man by the name of Paul Johnson?" she asked. "I need to find him."

Recognition flickered in his eyes, but it was gone in an instant. "Closest I can think of is a track coach named Gary Johnson. But I'll think about the name, and ask around if you'd like."

"Please do. I understand he's someone my father dealt with at one time," she said, being deliberately vague.

The man was writing the name down on his desk calendar when Lisa heard a soft electronic tone. Moore pocketed his pen, then reached into his jacket pocket and brought out a small, high-tech PDA.

Lisa recognized the device instantly, having seen it demonstrated at last month's trade show at the fairgrounds. If she remembered correctly, the PDA wasn't even scheduled to be on the market until late in the year. It had global capabilities, recharged from any good source of light, was equipped with a digital high-res camera, and was connected via satellite. Most interesting of all, it had an encryption system that was nearly impossible to break unless one had connections at the NSA.

Noting her curiosity, he quickly placed it back in his jacket. "I'm afraid something's come up, so you'll have to excuse me," he said, escorting her back into the lobby. Simon turned quickly to go back into his office, and bumped right into her.

"Sorry," he muttered, stepped around her, and disappeared behind his closed door.

Lisa looked for Hunter, but he wasn't in sight so she headed out the front door. His truck was parked across the street in plain view, but he wasn't inside.

She walked to the corner, then heard the sound of a scuffle in the alley.

Two husky men in business suits had Hunter by the arms, dragging him toward a large trash container behind the bank. He was protesting in Navajo, pulling halfheartedly and maintaining his cover as an old man, at least for the moment. If they intended on roughing him up, they were in for a surprise.

One man let go, and the other swung Hunter around, slamming his back up against the big metal container. As the first man drew back his fist, Hunter kicked him hard in the stomach. The man stumbled to the ground, gasping for air.

The second man brought out what looked like a leather slapper, a form of a club. Seeing the first guy getting up now, Lisa ran straight for the man, using the *kiai,* the yell of the spirit known and used by martial artists everywhere to confuse and distract.

The man spun to face her, his fists up. She deflected his punch with her arm, then spun and delivered a powerful kick to his neck.

Gagging and struggling to draw in his next breath, he fell back, grasping his throat. She thought about clobbering him with her tote bag, then remembered the computer inside.

Hunter had the second man in a wrist lock. He slammed the man headfirst into the side of the metal container, then let him drop.

Grabbing Lisa's hand, he raced with her out of the alley, across the street and into the truck.

Chapter Four

As they sped away seconds later, Hunter looked over at her, admiration in his gaze. "Good defense. Deadly—but nicely done."

Lisa nodded, reaching for her inhaler. As she used the spray burst, she felt the tightness in her lungs ease almost immediately. "When I fight, it has to be quick and dirty," she said, then continued. "Cool codger disguise. But why did they haul you into the alley and try to work you over?"

"Maybe they made me. Or maybe they thought beating up an old man would be fun." Hunter hit the open highway, his gaze on the rearview mirror. "They're not giving chase. We're okay—for now."

"They weren't in any condition to come after us," she answered.

He unbuttoned his long sleeves, one at a time, folding back the cuffs almost to the elbows. "Hot work, pretending to be a member of my grandfather's generation."

His shirt hung open, most of the buttons gone,

and she could see the sheen of perspiration that covered his upper chest. His strong hands were clenched into tight fists around the steering wheel.

"Are you okay?" He took one hand off the steering wheel and touched her arm lightly.

"I did okay back there and that's all that matters. Sure I have my vulnerabilities, but I'd be willing to bet you have some, too."

He smiled at her, then shifted his gaze back to the road. "Maybe so, but they're not as easy to spot."

"I'll have to look closer next time. It'll keep things more balanced between us," she said.

He nodded. "Balance is a good thing. It brings harmony. My people believe that you need both to walk in beauty."

Having lived in the Southwest most of her life, she'd often heard about the "Navajo Way." It was a philosophy that made sense to her. "Your people are light-years beyond everyone else in the ways that matter most."

"There, we agree."

Hunter had a devastatingly handsome smile. She felt its impact all through her. "Let me fill you in about what I found at the bank," she said, concentrating on work again.

"Hold that thought. The way we got away…well, it was too clean, too easy. They could have clocked me with that club when I was still playing old man. Instead they played the old schoolyard bully routine, telegraphing their punches. Now that I think about it, the whole thing was too…planned. They wanted us to *think* we fought our way out of there."

She considered it. "Simon must have known I was there the moment I accessed the box. My name was on the safe deposit box rent form, and in their system. But I'm not sure how he connected you to me, or how he saw through your disguise."

"Maybe an outside camera recorded us leaving from the same vehicle. Or security in civilian clothes got a look at my face. He might have noticed us talking, too. Considering the guy is high tech, it's also possible that he used a directional mike," he added.

Lisa began searching the interior of the truck, checking below the visor, around the cup holder and feeling beneath the dashboard.

Hunter caught on quickly and helped. After their search revealed nothing, he glanced over at her. "Do you think Simon could be connected to whoever broke into your house?"

She thought about Simon's PDA and what her father had said about the state-of-the-art one Paul Johnson had used. Lisa put a finger to her lips, indicating he shouldn't speak.

"Pull over. I think we have a flat tire," she said for the benefit of anyone who might have been listening.

Hunter glanced in the rearview mirror, then pulled off onto the shoulder of the highway and stopped. They opened both doors, then, together, searched the interior of the truck completely, now checking behind and beneath the seats as well. Finding nothing, they began to check around the outside of the pickup.

Hunter ran a hand beneath the front bumper, and she checked the tire wells and undercarriage. "Open the hood, could you?" she asked, then, together they searched the engine compartment.

"So I guess that's it," he said.

"No," she said quickly. "One more place."

She went around to the back of the truck, bent down, and felt behind the vehicle tag. A second later, she brought out a small tracking device she recognized as an expensive, fairly new model on the market. "Five hundred dollars minimum for a GPS device this small," she said, then dropped it on the asphalt and ground it into the pavement with the heel of her shoe. "Now we need to find someplace safe where I can go over what I found in the safe deposit box."

"We can use my place. I bought a house from a friend several weeks back. The paperwork is still in the tribal system, so there's no legal trail for anyone outside the processing agency to follow. It's on the reservation, west of Shiprock, about an hour away. We should be relatively safe there. Unfortunately, there's no place that'll be completely secure for us from now on. Not until we finish this."

"I know." She was in possession of information others wanted now, and that had pushed her and Hunter directly into the line of fire. "Let's get going. We should get off the main highway as soon as possible."

They drove for ten minutes in silence. She could see something was bothering him. Although it took effort, she didn't press, sensing he needed to work something out in his own mind.

At long last he reached out and placed his hand over hers, tracing a path over her skin with his thumb. It was a casual touch, but it sent sparks straight through her. "Your father was a fighter. Like me, he knew who he was and what he wanted from life. But you're more vulnerable than either of us."

Seeing her start to protest, Hunter held up a hand. "No, I'm not referring to your asthma. This goes beyond that. You've set out to prove your father's innocence. But are you prepared for whatever you find? Men like your dad, who have their own agenda, sometimes are tempted to see what they're trying to do as above the law, and lines can get crossed."

She had no quick answer for him. The truth was that it would have been just like John Garza to try and get the thieves to come out into the open by making himself the target. He'd loved to court danger and he would have welcomed the opportunity to break some rules for a greater good.

"My father was many things, but above all, he was an honest man. I'm as sure of this as I am of the next sunrise."

THEY ARRIVED AT A LARGE, custom-designed home seventy minutes later. It was one story and had a six-sided, hogan-shaped room with a large window facing the parking area. "This is it," he said. "Keep in mind that it's a work in progress, and I still have a lot of remodeling to do."

There was a large dish antenna on the roof, and a second collector she didn't recognize. Hunter obviously had some sophisticated communications gear—not just great TV reception. She was curious to see the inside. Homes held the stamp of their owners, even new ones still in the process of change. The interior would reflect better than words ever could, the person who'd chosen to make it home.

As she stepped out of the truck she looked around. She could barely make out another house in the distance. "You like your privacy, I see?"

"I demand it," he answered. "That's why I'd never make a good city dweller. The family who lives over there raises sheep and horses. They mind their own business, and I do the same."

"You're so outgoing and friendly," she quipped.

His grin was slow, lazy and quintessentially male. "I can be *very* friendly. It all depends on the company."

Knowing Hunter was flirting, that it probably was second nature to him, didn't stop her heart from beating a little faster, nor the thrill of awareness that shot through her.

As she stopped by the east-facing main entrance, Lisa saw the small circular carving on the upper right-hand corner of the door. It was hard to discern because it was crude and small, but the image held a strong resemblance to a drawing of flames bounded inside a circle that she'd seen in her father's diary.

"This carving…" She pointed, then noticed his back was turned as he unlocked the door.

He motioned for her to enter. "You say something?"

"Never mind." She admired the large, hexagonal-shaped room before her. The walls and ceiling were finished in rough-cut lumber stained a rich brown, not the traditional logs, but the design was beautiful. The ceiling beams were all lined pointing upward to the high center, where a large stove pipe extended from top to bottom. In the center of the floor was a large wood stove, which provided heat, at least for this part of the house. Interior lighting came from fixtures beneath a small panel that provided indirect illumination along the joint between wall and ceiling.

The flagstone floor was bare except for a large sheepskin rug between the front entrance and the stove, and a simple square wooden table and four matching chairs had been placed in front of the large window. Beside the other walls were two easy chairs covered in leather, a small desk, and a beam-framed doorway leading down a hall. Two of the walls held small shelves filled with books.

"Traditional hogans are this shape, and many modernist Navajos, like I am, end up incorporating the design into our homes. But don't let it fool you. A true medicine hogan is nothing like this," he said, then with a wave across the hexagonal room, added, "Make yourself at home."

She chose the table by the only window, and placed her handbag down. "The PDF that Moore was using is a state-of-the-art gadget," she said, remembering. "If that and the tracking device are indicative of how well our enemies are funded, we have a tough road ahead of us."

"I don't doubt it," he said.

"I scanned all the information I found in the safe deposit box into my laptop, but there's a name I'd like to run past you—Paul Johnson," she said, and filled him in.

He considered it, then, at long last, shook his head. "I haven't heard of him—which makes me think he may be using an alias. I know the names of most criminals connected with the theft of Indian artifacts."

"Because of your ties to the tribe? Are you in law enforcement?" she asked.

He waited a beat before answering. "I'm not in law enforcement, but I try to keep current on anything that affects the Diné."

She met his gaze, but all she saw in the dark eyes that held hers was the enticing allure of the unknown. "Hunter Blueeyes, I'd like to know more about you," she said honestly.

"You already know all you need. Your father trusted me because he knew I'd have the skills, training and the contacts to help you."

Hunter was a man of secrets—secrets he wouldn't share. The question now was how much information should she share with him? Common sense dictated that she only give him what he absolutely needed to know, nothing more. The only problem was deciding where to draw that line. "Give me a chance to go over this. My dad intended it for my eyes, and I'm going to respect that."

"Fair enough. In the meantime I'll try to find out more about Paul Johnson."

He stepped out of the room, and Lisa heard his footsteps echo down the hall. Alone, she called her mom on the cell phone just to say hello and check on her. Then Lisa contacted Happeth at the Albuquerque office. The connection was weak, but at least she got through to Albuquerque.

"It's Lisa. Anything new in the office?" she asked.

"If you mean, new clients, no," Happeth said. "But maybe it's too soon."

"I meant to tell you, if you want to take time off

to do a job search, do it, Happeth," Lisa encouraged. "You've been more than loyal to Dad and me."

After saying goodbye, Lisa powered up her computer, then went through the pages she'd scanned, one by one. Archeology had been her father's hobby, which had naturally led to his security work with the university's anthropology department. One of the pages in the thick journal had been filled with a long list of items—everything from Apache arrows to something he'd called *k'elwod.* She was pretty sure it was a Navajo term, but she had no idea what it meant.

As Lisa studied the pages, it appeared that much of the information wasn't related at all to the missing dagger, at least directly. Yet instinct and a thorough knowledge of her father assured her that there was an important message hidden within the notes and comments. Her father wouldn't have taken such care to protect the diary otherwise. Undaunted, she continued to search for the key that would uncover more clues.

Lisa methodically went through each page, but nothing caught her attention until she reached page 28, a number that corresponded to her age. Written within the text describing a method for flaking off obsidian to shape an arrowhead was a totally unrelated riddle. She read it over carefully, knowing in her heart that this was something her father had intended her to find.

In the brightness nothing's hidden,
Questions raised, answers given.
Born for blood, circle's bidden,
In the four, power's evened.

She leaned back and stared at the four lines. She'd always been terrible with riddles, anagrams and the like.

"Oh, help," she muttered in a barely audible voice.

HUNTER WENT TO THE communications room, entered through the back of a bedroom closet. The house, with hidden spaces concealed by the unique architecture, was much more than a one-of-a-kind home. This special room held many surprises. In a compartment behind a cork bulletin board, which lowered down to form a desk top, was an emergency stash of weapons and ammunition. And beside it was a special laptop with encrypted files and a satellite phone. He also had a com link that would get him in touch with someone in the Council anytime—day or night.

He brought out the laptop, which was always on, and typed an encrypted message. The proper response came in a matter of seconds as a coded series of letters flashed onscreen.

The letters, in a simple code, corresponded to a phone number. He made the call and, although they never used names, he recognized the male voice at the other end instantly. Hunter brought *Hastiin sání* up to date.

"Find a way to get the woman to trust you," *Hastiin sání* said. "Whatever it takes. Though she'll probably never thank you, in the long run, you may be saving her life."

"Understood," he said gruffly.

Almost as if he'd read Hunter's thoughts, *Hastiin sání* added, "The debt you owe her father must be secondary to your duty to the tribe…and the Council."

Hunter said nothing. He'd already made up his mind to try and find a way to honor both commitments.

After a brief silence *Hastiin sání* added, "You're interested in this woman. That will create a problem."

"No, *Hastiin sání,* it won't." He'd guarded his tone and words well, but it was hard to slip anything past the Old Man. "The woman has courage and a high sense of duty. I find that worthy of my respect. But that's all there is to it."

Even as he said it, he realized it wasn't completely true. He'd always liked strong, capable women, and Lisa was one of a kind. Back in the alley, she hadn't hesitated to get into a fight with a man who'd outweighed her by a considerable amount. And danged if he hadn't enjoyed seeing her take the big boys on.

You had to love a woman like that—fearless and disciplined, too. She hadn't learned those moves overnight. She had the guts to follow her own code of ethics…a code he'd certainly be trampling over when it got down to it.

The realization stopped him cold. He'd have to betray her sooner or later. His priority was the dagger. But even if taking it from her proved necessary in order to save her life, Lisa would never understand. Although the oath he'd taken as a member of the Brotherhood of Warriors defined him, she was fighting for her father, and her loyalty was to him.

"I need information on a man by the name of Paul Johnson," Hunter said.

There was a pause at the other end, and Hunter realized that the name had been recognized.

"We don't have much to give you, except that he's from our tribe, and that he works for Carlos Trujillo."

Hunter recognized that name instantly. "Makes sense. Trujillo's organization makes him the only fence in the area with the connections to handle an item as hot as *Hashkéts'ósí,*" Hunter replied, using the Navajo name for the dagger.

His superior grunted in agreement. "Trujillo is cunning and ruthless, but we're getting close to bringing him down."

That meant that the Council had an ongoing operation, and probably one or more warriors had infiltrated Trujillo's organization.

As he recalled his first experience going under

deep cover, his gut tightened and his fists clenched. Four years ago, he'd been sent to infiltrate the L.A. gang who'd been trying to expand their operation by muscling into New Mexico and the Navajo Nation. He'd managed to get strong evidence against several gang members when everything had suddenly gone wrong. Somehow his cover was blown and they'd uncovered his real identity.

They'd come after him at home one night. Using the threat to his wife, Amelia, the Hermanos Locos had tried to force him to divulge the identity of the other warriors in the Council. Amelia, who'd had a weak heart, had suffered a fatal heart attack that night long before help could arrive.

Her death seemed like a lifetime ago. There were days now when he couldn't picture Amelia's face clearly in his mind anymore. Yet her loss had become like a permanent shadow over his soul, and had left him a changed man. Women had come and gone from his life since then, but he'd sworn never to have a serious relationship again. Enough innocent blood had been shed.

Hunter closed the compartment, then left the communications area and returned to the hogan room. Lisa still sat where he'd left her, staring at her computer.

"What did you get?" she asked, turning her head as he came in.

"My contacts don't know much about Paul Johnson. All I've got is that he's believed to work for one of the major fences in this area. But your father wouldn't have warned you about him unless Johnson was a major player—and dangerous."

Lisa nodded. "What does *k'elwood* mean? It's Navajo, isn't it?"

He paused for a second, trying to make out the word.

Realizing that her Navajo pronunciation left something to be desired, she spelled it out for him.

"Navajo is a complex language," he said slowly. "Roughly, that means 'he kept running after an interruption that nearly stopped him.' Where did you come across it?"

"Is there an artifact by that name?" she pressed, not answering right away.

"Not that I've heard of. But you're going to have to give me more."

She nodded, lost in thought. "My father loved puzzles and riddles—anything that taxed his intellect and made those around him have to think. In his maze of seemingly unrelated notes, I believe he's telling me exactly what went down. He talks endlessly about everything from Apache arrowheads and obsidian blades to Sandia Cave and Folsom points. But when he talks about *k'elwod* he never mentions what it is. It's just thrown in there with no explanation or obvious references."

"May I see?"

She waved an invitation for him to join her by the computer. "See how he starts by talking about some arrowheads he found, dropping every minute and boring detail he could think of. At one point, he actually describes the pack rat he saw while photographing a new find."

Hunter gave her a puzzled look. "There aren't any pack rats in the region he's describing," Hunter said slowly. "I think he was trying to tell you something else."

"Something tied to the Navajo word…" she said thoughtfully.

"Maybe the connection isn't a literal one. Think of the habits of a pack rat. They'll haul away whatever catches their eye. But the thing about a pack rat, is that it frequently *leaves* something behind. It may take someone's diamond ring and leave a piñon nut in its place—but the point is that it's a trade of sorts."

"That suggests that my father traded something for the real dagger—undoubtedly, the replica—and then had to make a run for it," she observed, nodding. "It makes sense."

"But we already knew that. This clue, if that's what it is, doesn't get us any closer to the dagger," he answered automatically. Noting the flash of pain in her eyes, he berated himself for not having used more tact. She was still mourning the loss of a loved one. "I'm very sorry. I wasn't thinking. He was your father and partner and you must miss him a lot."

She nodded. "Work was Dad's passion. He loved taking on a complex case, then working to set things right again. He was a fighter through and through. He didn't know how to give up."

"Your father made it his life's work to restore balance and harmony—the *hózhq*. May the same be said about me when the time comes," he added gently.

Hunter saw the long searching look she gave him and wondered what she saw when she looked at him that way. Inside that tough shell of hers beat the heart of a romantic out on an impossible quest. He was the opposite, a realist…but he liked seeing himself reflected in her soft hazel eyes.

"We're sorting out the clues from the camouflage, and that's progress at least," she said, unaware of the direction his thoughts had taken. She stood up and stretched, wandering about the room. "There are no photos in here at all. Is that due to a tribal custom?"

"No, not at all. Lots of Navajo families keep photos of loved ones in their homes. We're no different than anyone else on that score."

"Then why…?"

"Why don't I?" he added, finishing her thought. "I take my memories, my mental photos if you will, and sculpt them. I have a studio in town, but the pieces I keep at home are more personal, so I don't display them in the front room."

"I'd love to see one of your pieces someday," she said. "I never dreamed you were a sculptor."

"It's my day job," he said. With a quirky half

smile, he stepped into the hall and gestured to the other end.

She followed in the direction he'd pointed. Inside a *nicho,* a niche built into the wall, and surrounded by soft diffused light, stood a beautiful twelve-inch wood carving of a mother nursing her child. The details of the piece were exquisitely rendered. It was as if he'd breathed life into the piece.

"Was it inspired by someone you know?" she pressed softly, her soft gaze on him.

"Knew. My wife passed away. That was…what could have been."

Chapter Five

Lisa felt her heart go out to him. She'd known pain, but not like this. The sculpted piece was an agonized memory, a cry from his heart. "How long ago?"

"Four years. Some people came after me, but she ended up paying the price," he said, then almost as a challenge, added, "So you may not be as safe with me as you think."

"I'm safer with you than I would be with anyone else," she said, as if she'd sensed what lay beyond his words. "You won't fail a second time."

The words ripped through him, but he held himself perfectly still and forced himself to hold her gaze with a steady one of his own. "You're absolutely right about that."

"What happened to the men who were responsible for her death?"

"Catching up to them wasn't hard. But off the reservation I was alone. They ambushed me. If it hadn't been for your father…" He shook his head. "Let's just say it got bloody."

She remembered her father going through a review process after a shooting. Her dad hadn't spoken about it then, and talking about it now seemed pointless.

Although she missed her dad terribly, accepting the loss of a parent was oftentimes easier than accepting the death of a beloved spouse. On one level or another, a parent's death was expected. It was the natural order. Yet the death of a spouse, particularly to murder, delivered two crushing blows.

Understanding his pain because she'd known her own, made her want to reach out to him. The desire to soothe and support was the essence of being a woman. But giving and accepting comfort would be dangerous to both of them. Distractions could cost them their lives.

"What else did you find in your father's notes?" he asked, his voice rough as he brought his thoughts firmly back to the business at hand. "Can I read through the scanned pages?" he asked, leading her back to the front room.

She hesitated, uncertain if she should honor his request or not.

"I thought you trusted me." His voice held an unmistakable challenge.

"I do trust you—to a point. But you're like a closed book, Hunter. I still know very little about you."

"You already know more about me than some people I've known for years," he answered, leaning against the door jamb, his eyes focused solely on her.

"I know you're a skilled fighter with good investigative skills." Her heart was beating a million times a minute under the intensity of his gaze. "But I don't know where you trained, or who you really work for. Sculpting's your day job, but there's a lot you're not telling me. You've got your own agenda," she added, mostly to gauge his reaction.

Something flashed in his eyes, but it happened too quickly to reveal much of anything. "I'm here by your side, and I *will* keep you alive while we search for the dagger. That should be the only thing that counts."

"But it isn't. I'm a security analyst. I'm trained to look beyond what's apparent on the surface. Right now, instinct tells me that we should remain on a need to know. It'll be a way of keeping both of us—and the information—safer. We can't give up what we don't know, not even by accident."

It was sound logic he'd used himself when he'd been forced to recruit an agent or informant outside the Council. "Your father's writings are the key to finding the dagger. So you tell me. What's next?"

"I believe that this riddle holds some answers," she said, and showed it to him.

He stared at it, lost in thought for a long while, then finally shook his head. "He obviously felt it was something you'd know how to decode."

"But I have no idea what it means," she said, exasperatedly running a hand through her hair.

"Do something totally unrelated to that for a while. It'll come to you when you least expect it. Sometimes when I'm sculpting, things don't go as planned. The only sure-fire way to get frustrated and accomplish nothing is to force it. Inspiration comes at its own time and can't be rushed... though certain things *can* spark it." He brushed his palm over her cheek then lower to her neck, his thumb caressing the pulse point there.

His soft-spoken words felt like an intimate caress. Hunter wanted her and she could feel her own body respond to that intuitive knowledge.

On a mindless, primitive level, she wanted him, too, but she wasn't wired for casual sex. Her heart demanded far more than that to be satisfied. Unable to focus under his steady gaze, she forced herself to walk away from him, putting distance between them. "Why don't you show me the rest of the house?"

He smiled and nodded once, accepting her response. "In reality it isn't as large as it looks from the front," he said, leading her down the hall.

Her training as a security analyst made her observant, and she noted the vents and subtle dimensional differences between walls and rooms that suggested hidden spaces—perhaps even small rooms behind concealed entrances. One room was a den and office combination, but the TV was much too unsophisticated to match the antennae array on the roof, and she'd seen no computers anywhere.

As they stopped by the last doorway at the opposite end of the hallway, he studied her expression, then spoke softly. "You've seen far more than I actually showed you. But I thought you might."

"Thank you for trusting me. That means a lot," she answered honestly. He was a man of many secrets. The knowledge filled her with wild curiosity... always a sign of trouble. "What's in there?" She pointed to the only room still ahead. The door was shut.

"My studio," he said, then opened the door.

The room was bathed in light from two sides that held floor-to-ceiling windows. It seemed in sharp contrast to the security measures elsewhere, and she mentioned the fact immediately.

"A practical romantic," he chuckled with a killer smile. "But to answer your question, that isn't ordinary glass."

"Nothing about you is ordinary, is it?" she said in a whisper-soft voice.

"I could say the same about you."

She walked to an exquisitely carved wooden

sculpture on the table in the center of the room. It was about two feet tall and depicted a blindfolded Indian warrior standing upright, hands tied behind his back. The warrior's chest was bare, muscles rippling, and the sheen of the finished walnut added to the realism of the piece. "I get the idea that he could break free. He looks strong enough," she said in awe.

"I call that piece Honor," he said, his voice reverberating with conviction. "Life isn't always about what we can do. It's also about what we don't do, even when we could."

She started to touch it, then pulled her hand back. "Sorry! The oil from my hands…"

"Won't hurt a thing. It's sealed. Go ahead, touch it."

She ran one finger over the figure's torso, feeling its smooth texture and its sharply defined muscles, signifying unyielding strength. The dark brown wood allowed every detail to show. The piece was all about power kept in check and strength that endured despite the circumstances. "The warrior…is it you?"

He tilted her chin up with one finger, captured her gaze, and held it. "You've seen enough for today. Now it's time to take care of our more basic needs."

Her breath caught in her throat and, this time, it had nothing to do with asthma. "Pardon?" she managed in a thin voice. She was aware of Hunter in ways she couldn't even put into words. His talent and intelligence, his confidence, even his scent called to her. As he rubbed his knuckles over her cheek, a wicked smile on his face, every inch of her skin became vibrantly sensitized and she yearned for more of his touch. But she was too levelheaded for this.

"I was only suggesting we have dinner—unless, of course, you have a better idea."

"Uh, no," she stammered, then tried to cover by pretending to clear her voice.

He took her hand in his for a second or two. "You're beginning to do crazy things to me, too," he said in a near whisper, then, letting go of her, led the way out of the studio and back up the hall.

Still shaky, she took a deep, steadying breath, then followed, closing the door behind her. By walking out first, Hunter had reminded her of the cultural differences between them.

In what was referred to locally as Anglo—white—culture, having a man walk out first would have been considered rude. Yet as her friend and sometimes employee Bruce had explained it to her once, a Navajo man preferred to lead because, in case of danger, he'd be the one to confront it first. She wasn't sure how white customs had evolved, but at least in this case, she could see the logic of the Navajo way and was more than happy to defer to it.

DINNER WAS NAVAJO TACOS—fresh fry bread smothered with pinto beans, chili sauce, lettuce and tomatoes, and heavily sprinkled with grated, sharp cheddar cheese. The scent was heavenly.

"I don't get to cook often, so when I do it's a special treat," he said, refusing to let her help during any of the process.

"I would have never suspected you were also a talented chef. You're a man of hidden talents."

He gave her a purely masculine grin. "I'm *trying* to behave, and there you are tempting me."

She choked. "No, I meant—"

He laughed. "Relax." He opened two cans of cola, then set them on the table. "Sodas taste better in the can," he said, then added, "Plus, I've never bothered to buy glasses."

As they ate, Lisa found herself relaxing. It felt good to be in the company of an interesting and thoroughly masculine man, and to be his center of attention. A little voice at the back of her mind warned her to be careful, not to let her guard down, but she shut it out. For now, normalcy felt like an exquisite luxury.

"So tell me. I know you're a security analyst, but what do you do when you're not working?" he asked, sitting back and relaxing after he'd finished his meal.

"My father tried to talk me into playing golf with him, but except for the walk, I was bored. I prefer to train in the martial arts."

"That's part of working—a job skill. What do you do to relax?"

"I play computer games. It's my one addiction," she added with a smile.

"Let me guess. You like shooter games, blowing away the bad guys?" he asked, laughing.

"No, not at all. I enjoy the quest or mystery games where you have to solve something or figure out how to get out of the maze and go rescue the good guys. Like that," she said, then added, "But after this is all over, I may need a break from those."

Reality rushed back into her thoughts, and the shadow that had covered her heart from the day she'd found her father's body crept over her again. "We each have our own darkness to deal with," she said, leaving the table and standing near the window. It was night now, and all she could see was her own reflection in the glass. "Does it ever go away—the sense that there was so much more you should have said or done…?"

"To push back the dark, you have to let in the light," he said, pulling her away from the window and into his arms. "Trust me," he whispered, lowering his head and taking her mouth.

His kiss was a blend of passion and tenderness. She'd expected a whirlwind—speed and flashes of lightning—but those would have consumed them in a matter of heartbeats. This slow fire burned through her defenses more thoroughly than she'd ever imagined possible, leaving her open and receptive to more.

She welcomed the intrusion of his tongue as it

danced with hers. His need pressed against her, and though she knew it was time to pull away, she didn't want the searing heat she'd found in his arms to end.

She moved into him, but he suddenly froze and eased his hold. The muscles on his chest and shoulders tightened and his eyes darted away from her face to an area just beyond her. "We've got company outside. Don't react. Just move with me away from the window, like normal. Then get ready to run."

He turned off the lights casually, pulling her into the darkness. As he did, gunfire erupted outside and bullets thumped against the window.

She ducked low instinctively, but he tugged on her arm. "The bullets won't penetrate—not unless they have a fifty-caliber machine gun out there. But we've got to make a run for it now."

"My laptop. My bag. Medications—they're all on the floor beside the table."

"Go," he said, releasing her hand and extracting a forty-five pistol from the desk drawer.

As she raced to gather her things, she could hear the rounds impacting on the bullet-resistant glass. She knew there was no need, but instinct compelled her to stay low.

She grabbed her tote bag and raced back to the hall. "How did they—" she called out, but he grabbed her by the hand and pulled her along with him.

"Later. Move."

"The truck's out front!" she protested as they moved down the hall. "How do we get to it?"

"Forget the truck. Stick with me." He led her into his bedroom, pressed the light-switch plate instead of the switch, then led her to the closet.

"Hide in the closet?"

"Be patient." As he opened the door, the clothes on hangers parted, revealing an opening at the back. Beyond, she could see light and another enclosure.

They passed through the closet into a small, concealed room with a cork bulletin board, a few vents and little else.

Hunter pushed the inside wall switch, and the back of the closet closed. "It can't be opened from the bedroom now, not without explosives."

"Now what? We wait them out?"

Lowering the bulletin board revealed several weapons in a rack. Hunter grabbed a shotgun, a bandoleer of extra rounds, and two extra magazines for the pistol. Then he raised the board back into position.

He stepped over to another switch plate, turned the plate clockwise, and the hardboard wall on the opposite side started to move. She felt a rush of cool air. Beyond was a tunnel—very much like a mine shaft.

"This was the perfect site to build a house like

this—one with a concealed exit. I've got a vehicle parked and ready at the other end, if we decide to leave."

She heard the faint sounds of pounding. "They're trying to break down the front door."

"They'd be better off ramming it with a truck. Simple entertainment for simple minds, I suppose. It'll be a good diversion for us."

He hurried out with her into the tunnel, flipped on a switch and a light came on overhead. On a wooden rack was a battery-powered lantern and a large flashlight. He turned the switch plate, and the wall panel closed behind them. "Stay here," he said, taking the flashlight. "I'm going out one of the exits and outflank them."

"I'll go with you."

"It's a firefight. Can you use a gun?" He held out the forty-five, butt first.

She hesitated.

"Never mind. If you have to think about it, you'll just get yourself killed. Stay here."

She bristled at his tone. "There's more than one way to fight."

"Against men with rifles and pistols? The laws of physics are against you. Don't risk your life— and mine—with heroics."

He hurried away, then disappeared up a side tunnel fifty feet away. Lisa grabbed the lantern, turned it on, then followed, unwilling to just wait. Fifteen feet up the side tunnel, the shaft forked into two. The light was dim here, and with only the hand lantern providing any illumination, checking the ground, trying to spot his footprints was tough.

Deciding he'd gone to the left, she continued, but the shaft divided again less than a hundred feet ahead, this time in three directions—one of them down a vertical shaft with a metal ladder. The underground network was a maze. She reached a solid wall of bedrock and noted the vent overhead. Above that, perhaps, the black night sky stretched out. It was then she heard the faint wail of a siren.

The neighbor must have called the police after hearing gunfire. At least they'd have help now. She decided to go back the way she came, and was passing the vertical shaft when she heard running footsteps behind her, in the area where she'd just been.

Lisa turned off the lantern, pressed her back to the wall and waited, ready, in case it wasn't Hunter. She'd been trained to disarm an opponent in ten seconds or less. But they had to be within reach, of course.

A heartbeat later, the footsteps stopped, but she could see light. "Stand down, it's me," Hunter said, appearing from a side tunnel, his flashlight aimed at the floor of the mineshaft. "Why didn't you stay put?"

"Where were you?" she answered, avoiding his question.

"I made it outside, but by that time they'd

scattered. A siren can be heard for miles around here, and our attackers were getting nowhere. The door was still intact, and the window hadn't been breached, though it's got a hole in it the size of a melon. We'd better leave too unless we want to get stuck with the police, answering a million questions."

"In our case, the officers won't be much help," she agreed. "But where to? Do you have another place in mind?"

"Yeah. Although I'd prefer using my other vehicle, we can't just drive out and hope to stay under cover. Our best bet is to remain on foot and get lost up in these foothills until everyone gives up. Then we can leave the area completely. The ones after us will lay low too, but once the officers are gone, they'll regroup and come back for us."

"So we hike out. Let's get going," she said, determined to remain upbeat.

He took her hand and they exited the mazelike network of what had once been an old coal mine by climbing up a ventilation shaft. Moments later, they emerged in the middle of a cluster of pines atop a small ridge, based on what she could see in the moonlight. The combination of the evening hour and the thick cover of vegetation hid them effectively. Yet despite all the walking they'd done, they hadn't traveled very far. She could still hear the wail of police sirens, and could easily locate the highway in the distance from the flashing red lights.

Making a spur-of-the-moment decision, they headed in the general direction of the main road. They walked on a parallel course to it, making sure to stay far enough away to remain hidden. It was downhill at first, but then they encountered a gradual uphill slope. The pace he'd set for them, scrambling up fifty yards of very soft ground, was more than her lungs could handle. Wheezing slightly, she stopped and reached into her bag for her inhaler.

"We have to slow down," she said, hating to admit that she couldn't maintain this pace. Using her inhaler again, she added, "I can go anywhere you can, but not at this speed. The great outdoors, at this altitude especially, isn't exactly ideal ground for an asthmatic."

"Let me rethink our route," he said, then after a few moments added, "We'll go slower, down one of the canyons. The distance is greater, but the hike will be a lot less stressful and there'll be a minimum of climbing."

Her breathing finally evened again, and she nodded. "I'm good to go."

As they continued, slow but steady this time, her thoughts remained on what had happened back at Hunter's home. "*How* did they find us?" she voiced at last. "We were *not* followed. We would have seen them ten miles off, at least for the first part of the journey." She looked over at the small irrigation ditch, where water was flowing at a brisk pace at the moment. They could make good time now since there were paths on both sides of the water.

"You're right," he said, and paused. "It doesn't add up."

She remained silent, deep in thought. "Back at the bank, Moore brushed by me while I was standing near the door."

They exchanged quick glances.

Hunter stepped behind her and ran his palm over the seam and collar of her blouse.

His touch was electric, and she had to force herself not to shiver.

"You're clean," he said.

Lisa reached into her purse and checked everything inside for a tracking device of some sort, but found nothing. Her gaze then fell on her cell phone and she froze.

Lisa took it out and glanced at him. "You don't think…"

"There's no tracking device on you. That's the only thing that might explain how they found us."

"I called Happeth from your place," she said, and explained.

"If they found a way to track that phone's GPS, we've got to put it out of action." He took it from her, and dropped it on the ground.

Before he could smash it with the heel of his boot, she grabbed his sleeve.

"Hang on! I have a *much* better idea." She reached into her purse again and brought out a plastic container that had held a sandwich at one time, then placed the phone inside. Snapping the lid shut and checking to make sure it was airtight, she walked to an irrigation ditch, then bent down and set the container in the fast-moving stream.

He laughed out loud. "Great thinking. That'll get them off our tail for a while. And if it makes it past the fields, the river is just beyond."

"Let's get cracking and put some distance between us and the phone anyway." Instead of following the ditch, they moved perpendicular to it now. The terrain was more uneven, but not as steep as before and she was able to keep up with him.

"That was good thinking, what you did with that phone," he said after they'd gone another half mile. "But I've been thinking, it would take some seriously expensive equipment to track someone's cell phone."

"Not if you have the right connections. Local rescue agencies can locate people who've had an accident and don't know their own location. All they need is your cell phone number. If the phone's in use, pinpointing the origin isn't that complicated."

"And getting numbers that aren't listed isn't

hard," he admitted. "I've done that myself. It's not what you know, but who you know."

"Yeah. But what about *your* phone? I know you carry one," she added, gesturing to the slight bulge in his windbreaker pocket.

"The number isn't linked to my name, and the GPS has been, shall we say, tinkered with. In addition to that, all my calls are prepaid."

They reached higher ground a full forty minutes later after a gradual climb. Hunter stopped, wanting to take a look around. It was a clear moonlit night, and they could see for miles. No vehicle lights were visible anywhere, not even in the direction of the highway. "I don't think they've been able to track us. Why don't you stay here while I jog uphill a bit more to make a phone call? Hopefully I'll be able to get a signal from there." He pointed toward the highest feature of the mesa they'd just climbed.

"You haven't just been trying to get away from the others, have you? You've actually been traveling *toward* something, right?" Though she was physically fit, she felt achy and tired from their journey, but he didn't look even winded.

"I always have a plan," he said and gave her a thoroughly masculine grin. Before she could reply, he moved off.

She watched him make his way through the thick underbrush, scarcely making a sound. He took her breath away—but in a good way. Around him she felt beautiful…and desired.

But instinct told her that he was trouble with a capital *T.* Inside Hunter Blueeyes beat a heart of fire—and secrets.

Chapter Six

Hunter returned a short time later. "We need to keep moving. They might have night vision binoculars, and even after ditching the phone we're vulnerable out here."

"Who came after us, Trujillo or Paul Johnson?" she asked.

"It wasn't Carlos Trujillo," he replied. "I'm certain about that. Carlos is as elusive as an eel. He keeps a low profile, and *never* gets his hands dirty. This man your father mentioned, Johnson, undoubtedly works for him, part of a team of hoods Trujillo can draw from."

They continued hiking in silence for another twenty minutes. She was dead tired, but he showed no signs of stopping anytime soon. Worst of all, nothing around them looked even remotely hospitable and like a safe place to hole up in for the night. "Are we there yet?" she muttered.

He chuckled softly. "Not unless you want to take a chance and camp out tonight."

"I'd rather not spend the night anywhere that doesn't come equipped with solid walls. It was walls—well, bullet-resistant glass—that stopped that hail of bullets."

"Yeah, good point," he said. Looking upward at the clear night and the stars twinkling above, he added in a faraway voice, "Maybe someday after this is over, you and I can share a night like this in the open, with nothing between us except the moonlight."

His voice sparked a fire, filling her with a powerful—and dangerous—yearning, considering their current circumstances.

Almost as if he'd had the same thought, he glanced away. "We're about three miles from the safe house now."

"The last one was your own home, and it was far from ordinary," she commented. "Will it be like that here, too? And what are these places? I mean, how many private homes other than those belonging to ex-presidents have bulletproof windows?"

He continued in silence for several moments, then at last spoke. "It's all a part of why your father knew you'd be safe with me. I can't say any more than that."

She'd already ruled out the possibility of Hunter being an active agent in some federal or state agency because they were here together now on a private venture—her own mission. If he had been a P.I., he would have had a business card and there would have been no need for secrecy. The thought of a Navajo mafia seemed ludicrous, so all that left was the tribe. Did they have a secret agency? Whatever the case, not knowing about your partner could be dangerous, when bad guys involved in theft and murder were gunning for you. But she wouldn't ask him again. She'd have to find the answers on her own.

They arrived shortly afterward at a small wood-frame-and-stucco home, well maintained but quite ordinary looking. A four-wheel-drive SUV was parked on the east side of the house.

"We're going to be somebody's guests tonight? Who lives here?" she asked.

"No one will be home right now. But since you've asked about identities, there's something you really need to know about Navajos and the use of names. Navajo ways teach us that names have power, and to use them casually depletes that person of a source of power he can drawn on in an emergency. The modernists among us don't mind so much, but traditionalists do. Most of the time you'll know traditionalists by the way they dress, and especially how they act."

"Should I stop using your name? If so, what do I call you?"

"It's okay to use my name. I'm what our tribe refers to as a modernist. I'm more flexible in my cultural practices," he answered.

She nodded slowly, agreeing silently with his assessment of himself.

"No one should be here but us, but don't take anything for granted. Stay on your guard until we check out the place," he said.

"So the people who live here knew we were coming, and that's why they left? Why? Were they afraid we'd place them in danger?"

He paused, trying to come up with a cover story that would satisfy her without compromising what he was sworn to protect. "It's a safe house, available when necessary. We don't need to know who lives here."

"But how do you know it's safe, if you don't know who lives here?"

He closed his eyes, muttered something under his breath, then looked at her. "You ask too many questions. Let's go."

"What about the key? It can't be very safe if the door's been left unlocked."

"I know where to look for the key."

"You really play your cards close to your chest, don't you?" she mumbled, not expecting an answer.

"You're not exactly being open with me, either, Lisa. 'Need to know.' Isn't that what you said?" He held a finger to his lips, signaling her to grow silent, then led the way into the yard.

Hunter opened a metal gate in the field fencing that outlined perhaps an acre of land, then closed

it again once she'd followed him onto the property
The mistrust between them weighed heavily or
him. It had been a long time since he'd been witl
a woman he liked as much as Lisa. The spark
between them were real, and it seemed a shame t
smother that beneath a mountain of suspicion.

They reached the porch, and she waited as h
walked around the side to retrieve the key, whicl
was hidden beneath a rock. When he returned, h
saw her studying the carving on the upper right
hand side, feeling the design with her fingers in th
moonlight.

"There was one like this on your house. It's a
insignia of sorts, isn't it?"

"Navajo families are proud of their heritage," h
said, not really answering her.

"There's more to it than that."

"Stay close to the door while I go inside t
check things out," he said, not commenting. She'
already put too many things together.

Weapon in hand, he went through the hous
quickly. The layout of all their safe houses wa
known to him, so things went smoothly. Assure
there were no surprises waiting for them, h
returned to where Lisa waited. She'd turned he
back to the door, studying the land around then
wary of another ambush.

She was a good ally—observant, smart, and sh
possessed tactical skills that could come in hand

And, like him, she never quite lowered her guard. Under other circumstances they would have been good friends—and more. He would have seen to it. There was something about this woman that tugged at him. He *wanted* to protect her, it wasn't just a job. It had been that way from the moment he'd first laid eyes on her.

Hunter expelled his breath, exasperated with himself. *That* was what being near her did to him. It scrambled his thinking. "I need to go to the communications room," he said gruffly. "Why don't you see if you can figure out the riddle your father left for you? If it has a personal connection, I won't be able to help with that, and it has to be done."

Seconds later he closed the paneled door to the tiny com room, accessed in this house via the laundry closet. He took a seat in front of the computer, typed in his code word, then a password, and logged on. He needed information quickly. He already knew they wouldn't be able to stay here for long. They'd thrown their pursuers a curveball, but the enemy would regroup quickly. The roads were being watched, and once the ones after them realized they were still in the area, they'd check every house, including this one. At best, depending on how many men were actively involved in the search for them, Hunter figured he'd bought them half a day.

A second later, Hunter saw the answering

password appear on the screen before him. H
typed in a question. Who in Trujillo's outfit woul
have the know-how and contacts to trac
someone's cell phone?

There was no answer for a long moment, the
the typed response came on the screen. The answe
to that will require a face-to-face. Be ready. You'
know the signal.

What supplies are available at this location
Hunter typed next.

Everything you need is on the way. Focus o
your job, not your partner.

I know about priorities, he typed.

Yeah? What about Marilu?

He burst out laughing. Now he knew who wa
at the other end—his brother. Marilu had been
girl he'd been paired with to do a group projec
back in eighth grade, and he'd fallen head ove
heels in love with her. He'd almost failed U.S
history because he hadn't been able to think c
anything but Marilu.

Hunter chuckled softly. The truth was that he'
always been a one-woman man...at least on
woman at a time. His brother was the opposite. Win
had always found safety in numbers.

Stay focused, bro, Wind typed in.

His thoughts drifted for a moment to Ameli:
and he knew he could never allow his relationshi
with Lisa to grow into something more substantia

Unlike Amelia, Lisa knew how to fight and could be a deadly opponent, but she was a beautiful woman with the right to demand more than he had to give. She deserved better than a part-time lover who would eventually walk out on her. All he had to offer her, ultimately, was betrayal.

Watch your back. And wait for the signal.

I'll be around, Hunter typed in, then signed off.

LISA'S CONCENTRATION WAS TOTAL, her gaze on the words on the computer screen. The answers her father had left for her were there, but the more she twisted the riddle around, the less sense it made.

Minutes stretched out, but there was no blinding flash of understanding and revelation. She sat back, studying the words, hoping that an idea would come to her, but no matter how hard she tried, nothing came.

At long last, frustrated, she wandered around the room, needing a break. As it had been at the other house, there were no photos here. Homes were meant to echo the personalities of their owners. Color choices, furniture and even knickknacks often had much to say. But these safe houses whispered only secrets.

Wandering down the hall, she avoided the room she'd seen Hunter enter and continued looking around. One of the back bedrooms had been turned into a home library. The shelves were ceiling-high, totally filled with books of all sizes. Liking the cozy feel of the room, she went inside. Books somehow made this room feel friendlier and less impersonal.

She studied the titles, most of them hardcover nonfiction, and found collections on a variety of subjects, ranging from anthropology to physics. As she moved on to a section filled with historical volumes, she found one leather-bound work by a Navajo author, judging solely by the name. Lisa pulled it from the shelf and saw that it appeared to be the memoirs of a white woman who'd married a renowned medicine man.

Lisa went to the large chair beside a floor lamp and sat down to read. As she opened the book to the first page, a small sketch caught her eye. It was a replica of the carving she'd seen on the door of both safe houses.

According to the author, the insignia was said to be the recognition symbol of the legendary Brotherhood of Warriors. Stories about the warriors connected to the Council abounded, though no one had ever been able to separate fact from fiction, or rumor from reality.

It was said that the Brotherhood of Warriors were trained in all forms of combat. Only the best of the best could survive the rigorous physical and mental training they'd endured to become members of the Council. The warriors were said to acquire total control over their minds and bodies—a fact that made them exquisitely skilled lovers, able to not only give and take pleasure, but prolong it.

A shiver coursed up her spine. If there really was a Brotherhood of Warriors, she was sure Hunter was part of it.

Hunter came into the room just then, glanced down at the book she was holding, then gazed back into her eyes. "Find something interesting to read?"

"Very," she said, feeling her skin prickling with awareness. "Ever heard of the Brotherhood of Warriors?"

"Sure. I heard the stories while growing up."

She studied his face, searching for more of an answer, but short of the amusement in his eyes, he revealed nothing.

"It's an interesting legend," she said. "The members of their Council are said to be protectors of the tribe."

He nodded. "That fits the stories I heard."

"They were supposed to have all kinds of… interesting abilities," she added.

"Which one in particular caught your interest?" He brushed her face with his palm.

Her stomach fluttered as she felt the sparks his touch left in its wake. With effort, she tore her gaze from his and shut the book. "Never mind. I'm sure it's all fantasy. No one's *that* good." She put the book back where she'd found it and sighed.

Hearing it, he chuckled softly, the sound deep

and masculine. "Reality is far more interesting than fiction." He took her hand in his, then pulled her toward him.

Desire flickered between them, taking on a life of its own. Then an animal cried out in the darkness and as quickly as it had begun, the moment shattered. He moved closer to the window and stood perfectly still, listening but staying out of view from the outside.

Lisa tensed as she watched him, her own nerves on edge. But after several moments, he relaxed and, seeing it, so did she. "Life is also about choices," he said in a hard and determined voice, then moved across the room from her.

As she looked over at him, she realized that the fire she'd seen in his eyes had vanished…or had been brought under control.

"Have you learned anything new from the riddle your father left for you?" he asked.

"Not yet," she answered, getting back on track with effort. "The only thing I know for sure is that my father always had a plan. The fact that he left me a puzzle to solve makes me think that he suspected someone close to him would betray him. Someone who might also be able to get to the journal."

"Who?"

"I don't know. Maybe Paul Johnson can tell us."

He considered what she'd said. "Or maybe

Simon Moore or Arthur Duncan can," he said, then added, "No, nix that last one. I've known Arthur for many years. He's not a traitor."

"Simon Moore wasn't my father's friend, not as far as I know, and I don't think he knew enough about my father's plans to sell him out. Still, we were at the bank when you got jumped."

"What about your father's assistant?" he said after a pause.

"Happeth? She would have laid down *her* life for my dad's," Lisa said quietly. "I can't prove it, but I've always suspected she had a thing for him. She always went the extra mile—working late whenever he needed, even helping him duck a creditor or two."

"That makes her an even more plausible suspect. Rejection can make people do terrible things, especially when romance is involved."

"No, there was no relationship. My father would have never given her reason to hope."

"He was a man. Men appreciate the attention and often take advantage of an admirer. Be careful not to idealize him too much even if he was your father."

She shook her head. "No, you still don't get it. What I'm trying to tell you is that my father's mind was *always* on work. My mother learned to accept that over the years. Though I was his only daughter and always tried to get his attention,

I only managed to get close to him after we became business partners. Happeth never had a chance—except for seeing him at work."

Hunter took a deep breath as he weighed what she'd said. "Either way, your father's assistant is still an unknown. Don't trust her with any of the details of what we're doing."

"I'll be careful."

Hunter stood by the side of the window and looked out. He was wearing a dark, short-sleeved T-shirt, and Lisa could see the tension in his arms and shoulder muscles.

"Are you waiting for something?"

"We're going to be contacted—soon."

"By whom?"

"Friends."

She nodded. After a long moment, a thought occurred to her and Lisa added, "Does the Brotherhood of Warriors' symbol incorporate anything related to the number four?"

He gave her a surprised look. "First of all, they're legendary, so it stands to reason the sign is fiction and the product of imagination. But from what I've seen in books, the number four doesn't figure into it," he said, then after a pause continued. "Keep in mind your father's riddle was meant to lead *you* to something. He wouldn't have picked a topic you knew next to nothing about and only stumbled onto by chance."

"Good point," she admitted grudgingly. "But that riddle's making me nuts. The answer stays just out of my reach."

He forced himself to take a seat on the sofa. The signal would come at its own time. He could do nothing to rush things along. But he hated to wait. Although it was a contradiction of everything Navajo, patience wasn't something that came naturally to him.

Lisa glanced at Hunter, who'd lapsed into a long silence. "I never know what you're thinking," she said, stopping in mid-stride and giving him a long, speculative look.

"And that's what you want?" he asked, his voice a low rumble as he rose from the sofa and came toward her.

The intensity in his gaze and his purposeful stride made her back up a step, but she ran into the wall.

"Be careful what you wish for…" He pulled her into his arms and took her mouth, slowly at first, then hard and hungry. His kiss worked magic, seducing and demanding all at once. It was gentleness and passion, and promised so much more.

He took only what she surrendered freely, but the longings that spiraled through her made it almost impossible to hold on to reason. Her thinking became muddled as the fires that drove him swept through her defenses.

She heard nothing, saw nothing—but felt

everything—from his searing breath on her neck, to his hand as it slipped beneath her bra and teased her nipple.

Shivers ran up her spine. But it was too intense. She wasn't ready for this. She braced her arm on his chest, took an unsteady breath, then moved to one side.

Though he clearly hadn't wanted to stop, he let her go. Passion burned in his eyes. "Didn't anyone ever tell you that you shouldn't play with fire?"

It hadn't been a challenge…more like a warning. She was still trembling as she answered, "Lesson learned."

As she moved to the table they heard the shrill cry of a bird somewhere nearby.

Hunter's expression changed instantly. "That's the sign," he said.

"The what?" she asked dully.

"The cry of a hawk. Time for me to go meet someone."

As he moved toward the door, she reached for her purse. "I'm going with you."

"We'll be speaking in Navajo. You won't understand a word."

"You can translate for me."

"Not until later. The messenger will need to finish his business as quickly as possible, then leave."

"I'm still going," she said flatly.

The determination on her face told him it would

be a waste of time to try and argue with her about it. They left the house under the cover of darkness, and made their way to an area of higher ground about a hundred yards away, beneath some trees.

"Why didn't he just come to the house?" she asked, keeping up.

"From the proper vantage point we can check to see if he was followed. Inside the house we can't see anyone until they get close."

"What's to see out here? It's pitch-black now that the moon has set. An entire army could have tailed him."

"He'll have infrared binoculars with him, plus other equipment we might find handy."

"Like what?"

He held up one hand and signaled her to be quiet.

She listened, but the only thing she could hear was the drone of crickets.

"There. About fifty yards farther," he whispered with a satisfied grin.

Hunter was in his element out here, she suddenly realized. It was as if he and the land were one and the same.

A second man suddenly appeared from out of the shadows and joined them.

"*Yáat'ééh,*" Hunter said, greeting the other man with a nod.

From what she could tell in the half light, the other man was very close to Hunter's age, and there was a resemblance between them that she suspected transcended race. But it was the way they spoke to each other that really held her attention. The two men made eye contact, which Navajo strangers seldom did, and it appeared to be in the spirit of a good-natured challenge. Their conversation was fast, and the only words she caught were two names, Michael Barker and Paul Johnson.

When the talking stopped, the man handed Hunter a duffel bag and then their fists met, knuckle-to-knuckle in a male bonding type of acknowledgment.

Standing beside a juniper tree, she grew aware of the familiar tightening in her chest. Lisa turned away self-consciously, reached into her bag and took a puff from her inhaler. Then she concentrated on relaxing and breathing as deeply as possible. As second or two later she felt the constriction in her lungs ease. When she glanced back at the men, she saw that Hunter's companion was gone.

"I never heard him leave," she said.

"He's like that," Hunter said, then listened for a second. "We're okay. If he'd spotted any sign of danger as he moved off, he would have signaled."

"What's in the bag?"

"Let's get back to the safe house first," he said, then added, "Are you all right?"

"Sure, why?"

"You used your inhaler," he said, leading the way.

She shrugged. "I use my inhaler so I can stay fine."

"Could hiking though the woods, like we've been doing, end up sending you to the hospital?" he asked quickly, concerned.

"No. I *can* handle this. If I hadn't been sure of that, I wouldn't have come. I just have to take my meds, that's all. Asthma is only a limitation if you let it become that way."

"You'd better be right. I don't want anything to happen to you," he said gruffly, yet his expression was gentle. Looking at him now, she saw the other side of the warrior—the man who knew how to be tender.

Somewhere along the way they'd started to care for each other. Yet deep in her heart she knew they weren't right for each other. Hunter had too many other priorities and loyalties that would always come first. Secrets would always stand between them, an impenetrable wall.

When the day came that she gave her heart, it would be completely, and she wanted a man who'd do the same—a man who'd be willing to go into hell itself for her.

"What's troubling you?" he asked, reading her expression.

"Secrets…and my duty. I'm here to prove my father didn't steal the dagger. You're here to…" she said, then let the sentence hang.

"To honor my word."

They were inside the house again a few minutes later. He opened the duffel bag and extracted the pair of infrared binoculars the man had brought. There were also two pistols, clips of ammo, a topographical map of the area and a variety of shrink-wrapped meals, like the military MREs.

Hunter was about to zip it all back up, when something at the bottom caught his eye and he reached for it.

Lisa saw him pull out a cutout black-and-white photo, like one from a magazine or book. "Who's she?" Lisa asked, noting from the hairstyle that it dated back at least two decades.

He burst out laughing. "It's a joke. Her name is Marilu and I went to school with her when we were kids."

"And that's in there because…?"

"An inside joke," he said and shook his head. Next time he saw his brother he'd have to kick his butt.

Chapter Seven

"Our men lost them." The tall Navajo man's voice held no particular inflection.

"Whoever was in charge of that operation no longer works for me," he said. "Got that, Paul?"

"Understood." Paul Johnson remained perfectly still, his hands clasped in front of him. He could tell from the way Barker's knuckles had turned pearly white as he clutched the coffee mug that he was in a rage, and it wouldn't take much to set him off now.

"You've been with me for what, two years now?" Barker asked, pale green eyes that sliced through his subordinates now trained on him.

"About that, yes." He played the part of the inscrutable Indian to the hilt. To do or say anything that revealed his thoughts would only spell death.

"I want *you* in charge of the next operation. You won't let me down. Get me the papers and laptop the woman's been carrying. Then kill them both. They're too much trouble alive."

Paul Johnson said nothing for a long moment. "There's a better way," he said at last.

Barker glared at him.

Johnson didn't even flinch. "If you kill them, they're of no further use. We should bring them both in. I've studied Hunter Blueeyes. I know him like I know the back of my hand. I know which buttons to push. Given enough time, I can turn Blueeyes. He'll cave if we use the woman against him. Then he'll work for us."

"Why would he care what we do to her? He's just muscle she hired."

"To Blueeyes it's all about honor—there was a debt he owed the woman's father…there may be more between them now."

Barker's smile was lethal. "That's why I like you," he said. "Target the pair and bring them to me."

"They won't be easy marks. They may become… damaged in the process."

"And?"

Johnson nodded. "After we have them, do you want them brought here?"

"Yeah. And once they're of no further use to me, they die."

"Understood." At least he'd bought Hunter some time. The woman, too.

Hunter was skilled at evasion. He wouldn't be an easy mark. But his own experience was greater, and that would lead to their capture. After that, their futures, or lack thereof, would depend on his ability to persuade Hunter to play along. *Bá'óltáí,* the Council's teacher, didn't exist here, only Paul Johnson, and the Council needed him to remain under deep cover for a while longer.

HUNTER WANTED TO PUT LISA OFF. She had too much information already, but he couldn't fault her for refusing to be kept in the dark. If their situations had been reversed, he would have done the same.

"I want all the information your source gave you about Trujillo and his men. Quit stalling. We both need to know our enemies," she said, her voice cool and distant.

She was fire in his arms—and ice when he crossed her. He preferred the fire. "Here's what I've got," he said at last. "Their tactical leader—the man who calls the shots and gets his hands dirty so Trujillo doesn't have to—is Michael Barker. His second-in-command is Paul Johnson."

"I heard the names mentioned when you two were speaking Navajo," she said with a nod.

"Trujillo knows that tribal leaders will pay for the return of the obsidian dagger, so he wants to get his hands on it via Barker. He intends to sell it back for a fortune, or worst case, to the highest bidder. He's targeted you in hopes you'll lead him to it."

"I won't let that happen. But this tells us who was breathing down my father's neck. What I have to do now is prove it. Maybe if I use the dagger as bait in a sting that involves the police…"

He said nothing. She had her soul invested in this quest. If he ended up having to take the dagger back to the tribe before she could get the proof she needed and make its return public, he'd break her heart—and his own. The thought of betraying her twisted his gut.

"You can only do your best," Hunter said softly. "You don't have control over the outcome, not in something like this."

"I can't fail," she repeated firmly. "You, of all people, should understand that. You and I follow the same code—one where honor is more than just another word in the dictionary. That's what binds us both to this operation. You're here to repay a debt you owed my father. I'm in this to restore my father's reputation. There's no room for failure."

"I'm your ally, and I'm very good at what I do," he said, putting no particular emphasis on what he saw as a simple statement of fact. "If anyone can help you find that dagger, it's me. But there's something else you need to know. The stakes have gone up." He watched her as he delivered the last part of the message his brother had passed on to him. "Barker has a free hand, and he's given the order that we're to be brought to him. So, we'll have a bounty on our heads."

"I wanted to draw him to us, but this isn't quite

what I had in mind. I suppose he wants to beat any information I might have out of me?"

He shook his head slowly. It won't be that simple or direct. "Remember, he wants *both* of us. My guess is that he'll work me over to pressure you to cooperate and vice versa."

For the first time since they'd started, he saw fear in her eyes. She dropped down hard on the couch, but he wasn't sure if her knees had buckled or if she'd simply wanted to take a seat.

"Do you still want to continue?" he asked her softly. "Things have changed, and under the circumstances, there's no shame in bailing out. But be aware that you may remain Barker's target anyway. When Trujillo sends him after something, Barker doesn't stop until he's got it."

"I'm in, but if you want out, I'll understand. I'll find a way to do what has to be done on my own."

It took a beat for her words to sink in, and they stopped him cold. He stared at her, trying to decide what he wanted most—to throttle her or kiss her senseless. "You think I can't handle this?" he said, his voice low and challenging. Men twice his own size had backed down when he'd used that tone.

She looked at him directly. "I'm just trying to protect you."

Her simple words punched a hole right through him. No one in his entire life had ever said that to him. Knowing that this fragile lady with the strength of tempered steel wanted to keep him safe was almost his undoing.

"So what's your answer?"

"I'm in this for the duration," he managed through clenched teeth, pulling himself together. Nothing in his life had ever prepared him to deal with someone like Lisa.

"Good. I need you with me on this," she said.

Her eyes had filled with tears. She just looked at him as if he was the only man in the world who mattered to her. Truth was, he would have gladly crawled through fire to see that look in her eyes again.

EVEN AFTER AN HOUR HAD PASSED, she couldn't concentrate on the riddle. Her mind was still on the information they'd received. "The stakes are different now. They want war, so we're going to have to play dirty."

Hunter waited, wondering what she had in mind. As a security analyst, she'd made her career out of taking raw information and transforming that into workable plans. He'd learned to respect her intuitions and her ideas.

"We can't let them come after us on their own terms. We have to turn the tables on them by using a strong diversion—something that'll keep them occupied while we focus on gathering evidence and finding the dagger."

"What have you got in mind?"

"A plan much like my father's—only better," she said. "We'll need a very good replica of the dagger. One that can pass as the original, at least for a while. Do you know anyone with the skill to make one for us?"

Hunter considered it. "I know a man who can do that kind of quality work," he said after a moment. "It may even be the same person your father used. But first I want more details. What exactly do you have in mind?"

"We'll get a duplicate made—leaving the bezel in the grip empty where the diamond was set— making it look as if my father had removed it to sell. Then we'll have a tracking device inserted into it. When Barker's men catch up to us, we'll put up a good show of resistance, but allow them to take it from us. The idea is to make them believe we've managed to recover the original—but without the diamond—which they'll undoubtedly assume is in the hands of some unscrupulous jeweler. While they try to find out who has the diamond, we'll track them and compile a list and the locations of the players involved. It'll be a solid step toward finding out the real story behind the dagger's disappearance. It'll also buy us time to figure out the riddle and go after the real dagger."

"The replica won't fool them for long. Even if it's top-notch, we'll get only a few days respite. They'll come back after us."

"It may buy us more time than you think. I'm

betting they'll go to every fence they know searching for that diamond, and they may even begin to question the loyalty of their own people. We'll tie up their resources and, by the time they come after us again, we'll have had the chance to duck under their radar. They'll have a tough time figuring out where we went."

He considered it for some time and then nodded. "Okay. It's a risky plan, but right now everything we do—or don't do—carries a risk. Let's go for it."

HUNTER AND LISA SPENT MOST OF the night gathering information and preparing the type of specs a craftsman would need to make a copy of the dagger. John Garza's notes were helpful, but Hunter and Lisa had an additional advantage which was that few non-Navajos had ever seen the original dagger up close.

Shortly after dawn the following morning, they were ready to roll in the SUV that had been left at the house for them. Lisa studied the small carving on the upper right-hand side of the entrance while Hunter locked up. To all but the most observant, it would have passed as an imperfection in the wood, a knot. But now that she'd seen a detailed sketch of the Council's symbol, she knew it for what it was. The Council was the stuff of legends, but it was also real—as real as the man beside her.

Her heart skipped a beat, then went on double-time as she remembered the warrior's reputed love-making skills. From what she'd seen so far, she had a feeling the story might just be true. Curiosity tantalized her already active imagination, and she felt a spine-tingling shiver race through her.

"Are you cold?" he asked, having noted it.

She felt her cheeks burning. "No," she managed, miraculously keeping her voice steady.

Whenever Hunter looked at her, the intensity of his gaze felt like flames licking at her skin. She watched his hands fiddling with the stubborn lock, thought of how deft they were, and wondered how they'd feel on her bare skin.

As soon as the door was latched he glanced over at her, saw her looking at his hands, and graced her with his lazy, bad-boy smile. "Stay focused."

Realizing that somehow he'd guessed the direction her thoughts had taken, she straightened her back and forced herself to look directly at him. "I'm extremely focused."

"Yes, but on what?" Then he laughed.

She swallowed a sigh of sheer frustration, then cleared her throat. "Tell me about the man we're going to see," she said as they climbed into the SUV.

"He's a *bilagáana,* a white man, who lives just off the Rez. His name is Hal Taylor. He does the kind of quality work we're going to need. He looks like an ordinary 'good ole boy,' but don't underestimate him. He's as smart as they come. Everyone knows how he makes his money—pawning off fakes to museums and collectors—but he's never been arrested or sued. He's never even had charges filed against him because Taylor doesn't deal directly with anyone he doesn't know."

"Then how does he get his jobs?"

"Not the way we're going to go about this," he admitted.

"So what makes you think he'll see us?"

"Nothing's going to stop us. One way or another, we *will* see him."

It was a flat, ambitious statement, but she didn't doubt it for a moment.

The drive was long, heading east out of the foothills, but the desert at sunrise was beautiful. Everything the sun reached had the fresh glow of color that came from cool, clear air.

Although the landscape was often stark and vegetation in short supply, there was a different sort of beauty here. The wind- and water-sculpted mesas reflected all the colors of the rainbow. She watched a lone hawk soaring high above and cottontails sitting motionless, concealed from all but the sharpest eyes beneath the cover of gray-green sagebrush. Each creature was searching for breakfast in its own way.

"You're too quiet, Lisa. What's on your mind?"

"I was just watching nature taking its course," Lisa said. "I sure wish that one thing didn't have to die for another to live…that humans didn't have to compete against each other for their own survival in business, in life, like predators and prey."

"There's order and harmony in the circle of life," he answered softly. "Everyone and everything comes from Mother Earth and goes back to her someday so new life can spring from her again. Humans are included in that reality. Accepting that is how you learn to walk in beauty."

"I hate death," she answered in a barely audible voice.

He knew she was thinking of her father. "It's how you live your life that matters, but even death has a greater purpose. There's an old Navajo story that explains it better than anything else I've ever heard."

Lisa gave him an intrigued look. "Tell me more."

"It happened at the time of the beginning," Hunter said, his voice changing and growing distant as he remembered his mother's teachings. "The Hero Twins, two of the best known Navajo gods, walked the earth, fighting all the monsters that preyed upon man. The Twins thought they'd completed their task when they suddenly came across four strangers—Cold, Hunger, Poverty and Death. Cold, a shivering old woman, told the heroes that if they killed her, there'd be no snow and, consequently, no water in summer. The Twins decided to let her live and that's why we still have cold.

"Hunger, a wretched, skinny man, then introduced himself. He told the heroes that if they killed him, people would lose their appetites and there would be no more pleasure in feasting and eating. So our heroes let him live.

"Poverty was next. He was an old man in dirty rags. He told the twins to just go ahead and finish him off. He wanted to be put out of his misery. But he also warned them that once he died, old clothes would never wear out and people wouldn't bother making new ones. Everyone would be dirty, ragged and smelly, like him. The heroes thought it over and let him live.

"Finally they met Death. She was old, hunched over and frightening to look at. The heroes were sure that they should kill her, but she warned them to think twice. If she ceased to exist, old men wouldn't die and give up their places to a younger generation. As long as she continued to be, young men could still marry and have children who'd bring newness into the world. She claimed to be their friend, though they didn't realize it. They understood then that they'd have to let her live. That's why we still have death."

He paused for a long moment, then added, "Death finds everyone, good or bad, sooner or later. It's the legacy we leave behind that matters."

"My father loved his company. That's his legacy to me."

He shook his head. "The business may be what he left for you, but *you're* his legacy."

The truth behind his words wound its way to her

heart. "You're right," Lisa said, swallowing back her tears. "Your way of looking at things is...clearer than mine."

SILENCE STRETCHED OUT BETWEEN them as they traveled out of the reservation. The road continued on through the river valley, and in many places former farmland had been replaced with small housing developments and apartments. Here and there an alfalfa field or apple orchard remained, but it was clear that off the reservation, at least here to the east, population growth was overtaking agriculture. Farther west on the reservation, things moved much more slowly, and that was often a good thing.

Thinking about where they'd just been, and how much she still had to learn about the Navajo Nation, Lisa also realized how little she actually knew about Hunter. She shifted in her seat so she could face him. "Do you have family living on the Rez?"

There was a long pause before he finally answered her. "My parents have passed on. It's mostly just my brother and me now."

"So tell me about your brother. Is he older or younger?"

"Younger—by minutes. He's my fraternal twin," he said.

Twins? No matter how hard she tried she just couldn't even imagine anyone else like Hunter. "Are you two a lot alike?"

"Naw, he's real ugly," he said, laughing. "Actually, we're as opposite as two people can be. We've been described as Fire and Wind. Not a good combination, mind you, but both can get the job done in their own way." He paused and added, "You met my brother up on the hill."

"Our messenger," she said with a nod, remembering her impressions. "You're obviously the one described as Fire. He's Wind."

"Yes."

"Tell me more," she said eagerly.

"We respect each other, but there's always been a lot of good-natured competition between us. Otherwise, there's not that much to tell," he said, then added, "One Navajo never speaks for another."

"Okay, so let's concentrate on you. Tell me something about yourself, something not related to work."

He thought about it for a minute then continued. "The cougar and I are spiritual brothers. I carry a cougar fetish with me for protection. It allows me to draw power from the animal's essence. The spirit of the cougar is filled with single-minded purpose. A cougar knows what it wants and doesn't stop until he gets it." He brushed his knuckles against her cheek. "Your dad knew *exactly* what he was doing when he chose me."

His words sparked a thought that hadn't occurred to her until now. John Garza had never believed in leaving things to chance. Since he'd understood her better than anyone else, he'd probably known how Hunter would affect her. He'd always bemoaned the fact that she hadn't married. Had this been his way of playing matchmaker, even from the grave?

"Time to get creative," he muttered.

She looked over at him in surprise, then realized that he was talking about business.

"Up ahead is Taylor's house," he said.

He pulled over to the side of the road and parked. There were orchards on either side of a graveled road that led straight up a tree-covered lane toward a house several hundred yards away. A sturdy chain-link fence stood eight feet high around the property, and the lane was blocked by a reinforced metal gate supported by steel uprights. A control panel stood on the left side of the road, and there was a surveillance camera atop the unit.

Lisa recognized the security system as one their company had installed. "Taylor's using a system I'm very familiar with. He can see and hear anyone who pulls up, and unless you know the access code, the gate can't be opened. If he doesn't want to let us in, we're going to have to use other options."

"He won't invite us," he said flatly. "Taylor screens all his visitors."

"Then I'll access the panel and open the gate myself. There are ways of bypassing the access code in case of an emergency."

She stepped out of the car and walked over to the panel. It didn't matter that the owner could see her there. Taylor didn't know about the override, and there was nothing he could do without coming to the gate personally. Moments later, the gate swung open. "Drive through," she said jumping back into the car. "It'll close and latch again in twenty seconds."

Hunter stepped hard on the accelerator and went through.

"There are two more checkpoints. One's a laser beam that activates an interior alarm if a person or vehicle makes it past the gate without the access code being entered. There, up ahead," she said pointing to a device that looked like a water sprinkler attached to a garden hose.

They were halfway to the main house when they heard what sounded like a gunshot. Hunter swung the SUV to the left, pulling into a dirt track that paralleled an irrigation ditch. The rows of fruit trees blocked them from the view of anyone farther up the lane. "Grab the binoculars from under the seat."

He took the pair she handed him and climbed out of the car. "Slide behind the wheel in case of trouble. I'm going to take a look."

She did as he asked, then watched him in the rear and side mirrors as he moved back to the lane and aimed the binoculars toward the house.

Hunter returned moments later, getting in the passenger side. "Taylor has visitors. I recognized one of them, Evan Martinez. He's an ex-military sniper working with Barker."

"Are you telling me that the man we came to see is dead?"

Hearing a car engine approaching, he pushed her down behind the seat. "Duck!"

A few seconds later Lisa heard a car on the driveway racing past them, headed toward the highway. She turned and looked, but all that was visible was a cloud of dust.

"Stay in the vehicle," Hunter said, hurrying back out.

"No way. I'm going in with you."

She ran with him to the lane. A white car with a yellow New Mexico plate was already passing through the gate. Hunter raised the binoculars, but the vehicle, accelerating again in a cloud of dust, reached the highway and turned east, toward Farmington.

"Get the tag?" she asked hopefully.

"No."

They ran toward the modest, ranch-style home. It had plain, white stucco walls and a pitched roof, and was certainly not the residence of a rich man—or at least one who wanted to look well off.

The front door had been kicked open. It was a solid oak door, and from the boot marks, she guessed it had taken at least three kicks to break the wood around the lock. Hunter stepped inside, and she followed, regretting it almost instantly.

Straight ahead on the sand-colored vinyl floor, lay the body of a man, face up, an ever-expanding pool of blood around him. He'd taken a shotgun blast to the chest, judging from the size of the wound.

The memories of her father's lifeless body came flooding back to her. Blood. So much blood... She covered her mouth with one hand, turned and ran back outside. She was going to be sick.

Lisa stood for several moments with her back against the outside wall. It was the only way she could keep her head from spinning. Taking several deep breaths, she somehow managed to keep it together.

Still shaky, she came back inside a few minutes later. Hunter, crouched beside the body, looked back at her. "You okay?" he asked gently.

She nodded, not trusting her voice.

"I'm guessing Evan Martinez was ordered to get rid of someone who'd outlived his usefulness," he said.

"Wrong." An elderly man with faded blue eyes came out of the back room, shotgun in hand.

Hunter spun around in a crouch, pistol in hand, then relaxed and put away his weapon. "Taylor," Hunter greeted with a nod. "What happened here?"

"Barker sent his men here to work me over, looking for information, I guess. I can't handle being threatened, so I defended myself." He stood tall and resolute, his long gray hair tied back in a ponytail.

"What kind of information were they after?" Hunter pressed.

"They found out that I'd made the dagger John Garza handed over to the tribe and thought I might know where the real one was. They intended on getting it out of me—one way or another. But the truth is I have no idea what Garza did with the original. I never saw it. He gave me photos and specs to work with," he said, then began gathering his tools and tossing them into a small cloth satchel. "When I realized that they had no intention of leaving me alive, I decided to take at least one of them with me. So I fought back and won—for now."

Lisa was making a concerted effort not to look at the body, but the knowledge that it was there, not ten feet from her, was enough to give her the shakes.

"Sorry about the mess," Taylor said, glancing at her. "I don't much like dead bodies either, but it was either him or me. He got my vote."

She nodded, unable to say anything.

"I'm glad you're finally here. I've been expecting you. I met you when your company sold me the security system, Lisa."

Lisa nodded. "Now I recognize you. But you gave us a different name...."

"I do that sometimes," he said, continuing to pack up.

"You said you were expecting me?"

He nodded. "Your father commissioned me to make a gift for you."

"He never mentioned that to me," Lisa said.

He reached into the top shelf of the closet and brought out a small box. "Here, take this, and go quickly."

"What is it?" she asked, studying the package.

"Open it later. We don't have time for chitchat now," Taylor said. "I've got to get out of here, and so do you two. I doubt anyone around here will be calling the cops, but Barker's men will be back in full force. I'm going into hiding until things cool down."

"We were hoping that you could make another replica for us," Lisa said quickly.

"I won't be around my tools and supplies where I'm going, so you're going to have to find someone else."

"Could I have the photos and specs my father gave you of the dagger?" she asked, thinking fast.

Taylor nodded, then reached back into the closet's top shelf and extracted a manila envelope.

"Anything we can do to help you?" Hunter asked him.

He shook his head. "I handle my own affairs. But thanks."

Hunter hurried with Lisa back to the car. "We have to go. From what I know about Barker's men, Taylor's right. They'll be back in full force soon."

"But why would they come back here? If Taylor had the dagger he would have been long gone."

"They followed the same deduction process our people did, I'm sure," he said, jogging with her back to the SUV. "We knew that Hal was the only man with the skill to make a replica like the one used to trick the tribe. We'd figured that to make such an accurate replica, he must have had access to the original," he said, quickly getting into the SUV with her.

"We looked into every aspect of Hal's life back then—including his financial situation," he continued. "We found no leads there. Then we learned that your father didn't trust anyone completely. That was the cop in him. We came to the conclusion that Taylor never had the dagger in his possession. Nothing I found here today changes my opinion," he said looking around for any sign of Barker or his men.

She remained quiet for a moment as he pulled out from behind the shed and headed for the gate, which now stood open. Then she said, "You and I have to talk. I have some questions I need you to answer for me."

"Later. Right now we need to put some distance between us and this place."

MILES LATER, AWARE SHE HADN'T said a word, nor had she opened the box her father had left for her, Hunter finally pulled off the road and parked in a canyon. "Let's have it. What's on your mind?"

"I hired you on my father's recommendation. But you've been looking for the dagger, too, for someone else—maybe the Council?"

For a moment he simply stared at her. The woman could read him well, but this took him by surprise.

"When you explained why Trujillo sent Barker and his men after Taylor, you kept referring to yourself in the plural—'we' not 'me.' And certainly never you and I—us."

Lisa was too smart, and now Hunter realized his own words had come back to haunt him. He'd been concentrating on Barker and the danger, not on anything else, and he'd given away too much. It was damage-control time.

"When I said 'we,' I meant my tribe. That dagger means a great deal to us as a people. The *bilagáana* police working with our tribal police questioned Taylor. I know the details because I'm well connected, not because it was public knowledge. At the beginning they suspected that Taylor knew exactly what had happened to the dagger—that either your father had given it to him for safekeeping, or that he had a good idea what had happened to it."

"So what happened?"

"Taylor had evidence that supported his claim that he'd never been in possession of the dagger. The detailed photos and specifications he had to work with wouldn't have been necessary if he'd had access to the original."

What Hunter couldn't tell Lisa was that the proof had come as a result of an operation run by the Brotherhood of Warriors. They'd seen the photos that backed up Taylor's story, and had done a clandestine search of Taylor's home and studio.

"So that's why you didn't waste our time by coming here sooner. But instinct tells me there's something else you're not saying."

He paused for a long moment before continuing. "Judge me by my actions. From day one, I've done my best to help you accomplish what you've set out to do."

She nodded slowly. "All right. I'll accept your answer for now."

He wasn't sure how it happened or even when, but this woman made him feel things he hadn't even thought about since Amelia had died. And even with Amelia it had never been this…intense. He'd never even made love to Lisa, yet he already found himself trying not to give her a diluted version of the truth. Gut feelings like these could jeopardize the work he'd sworn to do for the Council.

As he glanced at her, he saw Lisa staring at the simple cardboard box, reluctant to even touch it.

"You have to open it," he said softly. "Your father had that made for you for a reason. Maybe it has something to do with where he hid the dagger."

"Or it might just be a gift."

Hunter watched her carefully. "But you don't believe that," he added, reading her tone.

She shook her head. "If this *is* a clue, then my

father already knew his life was on the line when he chose Taylor to craft it for me. What's really tearing me up is that my dad didn't ask anyone for help— that he didn't ask *me,*" she added, her voice trembling.

Hunter said nothing for a long moment. "Any man who is a man protects his family. Every instinct your father had would have told him to keep you out of what was happening and out of harm's way."

"I was his *partner,* not just his daughter," she protested.

"He loved you and that drove him to protect you, even at the cost of his own life," he said, remembering Amelia. "You mean that much to him. Focus on that."

His words touched her, and she brushed a tear from her cheek.

At long last Lisa opened the box, then gingerly reached for something nestled inside, wrapped in tissue paper. As she pulled the paper away she found a circular metallic case made of silver. She pressed the latch, and the lid opened.

"A compass?" Hunter noted, surprised.

"Sort of. It doesn't list the four points. Instead, in the direction for north it says 'strong body.' The other cardinal points read 'clear mind,' 'pure spirit' and 'devotion to family.'"

"What's it mean?"

"The combination sounds vaguely familiar. I've heard those before. And there's four of them…."

she noted. "Remember, the riddle mentioned the sign of four."

"Those clues are meant for you. *You're* the key," he insisted quietly. "We're on the right track."

As she turned the silver case over, she found an engraving in the back. "There's more," she said in a shaky voice and read what was there. "In The Absence Of Sun—Only Regrets."

"What does that mean?" he asked.

She thought about it for a long time before finally answering. "It could mean that he knew he was going to die and regretted things left undone," she answered in a strangled voice, fighting back tears.

Hunter tried to comfort her by taking her in his arms, but she pushed away. "No. We have to keep moving. We're targets now, and when my sunset comes, I don't want it to be filled with regrets." Her fierce desire to protect Hunter made her understand her father's actions even more, and she knew without a shadow of a doubt now that he hadn't killed himself. "Men aren't the only ones programmed to protect those they care about."

"I know." He didn't deserve her loyalty, and that knowledge was slowing blasting a hole through his gut.

She took a deep breath. "So, what's next?" she asked, in a faraway voice. "I'm out of ideas at the moment."

"There's another craftsman capable of creating a credible replica dagger," he said slowly. "I met him once. He's not well known, but I've heard he's even better than Hal—and honest. He does legitimate work for museums looking for good replicas they can display to the public. The problem is he's not for hire. He only takes on work that interests him."

"Leave it to me. I'll find a way to make this appeal to him," she said flatly.

Chapter Eight

Hunter made several phone calls on his cell phone, then considered his options carefully. He'd met *Hastiin Nééz*, "tall man" in Navajo, when he'd been working on another assignment for the Council. But that had been years ago. Independent spirits like *Hastiin Nééz* moved around as often as the mood struck them.

"I can go to the address I got from one of my sources, but it dates back a bit, so the chances he'll still be living there are slim," he said.

"What other choice do we have? We'll start at his last known address and work from there."

Soon they were on their way, headed west again toward the reservation. "Your father meant for you to solve the riddle he left you, and I'm sure you will, one way or the other. But I was wondering if maybe your mother could help speed up the process?"

Lisa shook her head. "Mom never wanted anything to do with Dad's work, and they never talked about it, at least when I was around. The only one who might know something is Happeth. Your phone is untraceable, so I could give it a shot. To minimize the risk I could keep it simple and ask her only one question—if she knows what Dad might have meant when he mentioned the sign of four."

"That should be okay. Even if she's working for Barker, she doesn't have your father's journal and the other clues." He handed her his cell phone. "Go for it."

Lisa made the call, and Happeth answered on the second ring.

After the customary niceties, Lisa got down to business. "Happeth, does the sign of four mean anything to you—or more to the point, to Dad?"

"A story by Sir Arthur Conan Doyle? Something with Sherlock Holmes?"

"No, besides that. Dad stopped reading Sherlock Holmes when Holmes picked up that cocaine habit."

"Your father did seem fixed on the number four lately," she said after a brief pause. "It was part of the doodling I found on his memo pads and desk calendar—four lines, the Roman numeral four, the number four. But that's all I can tell you."

"Thanks. If you happen to find anything else in his files or around the office that might give us a clue, give me a call."

"Have you made any progress?" Happeth asked.

"It's going slowly," Lisa answered vaguely.

"The office is very, very quiet these days," Happeth commented. "I've been making cold calls, but so far have only come across a few retail businesses wanting help catching shoplifters who've managed to elude their own security. Bruce is taking care of those jobs. I'm coming in late these days. I hope you don't mind."

"Happeth, you shouldn't be coming in at all," she said, feeling guilty about doubting her. Loyalty like hers was hard to find. "Go to a half-day schedule. Unless I manage to clear Dad's name, truth is, the company doesn't have a chance."

There was a long silence at the other end, then Happeth spoke. "Elena called wanting to know if I could help her. It seems her credit card was denied. I checked the business accounts to see if I could help her pay the overdue bills from this end, but the balance on hand is just enough to pay next month's rent and utilities."

The news worried her, knowing that it was just the beginning of worse times ahead. Her mother never wasted money. She'd come from a poor family and had always been careful with every cent.

After saying goodbye to Happeth, Lisa sat back in the seat, trying to figure out how to proceed.

"More bad news?" he asked quietly.

She nodded, and explained. "I have no idea what's going on."

"If you need money, I've got some set aside—"

She held up her hand and shook her head.

"Thanks for the offer. I appreciate it, but Dad had money in an emergency savings account for times like these. I just need to talk to my mom in private."

"I'll pull over." He continued a half mile farther to a rest stop, then pulled off the road and parked. Hunter got out, leaving her in the vehicle. "I'll stretch my legs. Take your time."

Lisa called home and got through to her mother quickly. From the strained tone of Elena's voice, she suspected her mother had been crying.

"Mom, what's going on?" she asked quickly. "Are you okay?"

Elena Garza cleared her throat. "I'm just a bit moody. It's the house. It's too quiet and too empty. I'm thinking of putting it on the market and buying something smaller, maybe south near Los Lunas."

"Mom, I just spoke to Happeth. She mentioned that your charge card was turned down. What's going on?"

"Your father normally paid the bills, you know that. But he must have missed some payments last month. Funds are very low because he made a substantial cash withdrawal just before he left for the reservation. Do you have any idea why?"

The replica. She'd suspected it hadn't come cheap. Now she knew for sure. "I think it had to do with his last job for the tribe, Mom. But Dad had several accounts. And there's my checking account. If you need cash…"

"No, I was able to get everything straightened

out for now. I transferred funds from our savings into my checking. But the life insurance company won't pay because the police report listed his death a suicide. At this rate, Lisa, I'll only be able to hold on to the house for a few more months. If I sell it, will you be okay with that?"

"Mom, it's *your* home. If you want to sell it, go right ahead. But be careful. You're still reeling from everything that's happened. Talk to some Realtors who come recommended by someone you trust, but don't make any irrevocable decisions right now."

Lisa placed the phone on her lap and tried to get her thoughts organized. The business account for Rio Grande Security Services was nearly depleted. Her mom's attorney had filed an appeal with the life insurance company, but that had been denied, apparently. The funeral costs had also been astronomical, despite help from local police officers her father had served with.

Her own savings were being slowly depleted as well, and having another replica made would cost some serious money. It would probably take the remaining balance in her account. But she had no other choice. She had to fight.

She motioned to Hunter, who was standing some distance away. As he slipped behind the wheel again, he immediately asked, "Is your mother all right?"

"Yes, for now," she said calmly. Pride wouldn't let her admit to anything more. She knew Bruce would remain as long as possible, even if her cash ran out, but the situation was at near crisis level, and it was clear everything would come right down to the wire. "I've got to prove Dad wasn't a thief and that he didn't commit suicide. Everything depends on my ability to see this through."

They'd driven about ten miles when a gold sedan behind them caught her attention. They couldn't go straight to *Hastiin Nééz*'s now.

"Speed up," she said.

He pressed on the accelerator and the SUV responded. The sedan, too, picked up speed, keeping pace.

"What's up?" he asked.

"We're being tailed."

He glanced in the rearview mirror. "The gold sedan? But how could they have found us?"

"Several cars drove past when we were parked at the rest stop, and this vehicle was probably seen at Taylor's home. Maybe one of Barker's men got lucky," she answered, not really believing it. "There's *no way* to track your phone, you're sure?" she added.

"Absolutely," he answered, wracking his brains, trying to figure out how they'd given themselves away.

Hunter turned down a side road and picked up speed. Moments later, as he watched, the sedan shot down the main road, never giving them a second glance.

"I think we're just getting jumpy," he muttered, disgusted.

They continued on, stopping for gas in the town of Shiprock, the largest reservation community in the area.

Ten minutes later, northwest of town, Lisa checked her side mirror. "That gold car is back. Maybe there was another vehicle watching Taylor's house, planning on picking him up in case he took off before the other got there. That lookout could have seen us coming—and going—and could have stayed with us."

"We're both trained to spot a tail. That gold car wasn't back there. Something else is at play."

He noticed an old farm road ahead, braked quickly, then cut hard to the right, sliding into the turn and racing up a dirt track. The sedan tried to follow, but fell back and soon faded from view as they crossed narrow, sandy washes and exposed sandstone outcroppings. "Bet he's high centered a few times already, or maybe gotten stuck in that first wash," he said with a satisfied grin.

He found a low area that had been a marsh during wetter times, and drove in that direction. They were invisible from the highway at this point. After going several miles back in the opposite direction, Hunter finally encountered a well traveled graveled lane and took it back to the highway.

Less than fifteen minutes later they spotted another vehicle behind them. This time it was a red pickup.

Hunter tensed up, his senses immediately alert. "He's pacing us, holding back so we can't do anything sudden. But there aren't many late model, expensive pickups like that one on the Rez, so it sticks out. That truck's got to be loaded with everything. See the antennae sticking up out the top? You could probably contact Mars on that thing."

"They've made our SUV, then, and have lookouts watching the highway. We've got to switch vehicles as soon as we can," she answered. "Our highway options are limited."

"Well, first things first. We need to ditch our tail. Grab your stuff."

She checked her bag, made sure the laptop and the compass were still inside, then glanced at him. "Set. What comes next?"

"I know this area like the back of my hand. My uncle has a farm about ten miles northwest of here, bordering the river. Eventually, we'll head there, but we can't lead whoever's behind us to him."

"That truck's got a big engine, good ground clearance, and four-wheel drive on that thing for sure. I don't see how we're going to be able to shake him unless he runs out of gas. But you'll manage it, I'm sure," she said without any uncertainty whatsoever.

The grin he gave her was filled with confidence and male pride. "Count on it."

Like the cougar, he had that intense look about

him now that left no room for doubt. Instinct told her that she'd never been in better hands.

Ahead was a sign that read Rattlesnake Field, and she could see a narrow paved road leading off to the left.

"Coming up is the old Rattlesnake oil field turnoff. I've been down that road a hundred times and that's where we're going now," he said, his voice hard and filled with determination.

Again he turned quickly without signaling, and once they were out of sight for a moment, he left the road and headed down an arroyo. It was impossible to see their pursuer, but that also meant they were hidden. After several minutes he shot out of the arroyo, roared up a hill, then came out on the Rattlesnake road again. The red truck was still behind them, a few hundred yards back.

"How could he know I wouldn't double back? This one reads my mind," Hunter growled.

She remained still, listening, then leaned forward and looked upward out the windshield. "No, he's no mind reader. He's got high-tech help. See it?" she asked, pointing to the sky.

He glanced up. "What?"

"The small plane—one of those remote models not much bigger than a kite. It's like one of those Predators the military and CIA has, only smaller. He's been using it to track us. Bet he's got one of those hobby shop radio links, too. If we had a multi-band transmitter, we could probably jam the thing and make it crash."

"It would take a machine gun to shoot the thing down. Any ideas on how to get rid of it?"

"Yeah," she said after a second. "There's a thunderstorm brewing just ahead. If you go into that, the plane will probably get some serious radio interference. That's if the wind doesn't shear off its wings first. But they'll still be able to follow us in that truck as long as they maintain a visual."

Hunter continued west, looking for a side road or route that would take them toward the dark clouds forming on this side of the mountains.

They crossed a gap in the ridge, and once they could see the route more clearly, Hunter broke his silence. "I've got a plan."

A one-lane bridge was ahead, crossing a wide, deep arroyo, and beyond the bridge on the far side was a sheepherder standing beside his horse. The youngster, wearing a baseball cap, was watching his sheep, which were scattered along the road beyond, feeding on plants that had grown larger because of the runoff from the road.

"How good are you on a horse?" he asked her.

All kinds of adjectives popped instantly in her mind—lousy, dismal, hopeless. Instead she forced a smile. "It's been a while, but I can stay on."

"Good."

Once they reached the bridge he slowed quickly, then braked hard, turning as they came to a stop.

The SUV blocked their end of the bridge perfectly, at least for any vehicle larger than a bicycle.

"Grab your things and get going," he said. "I'm disabling the truck. I'll be right behind you."

Hunter brought out his knife, jabbed all four tires, then popped the hood. Seeing that she was still there, he yelled, "Go! I'll catch up."

She started running, actually it was more of a jog, a pace she could maintain for a short distance, then turned to look. Hunter was ripping out wires by the handful.

She focused on the far side of the bridge where the young man on horseback was watching them curiously.

"Keep going," Hunter said, catching up to her. He still had several wires in his hand. "Let's get off the bridge, then stay as low as possible."

He tossed the wires down into the arroyo as they reached the far side of the bridge. "Stay out of sight just in case they get stupid and start shooting."

As he'd hoped, the ones after them stayed back, trying to figure out how to move the big SUV. Above he could hear a faint noise, more of a buzz, coming from the engine of the small airplane above them. It had a wingspan of perhaps eight feet, and he wondered how long it could stay up.

Hunter hurried toward the Navajo, who'd let go of the reins of his horse. The animal had started to graze immediately.

"*Yáat'ééh,*" Hunter called in greeting. Lisa was

close behind him, nearly out of breath by now, judging from her pace.

The young man beside the horse nodded to them, but said nothing. Hunter could see a rifle propped upright in a bush not three feet from the herder.

Aware of how things must have looked to him, Hunter reached into his back pocket and brought out all the cash he had—around one hundred dollars. "We need to ditch those men in the red truck. Can I borrow your horse?"

The young man looked at the bills and shook his head. "My horse is worth a lot more than that."

"We'll make sure you get it back in good health," Hunter said, looking back across the bridge.

Lisa saw what Hunter was looking at. The men over there were hooking up a rope or chain to the SUV. If they managed to tow it out of the way…

Lisa took off her watch. "This is worth quite a bit. It's gold," she said, showing it to him and noting silently that he didn't have a saddle on the animal.

That changed things. She prayed that if he did loan them the horse, she'd be able to stay on.

"My clan is *k'aahanáanii*," Hunter said, referring to his mother's people, the living arrow clan, "and I was born for *haltsooí dine'é,* the meadow people."

The shepherd nodded. "You aren't my kinsman, but my future wife is related to your born-for clan.

You can borrow my horse, but I'll need him back. Where do you want to go?"

"We need to get rid of that pesky crow," Hunter said, pointing to the circling aircraft. "So we want to ride into the storm," Hunter answered, wishing he didn't have to answer.

The young Navajo man nodded slowly. "Smart idea. Dodger is a good, steady horse. He doesn't mind rain. He sees it in the same light we do—a rare blessing. He's okay with lightning and thunder, too. But the winds…well, that's how he got his name. They frighten him."

He stepped over to the horse, slid off the saddle blanket, then grabbed the reins and handed them to Hunter. "When you're finished, will you bring him back? I live over there in the green house," he said, gesturing Navajo-style with his lips.

"I'll make sure he's brought back to you. And we'll take good care of him," Hunter added.

Hunter jumped on and held out his hand to Lisa.

She hesitated. "I'm used to a saddle, actually."

"Okay, we'll improvise," he said and jumped off. "You'll ride in front of me. Hold on to the mane, and I'll hold on to you." He lifted her up onto Dodger, then in one smooth motion got on behind her.

"You might want to head home with your sheep," Hunter advised. "You don't want to run into those men."

"I shoot wild dogs who bother my sheep, even

dogs with two legs," the young man said. Then he grinned widely.

Hunter nodded.

Lisa never heard him click or give the horse any cues but, a heartbeat later, they went racing into the storm.

Chapter Nine

Grateful that the animal had a very long mane, Lisa hung on, her legs wrapped tightly around the horse.

The animal and Hunter worked like a team. When Hunter exerted pressure with his leg, the animal would head in a different direction without any cues from the reins.

"This horse is smooth. But that surveillance plane is still tracking us," he said.

"It can't stay with us much longer. You can feel the wind already picking up. What I'm worried about is Dodger here. Will he be able to handle it without bucking or going berserk?"

The gelding tossed his head, his ears standing up tall and alert with excitement. Hunter eased up on the reins. "Just hang on to his mane, and don't squeeze him too tight with your legs. He might mistake that as a signal to gallop."

"Make sure you hang onto me," she said, her voice a little shaky.

Hunter's arms steadied her on both sides, and the heat from his body ribboned around her. Though the dust swirled around them, and the downdrafts of the thunderstorm whistled like an approaching tornado, she felt protected inside the circle of his arms. He pressed against her from behind, and she felt the impact of that intimacy all through her. Her senses achingly alert, she was aware of everything—from the wildness and power of the horse beneath them, to the raw strength and courage of the man who'd taken charge of it.

Rain began to fall, big cold drops at first, then a sudden burst in intensity, beating against their skin. Hunter slowed the horse, then stopped beside a trio of pine trees, allowing the animal to put his back to the downfall, which was coming in at a steep angle from the direction of the storm.

"Cold," she muttered as the rain pelted their backs.

"Any rain feels good on the Rez." Hunter pulled her against his chest, sheltering her from the downfall. The gesture was warm and welcome for more than one reason.

There wasn't really that much rain, not in a thunderstorm so small, and within the storm itself the air was nearly still. Lisa looked back in the direction they'd come and saw the fragile airplane being buffeted by the leading edge of the storm. Whoever was guiding the aircraft by remote control was obviously losing control. The craft, facing into the wind, was nearly motionless relative to the ground for a few seconds. Then both wings sheared off at the body, fluttering away like runaway kites. The fuselage nose-dived, spinning down, out of control. It crashed behind some trees a few hundred yards away.

"Finally," he said. "Even if they have a backup drone, they can't launch it now. Let's ride out the back side of this storm."

The rain was already dwindling, and five minutes later stopped completely as Hunter led the horse toward the west, perpendicular to the current prevailing winds. The sun reappeared, and they began to quickly dry off.

"All that wind and thunder, yet so very little water actually made it to the ground," she commented. "New Mexico is famous for this," she said, patting the horse's neck.

"We need to make it to my uncle's place—my mother's brother. It's just a few miles from here."

They rode at a more leisurely pace now that they were out of danger, but having time to think made it worse. Hunter's nearness had heightened her desire. Adults seldom got everything they wanted. She knew better than to indulge in too many fantasies. Yet whenever he shifted and his thighs pressed against her, her stomach would flutter and a thrill would rush through her.

They reached Hunter's uncle's place thirty minutes later. Nobody seemed to be at home. The tiny wood frame house was locked up and the horse stall was empty. "The truck and the horse trailer are gone, so my guess is that they've gone off into the mountains, maybe to gather piñon nuts. It's a good year for them, so I've heard."

"What do we do now? We'll need a vehicle of some sort," she said as he helped her off the horse. "They'll find us eventually if we can't get out of the area."

He knew what he had to do—get in touch with the Council. They'd send another vehicle in no time at all. "For now, we'll stay put. My uncle never locks the back window because he's in the habit of losing his keys, so I'll climb in that way, then open the back door for you. Once I make a few calls we'll be on our way again. But first, I need to brush off the horse so he cools down and give him something to drink. My uncle usually has some sweet feed too, and I'll give Dodger some of that for quick energy."

"Okay. I'll help you get him settled."

After taking care of the horse, they went to the house. Once they were both inside, Lisa went in search of something for them to drink, and Hunter went into his uncle's office. There was no computer there, and no telephone line, but Hunter had his own cell phone and quickly dialed the emergency number. *Hastiin Sání* answered.

Hunter briefed him quickly, then added, "We need another vehicle and some cash. Also, we have a borrowed horse that needs to be returned. I'll need to know where I can find *Hastiin Nééz,* too."

"Expect someone within the hour," he said.

Hunter closed up his cell phone, then set it up to recharge. At least there was electricity here, a luxury absent from too many Navajo homes. He was lost in thought when Lisa knocked lightly on the open door and came in. "I found some soft drinks in the refrigerator," she said, handing him one.

He took the cola, glad for anything to moisten his parched throat. "Are you holding up okay?"

"I expect I'll be sore tomorrow, but I'm fine."

Hunter noticed how she kept her distance from him. He didn't blame her. What was happening between them went against all reason. All through-out that infernal ride, he'd felt her softness pressing against him and it had practically driven him crazy. The desire to have her, especially after she'd pressed up against him during the rain, was still blasting through him. He'd have traded ten years of his life for some mindless, crazy, hot sex with no strings attached. He was capable of that...but not with her. Everything with Lisa Garza was different.

"We'll be going to see the man you mentioned, *Hastiin Nééz,* next?" she asked.

"After we have a vehicle delivered. That's the plan. And if we do strike a deal, remember not to offer to shake hands. Traditionalists don't like to shake hands with strangers."

"Who's delivering all this to us?"

"I have friends on the Rez," he said. "That's how things get done here."

Forty-five minutes later, as he watched from the front room, two pickups, one with a horse trailer, came driving up. A woman was behind the wheel of the first truck, a man in the second. He recognized neither, and that made him uneasy.

"Problems?" she asked, sensing his mood.

"Not necessarily, but I don't know either of these people. Wait here, and stay out of sight."

"Why?"

"I'm a Navajo in the Diné Bekayah, Navajo land. You're an Anglo, and you're more likely to be noticed and remembered. Do I need to remind you that there are people looking for a Navajo man and a white woman?"

"Oh my, yes. How could I have forgotten about that," she said sarcastically.

"You handle yourself well in a fight, but I'd rather avoid one—or flagging our location."

"I'll stay here, then, out of sight."

"Isn't this where we began?"

Lisa made a face at him and he laughed. "I'll be back in a minute. If you see me run into trouble, try to steal the truck without the horse trailer while I keep them busy."

From behind the curtain she watched Hunter as he approached the Navajo couple. It didn't take her long to decide that they were the ones he'd expected.

The Navajo woman had beautiful almond-shaped eyes, and ebony hair that draped down past her waist. The man was of medium height with gray at the temples.

Lisa struggled to listen, but she didn't speak Navajo, so the conversation was lost on her. Hunter gestured with his head toward the horse in the stall, and the woman nodded.

The man, a fit-looking Navajo wearing jeans and a cowboy hat, handed Hunter a thick manila envelope. They argued about something briefly, then the man walked away, headed for the horse stalls. The woman joined him.

Hunter came in a moment later. "They'll return the horse for us. You and I are leaving right now."

She wasted no time getting her tote bag. "Did they happen to see anyone keeping watch on the roads or hanging around the area when they drove over here?" she said, meeting him by the door.

"No. I asked them that right away. But I think Barker's men are still out there. We'll have to take the back roads and avoid the major highways."

HUNTER KEPT HIS EYES ON THE stretch ahead. Avoiding the roads meant using dirt trails or in some cases going cross-country, but their truck was well equipped for the rough ride.

"What were you arguing about?" she asked.

Hunter hesitated. It had been Council business. He'd been asked—or more accurately ordered—to make a copy of the material she'd uploaded into her laptop from her father's journal, and also copy down the message on the compass. The Council would study the information and hopefully come up with a lead he could follow. He'd argued that a move like that would jeopardize the trust between them and blow the partnership if he were discovered. Yet, despite his protest, the Council's orders had been clear, and stood.

"Did you hear me?" she asked.

"Yes, I was just thinking of something else. Sorry. We weren't arguing. He just wanted to make it clear that he's renting me the truck, not just letting me use it," he said. That much was true.

"And he wanted payment in advance?"

"No, actually he brought *me* some cash. His, which is why he was insisting on getting it back with interest."

"Is this person a friend of yours?"

"In a way, but if anything happens to this truck, there'll be hell to pay. He's still making payments on it."

"I've noticed that you're not exactly gentle on your vehicles," she said with a tiny smile. "I don't blame him for worrying."

He nodded absently. "At least I've got *Hastiin Nééz*'s current address. By all accounts he's living in a house just off the reservation near the Hogback. The man doesn't like company and doesn't answer the door when he's working on a project, but I'm pretty sure I can get us in. A friend has cleared the way. But what happens after that is anyone's guess."

"Tell me everything you can about him. If you get us inside, I'll find a way to get him to accept the job."

THEY ARRIVED AT *HASTIIN NÉÉZ*'s place over an hour later, having had to take a route that passed north of Shiprock and down mostly oil and gas wells' service roads. Hunter parked beside a large, well-used Ford pickup with a big camper shell over the bed. The house was a very modern-looking structure with tall, wall-high windows. They could see someone inside, moving around.

Hunter turned off the engine and leaned back in the seat.

"What's going on? Someone's inside. All of a sudden we're too shy to go up and knock on the door?" she asked, eager to get started.

"Navajos consider that rude, even those who live in fancy houses instead of log hogans. We'll wait. When he consents to see us, he'll step to the front door and invite us in. He knows we're here and he's expecting me so it shouldn't take long. Once we're inside, don't stare or make direct eye contact. Some Navajos see that as confrontational."

She'd known about that last cultural practice, but not about waiting to be acknowledged before going to the front door. Of course, she'd never gone visiting at a Navajo Nation home before.

Lisa had done many difficult things in her life, but

waiting endlessly was among the hardest. Growing impatient, she shifted in her seat. "We're in a time crunch. Maybe I can go up—"

"No. Sit tight. Trust me, he's testing us."

An eternity passed and finally *Hastiin Nééz* appeared. *Hastiin Nééz,* "tall man" in English, lived up to his nickname. He was over six feet tall, which was rare for a Navajo, and had large biceps and goal posts for shoulders.

His furnishings were modest, and the large living room had been converted into a workshop with two heavy wooden tables and sturdy wooden boxes of tools against the wall. There were ceiling-high windows on two sides flanked by travertine *bancos*—built-in benches of locally cut stone. Light from outside, as well as the recessed lights inside, bathed the room in a soft glow.

"What can I do for you?" he asked, not looking directly at either of them, just as Hunter had predicted.

"I asked my friend to bring me to you," Lisa said, also remembering not to use Hunter's name out of respect for Navajo customs. "I would like to commission you to do some work for me."

"Not interested. I already have plenty of work," came the instant answer. He went to the workbench, turned on a small propane torch and, using tongs, began to heat a metal coin.

She'd been prepared for this. Hunter had already told her that *Hastiin Nééz* was a free spirit who liked changes in his routine. Also from what Hunter had said, it was clear he liked to take on difficult pieces that would test his skills.

"I understand," she said with a mock sigh. "You must have already heard what we want…. Considering the precision work that will be needed for this piece…well, I can see why you'd back away. You making a button, huh?" She looked casually over at his work.

He turned off the torch then, and just waited, looking down at his workbench.

She'd taken a risk, trivializing whatever project he was working on, but she had his interest now. What she did or said during the next few minutes would determine if she succeeded or failed.

So Lisa waited.

He waited.

Silence stretched out.

Finally the old artist cleared his throat. "Woman, I don't have all day. What's this work you've come to offer me?"

She took the photos of the dagger out of the envelope in her purse and handed them to him. "I hope you can work with obsidian. We need a replica of this to use as bait against some dangerous men."

He studied the photos of the dagger for a moment. "*Now* I know who you are." He said nothing for several minutes, but Hunter signaled for her not to interrupt the silence. So Lisa waited, and waited.

He glanced at Hunter. "You hope to find *Hash-kéts'ósí* and return it to our tribe?"

"That's the plan." Hunter had a feeling that *Hastiin Nééz* already knew about the Council, and more important, about his association to it.

"And you're hoping to use the copy to get someone off your back…so others must be after the real dagger, too," he said at long last.

It wasn't a question, but she verified it for him. "That's all correct," she admitted. "But the men we're hoping to deceive are not only greedy, they're also dangerous. They may retaliate." She wouldn't have felt right if she hadn't warned him.

Hastiin Nééz nodded slowly. "I can help you. I've been shaping points with obsidian since I was a child."

"We won't tell anyone—"

He held up a hand. "People will know my work. But I'll become a moving target—and hard to find. I'm getting restless anyway. I'll finish the piece and move on."

He studied the photos. "But the diamond in the handle poses a problem. I can get a good copy, but it won't fool a jeweler."

"No diamond. The dagger must be constructed to look as if someone pried off the real thing and left an empty socket in its place. Can you do that?"

He nodded slowly. "I can construct a silver bezel—the dish that held the diamond in place—then make it look as if it was tampered with. The quality you want, and the precise shaping of the obsidian blade will take many hours…it'll cost you." He scribbled a list of numbers, then added them up and handed her the piece of notepaper. "That's my price."

She stared at the sum. It would take every cent in her savings and checking account. "I don't suppose you'd take a credit card?"

He grinned widely.

"I'll take that as a no," she said slowly. "And there's one more thing." She reached into her pocket and brought out the GPS transmitter she'd removed from her laptop when they'd been at Hunter's uncle's ranch. This particular model, powered by its own long-lasting battery, was the one favored by her father. They'd used them in case one of their company laptops was ever stolen. With a range of ten miles, the laptop could be tracked if you knew how, even if not powered up. But the GPS itself had to be activated before it could be located, and that could only be done remotely after sending the correct codes—codes only she knew now.

Lisa held up the transmitter, no larger than the refill cartridge for a pen. "Would you place this inside the handle for me?"

Hastiin Nééz took the device and looked at it closely. "A transmitter, huh? How fragile is it?"

"As long as you don't hammer it, heat it or dunk it in a liquid, it'll be just fine," Lisa said.

"Never seen one like that before," Hunter commented. "How do you turn it on?"

"It's on right now. Has a five-year battery." She looked back in *Hastiin Nééz*'s general direction. "Can you do this?"

"It'll take a little extra drilling, but I won't charge you for that," he said.

"Great. Then you've got yourself a deal," she said, and reached out to shake his hand. Then she remembered and quickly dropped her hand back to her side. "Sorry," she muttered.

He gave her an approving nod. "I'll need half up front, and the other half when it's completed."

"All right. I'll make a trip to the bank, then come right back," she said. "When do you expect completion?"

"A week," he said. "No, five days."

She shook her head. "We just don't have that much time."

Hunter joined her near the desk. "She's right."

"Do you have any measurements or scale drawings of the dagger?" the man asked.

"I knew you'd need them," Lisa said, handing him the envelope filled with the photos and specs she'd received from Hal Taylor.

He looked over them over, then lapsed into a long silence once again. "I've got an obsidian spear point I had planned to use for something else—a museum replica—but they didn't commission me for the job. So here's what I'll do. It'll be tricky, but maybe I can refashion that into the dagger's blade. The dimensions, size and shape of the spear point are already close and, thankfully, larger, not smaller. The silver for the hilt is not going to be a problem, nor is the antler, where I'm going to hide your little device. But if you want me to make the dagger appear authentic, one detail requires me to know what the tribe uses to polish the silver—to remove the oxidation. I can leave traces of that behind."

"My father's notes indicated that the silver was polished using just a soft cloth, baking soda and water," Lisa recalled.

"The old fashioned way. I should have guessed," *Hastiin Nééz* replied.

"What's the soonest you can have the dagger ready?" Hunter added.

"Tomorrow morning—if I work all night and manage to avoid breaking the blade. Come around dawn. I should be finished by then, and I'll want to leave here as soon as possible."

Hunter glanced at Lisa, who nodded.

"Done," he answered without hesitation. "But since we'll be back tomorrow, will you begin the project now without waiting for the money, then accept full payment in the morning?"

Hastiin Nééz considered it. "You'll guarantee payment?"

"Yes." He knew, as *Hastiin Nééz* did, that he spoke for the Council and that his word would bind them.

"Then it's no problem."

THEY LEFT A SHORT TIME LATER. "Thanks for backing me up in there," Lisa said. "He obviously trusted you more."

"I'm not a *bilagáana*. Most of us haven't fared too well trusting white people," he added with a shrug. "Particularly not when you look back at the past two hundred years or so."

"True, unfortunately," she conceded, looking around. "I'll need to stop by the First Security Bank—any branch will do."

"That's not a good plan," he said slowly. "I'm betting that bank manager Simon Moore can access your accounts without breaking a sweat."

"There're still quite a few branches here in New Mexico. No way they could have that many men."

He considered it in silence.

Sensing his reluctance, she continued. "I'll go inside the bank and make the withdrawal while you keep a lookout. Just in case they've got the capability to track my withdrawal, we'll put plenty of distance between the bank and *Hastiin Nééz*'s place. We'll pick the branch in Bloomfield, east of Farmington. The trick will be to work fast and get out of the area before they can figure out where we're going, then hole up until tomorrow."

"All right. But first we put a backup plan in place.

We're going to create a few illusions and provide enough evidence for a false conclusion or two."

The drive to Bloomfield took them less than an hour. Hunter made a quick stop by a hardware store down the street from the bank and bought a shovel, then they walked across the street to a sporting goods store, which sold mostly hunting and fishing gear, and bought an outdoorsman guide with detailed topographic maps of the county.

"What are you up to?" she pressed.

"I'll explain later," he said, pulling up into the parking area beside the bank, located near the center of the small community. "Work fast."

Chapter Ten

Hunter got out of the truck, but hung back as she went inside. He searched the street, vehicles cruising by, and even glanced up at the sky once in a while, but, for now, in a populated area, they seemed to be safe. He looked at the front entrance to the bank a few times, but couldn't see inside because of the tinted glass. His focus remained on the passing cars and SUVs. One wrong move and they'd both be dead.

Trujillo and Barker were very well connected with the local criminal elements. If they'd been marked for death, or a bounty had been offered to anyone who tracked them down, danger would close in very quickly. Barker would pay off street gangs—most of the communities had one or more, and these young hoods would spread the word. For those dealing in everything from drugs to stolen cars, being known as Trujillo's friend rather than his enemy paid off.

Hunter hadn't told her about that because he

hadn't wanted to add to the stress she was already under. He'd heard her wheezing when she breathed. Though she seemed barely aware of it, it scared him—for her. After Amelia's death a part of him had died. Though time had healed the pain, the emptiness inside him remained. Lisa's softness and her courage had touched him and pushed back that darkness. In this mission where honor directed their paths, he'd found something deeper…something he didn't want to define.

Lisa came out clutching her handbag a moment later. "I've never carried this much cash on me before," she whispered.

Just then Hunter spotted two tough-looking kids with gang tattoos cruising by slowly for the second time. Both were looking right at Lisa. "Keep your eyes straight ahead," he said, leaning over to whisper in her ear. "If they pass by again, or stop their car, let me handle it. You safeguard your bag."

The car, an older-model green sedan with primer paint on one fender and undersized wheels, pulled over against the curb and stopped. Seeing the kid on the passenger side reach for his cell phone while watching them in the side mirror, Hunter touched Lisa firmly on the arm.

"Move toward the truck, but don't run," he urged softly, seeing both young men getting out of the vehicle now.

The young men looked at Lisa, then Hunter. The passenger said something to the driver, a red-haired kid smaller than Lisa, and the boy walked almost casually back around and got inside. He drove off, tires squealing.

"Must be a false alarm," Lisa said, watching out of the corner of her eye as the one with the cell phone turned away, still talking to someone on the line.

They'd just reached their pickup when the green sedan suddenly came around the corner, tires squealing. The driver turned into the parking lot and slammed on the brakes, blocking their pickup and preventing them from backing out.

Hunter noticed that the teen with the cell phone was coming up behind him. Despite his age—the boy couldn't have been more than seventeen—that kid, unlike his companion, was big and husky, outweighing Hunter by at least twenty pounds. "You trying to disrespect me, Indian? Flipping me off like that?"

"No need to make up stories, tough guy. Walk away, while you still can," Hunter snarled, his eyes slicing into the boy.

"You wanna throw some blows? Chance to impress your woman?" the young man said, throwing his chest out like a bantam rooster.

Lisa saw the redhead opening his car door. He was moving slowly, and it was obvious the little guy wasn't in any hurry to fight. Lisa caught his eye and shook her head in warning.

But the guy on the sidewalk kept inching closer. "Okay, son. If you want to be humiliated in front of your friend, that's your call," Hunter said in a bored voice.

The boy lunged forward, throwing a quick jab from his waist in a surprise attack. Hunter deflected the punch with his left forearm, stepped into the move and slammed his fist into the boy's stomach, putting his weight and motion into the blow.

As the teen doubled over, gasping for air, Hunter grabbed Lisa's hand and ran with her to the truck. Seconds later they were heading west down the Bloomfield highway. "The tattoos on the kid said that he's in the *Sombras* gang. 'Shadows' in English. They have members all over the county, except for the Rez."

He glanced at the rearview mirror often, searching for a possible tail. Once he got closer to Farmington, he took a road to the right, circling the northern part of the city. A few times he turned off the main roads, circling blocks in neighborhoods, moving slowly and always checking the rearview mirror. "If we're on their radar, we've got to get off these streets and hole up."

"Do you know of any other safe houses in this area with the mark on the door…that insignia?"

He could feel her watching him, checking for a reaction. "The what…insignia? What are you talking about?"

She sighed. "Never mind."

"I need to get in contact with someone, but I can't do it while we have them on our tail."

She glanced in the side-view mirror. "Are you talking about the red sedan? It's been with us since your last turn."

"Yeah—two kids inside."

"With cell phones and probably armed," she said, completing his thought.

"Yeah, you're getting the picture," he said.

He turned a hard right, then a left. The sedan was still with them. "Unless I can shake these boys, they'll have others here backing them up soon. We have to make a move and I've got an idea," he said reaching for his cell phone.

His brother, Wind to the Council, worked nearby. Actually, Birdsong Automotive, owned by the local racing family, was a specialty shop specializing in high-performance engines, race car design, and custom body work for monster-truck shows. Their shop and test track, located on the old fairgrounds, wasn't far from their current location. Ranger modified cars for all kinds of track and off-road competition, and was a consultant for the Birdsong racing team.

Hunter dialed his brother's cell number. "I need backup," he said quickly. He gave him their location in short, staccato sentences. "Can you run interference—help me ditch a tail?"

"Hang tight, bro. I'll be there," Ranger responded. "Circle the neighborhood, coming back to Edgewood Lane, until I get there. I've got you covered. Just hit your brake lights twice when you're ready to make your move. Then I'll make mine."

"Gotcha," Hunter said.

"How soon can we get help?" she asked, as soon as Hunter put the phone down.

"In a matter of minutes." Less than five minutes later, heading north on Edgewood, Hunter spotted a wide, low, sporty blue model coming up behind the red car. Ranger had taken one of his latest creations—a custom model that street racers had been begging to test drive. The little unit could accelerate faster than anything off a drag strip and still corner like a sports car.

Ranger creeped up right behind the gang member's car and honked. The horn, taken from an old truck, was extremely loud and annoying. It was the perfect way of getting someone's attention.

Hearing the blare Lisa jumped and turned to look.

"Now the boys following us have something more to think about," Hunter said.

As soon as they crossed the railroad tracks, Hunter pumped the brake light twice, then suddenly accelerated. So did Ranger, who swerved around the gang member's red sedan, cutting right in front of them.

The kid behind the wheel hit the brakes hard. Ranger raced ahead, then spun the wheel and braked hard, reversing directions and coming to a sliding stop. Then he headed straight at them.

Again, he came to a screeching stop, facing them, inches from the hood of their sedan. Then Ranger did his second moonshiners turn, and raced off.

Hunter cut down the next side street, knowing he'd lost the rattled teens, and pulled to the curb.

"We can't leave him," Lisa said quickly, watching in the rearview mirror as the teens raced down the other street after Ranger. "What if they catch him?"

Hunter burst out laughing. "You can't catch the wind." Seeing the puzzled look on her face, he added, "That was my brother."

"So what's your plan now that the boys tailing us are off on a wild goose chase?"

"We go south through Farmington using the truck bypass, then take the back roads to Shiprock and head south. We'll hole up someplace out there for a while. We don't want to be anywhere close to *Hastiin Nééz*'s place, so I'm going to head to Narbona Pass. That's in the Chuska Mountains, southwest of Shiprock. There's a place there…. It's special to me." He'd never taken anyone there. Yet he wanted her to see it—more like experience it—with him.

"Let's go then."

THEY DROVE FOR OVER AN HOUR and a half before entering the mountains. The route had taken them up a narrow canyon that wound through the juniper- and piñon-covered foothills. A half hour earlier he'd pulled over to make a phone call, and, assured that they'd have supplies waiting, they'd continued on their journey.

"*Hastiin Nééz* will have protection tonight as he works—and for as long as he wants it, too," he said.

"Who'll be doing all this?"

He said nothing for some time, then finally answered. "Tribal officials, and their friends and family, most likely. On the reservation everyone knows everyone else's business and word's out we're trying to find the dagger. In this case, that's not a bad thing. The tribe stands behind what you're trying to do, and most Navajos will help us do whatever's necessary."

"To clear my father's name?" she pressed.

He shook his head. "To find the dagger," he answered. "But one, hopefully, follows the other."

"Our priorities are poles apart," she said in a heavy voice. "I know I can't change that, but I won't pretend it doesn't make any difference."

"We have to follow the same path and confront the same dangers. And the truth is that neither one of us knows what's at the end of the road. Just take it one day at a time."

She didn't reply. She was hoping that the GPS in the replica dagger would lead them to whoever her father had been hiding the dagger from—those who'd somehow arranged for his "suicide." Her father's only victory had been keeping that dagger from them. Of course, like Hunter, she was also hoping to recover the dagger. But proving that her father had done the right thing mattered most to her. She knew he wasn't a thief, and she wanted the world to know that, too.

"We both need to find the dagger. Following its trail will hopefully allow us to reconstruct what happened. Our goals aren't mutually exclusive," Hunter said.

"And after we find it, what then? Will I still be able to count on you?"

"We'll take the appropriate steps," he said. "I've helped you do what you need and kept us both alive. But I need you to trust me." He had no right to ask that of her, but, without it, the dagger's enemies would win.

He was focused on her now, listening for her answer, though his gaze remained on the twin ruts of the dirt track they were following.

"I trust you to follow your highest sense of right," she said at last.

He glanced at her, then back at the track, wishing he could offer more assurances. She was worried and with reason. "That's good enough for now." Hunter paused then in a slow, fierce tone, added, "I *will* continue to protect you—and we *will* find that dagger." He could assure her of that much, and he knew, on that score at least, he would *not* let her down.

"I believe we'll find the dagger, too, and not just because we'll never give up," she said softly. "Though evil sometimes makes more noise and seems to have the upper hand at times, good is stronger. Look at history. From the dawn of time, evil has attempted to defeat good, but all it ever manages is a temporary victory. Good endures and, ultimately, wins out."

"Your way of looking at it isn't that different from ours," he said in a quiet voice. "Navajos believe that evil is simply the result of something being out of control—out of balance, if you will. We restore harmony with the help of Sings and other rituals. We have ceremonies so we can restore balance to all aspects of a person's life. Once evil is brought under control it has no power. That's how a Navajo walks in beauty."

"Order and balance," she commented thoughtfully. "The rest of the world could learn a lot from the Navajo way of looking at things."

AS THE ROAD—OR WHAT PASSED for it—came to an end, she saw a thick grove of trees crowded within a narrow space less than a hundred yards wide at the mouth and leading up into the mountainside. Sandstone bluffs towering above suggested it was a blind canyon.

"We're here," he said, parking between two giant pine trees. "There's a cave uphill from here, and a spring. Supplies are there waiting for us." He led the way through a thick growth of pines, most of them at least a foot in diameter. They had to maneuver carefully to avoid being poked by the sharp needles, the branches were so close together. There was no trail, but Hunter was able to choose the best path, apparently from experience. Up ahead, there was a small clearing with tall, green grass and moss- and lichen-covered boulders scattered about. The space was like an amphitheater, with forest on one side, the open space in the middle and a half circle of head-high brush lining the base of the solid rock walls that extended to the top of a tall cliff.

"Right through there," Hunter said, leading her behind a bush onto a hidden path continuing through a narrow crevice in the mountain.

The brush was so tall and thick at one point she couldn't see anything except Hunter's strong back and the walls of the cliff on either side. Just as she started to become a bit claustrophobic and lose all sense of direction, the brush thinned out, revealing what appeared to be a dark slash in the side of the mountain.

They went inside the narrow gap. For several steps there was no room to maneuver, but suddenly the cave opened up, revealing an open area ten feet across and at least twenty feet high. It was cool and dry, and they'd be well hidden.

"No one can sneak up on us here. The terrain, the birds—nature itself—will give them away," Hunter said.

Lisa had never been an outdoorsy person. She wasn't sure if that was because asthma had held her back or, more to the point, the *fear* of getting an asthma attack far from medical help. But this place was enough to make her change her mind about staying indoors.

Lisa watched as Hunter walked to the rear of the cave and picked up a large duffel bag someone had left there for them. He brought it out into the light, then unzipped the bag and began to set out the supplies.

"Hungry?" he asked.

She shook her head, then froze, listening. "What's that? Water?"

"It's a hot spring not too far from here. Well, I guess it's more like a warm spring. The water's about one hundred degrees, give or take."

"Let's go see," she said.

"You go ahead. It's back in the direction we came, about halfway down the narrow path, on your right and through the brush. I need to get some firewood for tonight, so I'm going to look for some branches just outside the cave."

Aware of how cold desert nights could be, even after a hot day, she didn't press the issue. "I'll be back in few minutes and help you."

He shook his head. "No, go relax. Soak your feet in the spring. Take your mind off your breathing for a while."

"Yeah, I'm whistling like a tea kettle right now," she said with a half smile. "But it'll pass. I just need to increase one of my medications, that's all."

"Which brings me to my next question. How's your supply holding out?"

"It's hard to tell with inhalers—they're opaque. You kinda have to go by weight. But my guess is that they're still half-full, but I also have a spare of each. I have pills, too, enough for a month. I'm covered."

While he gathered branches for firewood, she went toward the sound of water. She walked slowly, at her own speed, stopping only to listen to the spring and confirm she was getting closer. She missed her life back in the city—a morning cup of coffee at her desk, doing her yoga breathing exercises at noon, dinners at her valley home in what passed for the country that close to Albuquerque.

Sadness enveloped her as she realized that everything would change. Even if she identified her father's killer and found the dagger, her dad was gone forever and nothing would bring him back.

Lisa wiped away her tears with the back of her hand. She was tired, that was all. This was no time for negative thoughts. There was too much that still needed to be done.

THE HOT SPRING, STEAMING slightly from the high humidity, was a dark blue-green pool about the size of a hot tub, resting against the cliffside. Colorful minerals dissolved and carried out of the ground by the warm water formed a crusty edge on the low side of the spring. Here, the water overflowed the hard lip of the basin and disappeared into the sandy soil within a few feet.

Crouching by the water's edge, Lisa placed her hand in the pool. It was barely above body temperature, and it felt wonderful. How long had it been since she'd taken a nice bath? She looked around. She was as alone out here as one could get. Hunter was off searching for firewood, and even if he decided to come looking for her, she'd hear him coming well before he arrived. What better way to relax than by soaking in a warm pool of water?

She stripped quickly, intending on indulging herself just long enough to ease her breathing and her aching muscles. Leaving her clothes by the edge of the pool, she stepped into the welcoming water.

Lisa found a nice, sunny spot against the cliff, enjoying the heat radiating from the rock as well as that of the water surrounding her. Closing her eyes, she relaxed, her thoughts and time drifting as she focused on nothing in particular.

Before long, she realized the shadows were lengthening. It was time to go. There were plenty of animal prints on the ground around the spring, and she knew some would come by at dusk and later in the night for water.

Lisa climbed out, then dried off, using her canvas jacket. As she reached for the rest of her clothes, she heard a low throated growl. The deep rumble made her freeze. Half-hidden by the surrounding brush, less than twenty feet away, was a cougar.

The big tan cat, with a battle-scarred face and intelligent green eyes, was magnificent. For a second they stood still, staring at each other. The cougar seemed as surprised to see her as Lisa was to see him.

Naked, she grabbed her things, slowly coiling her fingers around the clothes at her feet. When she stepped back, intending to leave and dress elsewhere, the cat growled a warning. Lisa froze instantly. She wouldn't be able to outrun it, nor was she in a position to fight it. She searched her mind for another option when she heard Hunter's voice.

"Don't move a muscle," came a harsh whisper from somewhere behind her, "and don't crouch down. Hold your ground. The bigger you appear, the less likely you are to be attacked."

She recognized Hunter's voice. Her first instinct was to cover herself, but fear and common sense prevailed. Forcing herself to do as Hunter asked, she remained perfectly still.

A heartbeat later, Hunter's voice rose in a song that seemed almost hauntingly seductive. It reverberated with power, and with promise.

The cougar stood rock-still for a moment, then backed slowly out of sight, disappearing into the brush.

"He'll be back," Hunter said quickly, his thorough gaze searing down her body.

She felt even more vulnerable now than when she'd seen the cougar, and she fought the urge to turn her back on him, or try and cover herself with her hands, afraid he'd see it as a sign of weakness.

"Turn around," she managed in a strong voice. She was trembling, but not from the cold. Feeling his gaze on her had awakened powerful yearnings. Her body felt as if pieces of her were melting under the fire in his gaze.

"Turn around, why? I've already seen...all of you," he murmured in a deep voice.

His gaze remained on her, devouring, ravaging. Everything about him screamed male and called out to the woman she was. Her heart pounding, she forced herself to look him boldly in the eyes. Her breath caught in her throat as she saw the fire smoldering there.

"Turn around! Now!" Her voice shook.

"Well, if you insist," he said, taking one last, slow look. "But I'd advise you to hurry. The cougar *will* be back."

She'd never dressed so fast in her life...nor with such reluctance. She'd wanted Hunter more than she'd ever dreamed possible—to feel his arms around her, his strength against her softness, to surrender to those fires.... She took a deep, shaky breath. Well, her asthma was certainly gone. Nothing like two quick shots of adrenaline to send it packing.

"What was that chant you sang to the cougar?" she asked as they headed back.

"It's called a *Hozonji*. It's a Good Luck Song

that's been in our family for many years. The songs are part of our inheritance, a gift handed down to each child. The Diné believe that *Hozonjis* have power."

"It was…mesmerizing," she said at last.

"It did what it was supposed to do, bring luck our way."

"The cougar…it was as if he understood what was expected of him, what you wanted him to do."

"Most animals will not attack a human unless extremely hungry, or cornered. But, in this case, there was even more than that at play. Remember that the cougar is my spiritual brother."

"Tell me more about your link to the animal."

"Cougars are secretive by nature," he answered, a ghost of a smile playing at the corners of his mouth. "They hunt alone. Although they can chase their prey, they prefer to stalk and use the element of surprise to bring their meal down. They also plan for the future. When they make a kill, they feed, then cover the carcass and hide it with leaves and twigs so they can come back to it later and feed again."

They reached the cave moments later, and she saw he'd made a small, hot fire. The flow of the air through the cave directed the smoke outside, which was a good thing, considering her asthma. "What made you decide to come looking for me?" she asked.

"I saw the tracks of the animal, some of them

over yours, and realized where they were leading to," he answered, then, after a pause, added, "But that's not the whole truth." His gaze captured and held hers. "I knew you'd gone into the water."

She sat down on the floor of the cave before her knees buckled. "How?"

"I just knew. Or maybe I hoped...."

He lay on the ground beside her, resting on one elbow. "You're a beautiful woman, Lisa."

His voice was like fine wine, seducing and weaving a spell around her. She needed him in a way that was as primal as the land around them. Desire and longing spiraled around her until she couldn't see or hear anything but him.

"You're in my blood," he whispered.

He leaned over her, pushing her back onto the ground, then covered her mouth in a kiss so achingly tender her defenses crumbled away. His lips were seductively soft and then commanding. He tasted and plundered, taking everything, inciting the raging fires inside both of them.

The voice that warned him to hold back, not to cross the line that could only lead to heartbreak, faded away. The need to make her his pounded through him. His blood roaring through his veins, he struggled to hold to one last shred of sanity. The job...a debt...but he was burning...logic vanished, giving way to the heat.

Suddenly he froze. "Don't move. Just listen." His eyes narrowed as he concentrated.

With her heart pounding in her ears she hadn't heard a thing except the soft moans that had come from the back of her own throat. She needed him. Why had he stopped?

"I heard a gunshot," he said, moving away from her quickly. "We can't stay here any longer."

His words penetrated the haze clouding her senses, and she sat bolt upright. "They're coming after us? Here? How?"

"It may have been just a poacher. It's not legal to hunt in these woods, but when people are hungry, they do whatever they have to do to survive."

"The cougar?" she asked in a tight voice.

"I don't know," he answered honestly. "But probably not. Now hurry. We can't take the chance that someone else—like those after us—heard the shot, too. If they did, they'll be coming in our direction double-time."

Hunter put out the fire as she gathered her things. Within minutes, duffel bag of supplies in hand, they were hurrying back to the truck.

Regret left her feeling hollow inside and achingly empty. She'd wanted Hunter—against all logic, against all reason. Even now, she couldn't quite shake free of the magic she'd found in his arms.

After loading their gear into the truck, they climbed in. Though the light was fading, Hunter drove without using the headlights, hoping to keep their exact location as hidden as possible. They continued slowly down the dirt road for a few minutes, neither of them speaking.

"I hope the cougar made it…and that no one had to go hungry," she added in a whisper.

They'd gone less than a quarter of a mile when Hunter reached for her hand, giving it a reassuring squeeze. "He lives to hunt another day. Look up," he said and gestured to a ragged ledge high above the tallest tree.

The cougar stood, bathed in the moonlight, watching in silence as they drove away.

Chapter Eleven

Hunter didn't stop until they'd driven for nearly an hour, heading east to the main highway, then southeast, out into open country. There was no cover here except for the rolling terrain and clumps of brush. They'd found a low spot in a wash where the truck could be hidden, but from ground level they could see for miles in every direction.

"We'll be okay for now," he said, parking with the front of the pickup pointing in the direction they'd have to take to get back out of the arroyo. "But we should sleep in the truck."

He didn't have to convince her. Even keeping her eyes open became a test of will. Lisa pushed the seat back, intending to rest for just a few minutes, but reality faded quickly.

The next thing she knew she was blinking against the rising sun. Daylight bathed the interior of the truck and they were out of the arroyo, moving toward the main highway again. At least the general direction was to the west, and the sun wasn't in her eyes now.

"Did you get any sleep?" she asked, coming fully awake and adjusting her seat.

"Some."

"Where are we going now? Back to *Hastiin Nééz*'s place?"

"Yes. I gave him a call while you were sleeping. The replica is finished."

"Any chance you can make a quick stop for coffee someplace?" she asked, rubbing her eyes. "We'll have to pass through Shiprock."

"Not a morning person?" he teased.

"This isn't morning. It's six forty-five. That still qualifies as dawn to some."

On a long hill leading into the reservation town of Shiprock, they made a fast stop at a roadside vendor and picked up *naniscaada* sandwiches— fried bread filled with eggs, sausage and bacon, but not rice, cheese, or lettuce, like the ones found outside Rez borders. Lisa couldn't decide which was better—the heavenly scent or the taste. Balancing cups of coffee, they ate on the road. Afterward she felt much more prepared to tackle the difficult day ahead.

"You haven't said much," he commented. "Are you having second thoughts about the plan?"

"No. I was just trying to figure out the details. Who will we be pretending to take the fake dagger to? It'll have to be someone who'll convince Trujillo and Barker we've got the real thing—that we went to retrieve it last night."

"I'm hoping the fact that I bought a shovel and a map will lead them to think we dug it up somewhere. The trick will be getting it from *Hastiin Nééz* in secret, then letting ourselves be seen heading back onto the Rez, pretending to return it."

"Any ideas?" she asked.

"Yeah. After we pick up the dagger, I'd like you to call Simon Moore and tell him that you'll be closing the safe deposit box later today and he should have the papers ready. Tell him that you finally have what you need to clear your father's name, and once you deliver that evidence, you'll be heading home. Don't give any more details than that. He'll contact people, and pretty soon, we'll get a reaction," he assured her. "By that time, we'll be on the main road leading into Shiprock."

"Going where? Our direction of travel can help us with the con if we play it right."

"I've got that covered. I'll let word out that we're on our way to see Roy Blackgoat, who lives near the turnoff leading to Window Rock. Roy's a very elderly and respected *hataalii*. No one will doubt that we've got the dagger then. The fact that we fell off their radar last night will just add fuel to the fire. They'll probably make their move somewhere along the highway south of Shiprock."

As they drew near *Hastiin Nééz*'s place, just beyond the Hogback, Hunter lapsed into silence. She could see him concentrating, alert to any signs of danger.

They made the turn to the north, and arrived just five minutes later. As they waited in the workshop, now almost empty except for the boxes stacked by the door, *Hastiin Nééz* retrieved the piece from a back room.

Lisa's heart was pounding. She'd never been more nervous. She'd be paying this man a huge sum—all her savings. Yet if things worked out, they'd finally be able to track the people most likely responsible for killing her father.

"I trust you'll find it everything you expected," he said, returning.

He unwrapped the obsidian dagger from the soft cloth around it, and placed the replica on the worktable before her.

Lisa's breath caught in her throat. It was an exquisite copy. The obsidian blade, with its razor-sharp, natural-glass edge painstakingly created by hundreds of small steps, looked deadly. The carved antler handle, with the silver knob, looked as if it had been used and worn down through the ages. The hilt gleamed, but the silver was slightly tarnished, as if the dagger had been out of its protective case for too long. The center where the diamond had been, lined with a tarnished silver bezel, showed simple tool marks that made it look like the unpolished, uncut stone had been hastily pried loose.

"Perfect," she said. "This is an absolutely amazing piece of work. Is the GPS device in the handle?" she asked.

"Yes. But you'll have to pry off the knob to remove it."

"Great work." Lisa brought out her laptop, turned it on, then started up the GPS program with the map overlays. A blinking dot on the simple map showed the location of the GPS. Assured it worked perfectly, she shut down the computer.

Lisa nodded to Hunter, who was talking to someone on his cell phone, then brought out the cash from her tote bag and set the money on the bench.

"Time for you to leave, then." The old craftsman took the bills and stuck them in his jacket pockets without counting them. "Once I load my gear, I'll be gone too. I've accepted new work that'll take me to a place of complete safety."

"Now you've made me curious. Where will you go?" she asked with a tentative smile.

"I'll be working for the governor," he answered with a smile. "He wants me to make a special medallion for him. It'll be a personal gift from the governor to the president of Spain when he comes to visit this spring. The medallion will have the Zia symbol and other designs that reflect our state's history," he answered, then added, "The governor has invited me to stay at the Governor's Mansion while I draw up the design. As I said, I'll be perfectly safe where I'm going."

Hunter thanked him, and hurried out with Lisa. "Now it starts. While you and he spoke, I called a friend who'll make sure word goes out that we have the dagger. Be ready. It's nearly an hour's drive to the *hataalii*'s place," he said, and added, "But you may want to leave that laptop someplace safe. We'll need it to track the dagger, right?"

"If anyone but me tries to access the computer they'll get nothing but a hard-drive mirror image full of useless old business files and a few phony new files I've inserted just to confuse them. The actual hard drive and its files are password protected, but I've hidden the menu so they won't know when to enter the password even if they manage by some miracle to figure out what it is. It's a safety feature I installed myself. There's no way they'll know they're being spoofed."

He nodded in approval. "We should leave the dagger where it can be found in a casual search, but we still need to keep the laptop as far out of reach as possible, agreed?"

She nodded, then made her call to Moore while Hunter was stowing the laptop under the seat, out of sight. The dagger, wrapped in a protective cloth, rested on the seat between them. Soon they were on the highway heading to Shiprock.

"We have to make this look good, so we'll have to give them a believable fight. We'll have backup coming, so don't worry. They'll have to grab the dagger and run, leaving us behind."

"I'm ready," she answered.

They'd traveled less than five miles when he spotted a tail.

"They picked us up at the turnoff to Kirtland, which means they've probably got someone covering every paved road leading in and out of Shiprock. I was expecting them to catch up to us between Shiprock and Gallup," Hunter said. "That stretch of highway has a lot less traffic," he said, placing his forty-five beneath the seat.

"Is that necessary? The goal is to let them take the dagger without anyone getting injured," she pointed out.

"Our backup is not in position yet. And there's something else you need to keep in mind. It's possible—though not likely—that once they've re-covered the dagger they'll decide to kill us both. The reason that's unlikely is because Trujillo will undoubtedly want to verify its authenticity before getting rid of us. But there are no guarantees. What I'm counting on, and what we need to hope for, is that they'll try to take us alive."

"They can *try*," Lisa said. "But there's no way I'm going with them."

"You're in the right frame of mind. We may

have to hold our own for a while until my brother and his friends show up. I hadn't expected Barker's people to move so quickly. Are you up to this, Lisa?"

She nodded. "I can hold my own in a fight. You know that. I can disarm an opponent who's carrying a club, knife or pistol. Let them bring it on." She glanced out the side mirror. "But it looks like luck's on our side. Whoever's back there isn't closing in on us."

"They're Barker's eyes—just snoops. They won't be the ones making a move. The dagger means too much to Trujillo. Barker would never turn over anything that important to some local punks. Judging from that low-rider-style car, they belong to that same street gang we encountered outside the bank in Bloomfield."

"So we'll be picking up another tail—the real bad guys—once word gets passed along the pipeline."

"Yeah," he answered. "And with two eastbound lanes and two westbound, separated by the fence and center median, they'll need three or four vehicles to pull it off. If that's their strategy, they'll be moving hard and fast, so stay sharp."

Her heart was pounding hard inside her chest, and the adrenaline coursing through her had heightened her senses. Lisa was terrified, but she'd see things through no matter what it took. "My father tried to protect the dagger. That's why he had the replica made, then hid the real one. His thinking and mine run along the same lines. I've studied his notes and thought long and hard about them. I'm not sure if I'm right, but I have an idea."

"Hold that thought," he said. "There's a big white SUV coming up fast from behind. They've just passed the low-rider car. Unless the SUV is full of hot-rodding kids, they're about to make a move."

"Those aren't teenagers back there," she said, glancing in the rearview mirror. She took a deep, steadying breath. Fighting was a matter of focus and timing. If she kept her wits about her, she'd do fine.

Hunter picked up speed as they continued along on the nearly deserted westbound lanes of the highway. He moved from the slow lane to the left-hand passing lane, going around an old man hauling firewood.

They continued on, and Hunter returned to the right-hand lane. Ahead, an eighteen-wheeler pulled out onto the highway. Closing ground way too fast, Hunter slowed, then swerved into the left lane again. But a quarter mile ahead, from a crossover spot in the center median, another white SUV suddenly pulled out in front of them.

Hunter let off on the gas, touching the brakes, and Lisa looked in the rearview mirror. Both lanes behind them were blocked, with cars coming up fast.

Hunter was forced to hit the brakes again to avoid rear-ending the SUV, and now unable to cut right without running into the semi. "They've boxed us in," he warned. "Hang on, I've got to make it look good." He slammed on the brakes harder this time, then inched to the left down into the shallow drainage ditch in the median.

"Look out for the fence," Lisa said just as they scraped a metal post.

Hunter held the truck steady, but couldn't accelerate quickly enough to get through the gap. Then the SUV ahead inched over to the shoulder, squeezing them even closer to the fence.

"Hang on!" Hunter yelled, swerving back up onto the highway. For a second, he had a shot at slipping between the SUV and the semi, but he held back. Escape wasn't part of the plan.

Then the semi came over the center line, and Hunter had to stand on the brakes to avoid ramming the tractor trailer. They skidded to a stop, tires screeching as the seatbelts dug into their shoulders. The cars behind them slid to a halt, blocking the rear. They were hemmed in from all sides.

Hunter glanced over at her quickly. "I'm not pulling my gun. Just try to keep your back to the truck if they decide to get physical. If they'd wanted to kill us, we would have been dead already."

As Hunter reached for the door handle, one of the men from the car directly behind them suddenly appeared beside the driver's door, his pistol aimed at Hunter's face.

"Let me see your hands."

Hunter placed his hands on the top of the steering wheel, and Lisa held hers up at shoulder level, palms out.

"Get out, hands above your head," the same man ordered.

Two men from one of the cars that had trapped them were moving back down the highway, probably to keep any civilians from interfering, and another two were standing in the median, in case someone tried to cross over from the eastbound lanes.

They were badly outnumbered, but Hunter wasn't worried. Wind and the others wouldn't be far behind now, and his brother would know exactly how to deal with them.

Hunter spotted Barker immediately as he and another man stepped out of the white SUV ahead of them and walked toward Lisa's side of the truck.

Barker was tall and lean. An ex-soldier, he was highly trained, and his movements were fluid, meant to conserve energy. Hunter had seen the man with him before, too. Evan Martinez was just short of six feet and built like a wrestler.

They'd gone at it in the past and Hunter had learned back then that the man's bulk was deceptive. Martinez was capable of lightning-fast moves. He was a skilled fighter and showed no mercy.

The man with the pistol aimed at Hunter's face was just extra muscle, near as Hunter could tell, but he was the one showing a gun at the moment.

"Move now," Martinez growled, coming around to Hunter's door. "And don't get cute and give me a reason. There's nothing I'd like better than knocking your head off."

"Dream on," Hunter answered in a bored voice, reaching down to open the door. He slipped out of the pickup slowly, and saw Lisa doing the same. One other man, the one who'd blocked them from the front, had remained inside the second SUV. His face was in shadows, and partially hidden by a baseball cap low on his head. Though Hunter tried to get a look, the man was making sure he remained unidentified. Hunter closed the door to the pickup casually.

Barker had brought Lisa around to the driver's side and she now stood beside Hunter, her back to the pickup.

"The dagger," Barker demanded, stepping toward Hunter.

Hunter looked at Lisa, who shrugged.

"It's on the seat," Hunter answered without emotion.

Barker signaled the man with the pistol. The man put the pistol in his pocket, looked at Hunter and Lisa, who were blocking his way, then decided to go around the truck to the other side.

Hunter studied Barker and Martinez, and noticed that the semi driver was approaching from the front. Barker would be impossible to take down quickly, but it could be done.

Although Lisa's skills were impressive, he knew she wasn't up to opponents like Barker or Martinez. The truck driver would be no problem, he looked more curious than anything else, and the muscle with the pistol would be distracted while getting the dagger.

Evan Martinez would have to be Hunter's first target. He had the look of a man spoiling for a fight.

Barker stepped over beside Lisa and grabbed her arm. "You're coming with us."

She drove her elbow into his middle and turned to face him, her arms in fighting position. "Do *not* touch me," she said, biting off the words.

Barker laughed, shaking off the blow. "Seems like your daddy taught you a few moves. But don't do that again unless you want some broken bones to mess up your face."

Until that very moment she'd never thought it was possible to feel evil, but it oozed from this man like some foul body odor. Lisa took a step back, keeping her back to the truck. She saw the letters of a tattoo on his forearm, *B T R H,* and wondered what they meant, but there was no time to dwell on it.

"Come on now, sweet cakes. Into my SUV. Don't make me have to use force."

"Perverts like you enjoy hurting women, I bet," she said.

His gaze suddenly went from controlled to cold, making her regret her retort. Then Barker smiled. It wasn't a friendly gesture. It was more like a leer, and it made her skin crawl.

"Just come along," he said. "Save your pretty cheekbones."

The sound of squealing tires on the eastbound lane distracted Barker for an instant, and Lisa spun and kicked out. The man blocked the kick and countered. She ducked to the left, and his boot struck the side of the pickup instead of her face.

By then Hunter was fighting the truck driver and the guy built like a stump, circling them constantly to keep from being outflanked. Lisa knew Hunter had his hands full, with the stubby guy blocking every strike.

This fight was hers. Lisa stepped out from the truck to get some maneuvering room. As Barker advanced, she tried to sweep his legs out from under him, but he evaded her and kept coming.

"You've got the dagger. Let us go," she said.

He didn't answer. Instead, Barker feigned a move to her left and moved in low to her right. Ducking under his arm, she danced around him and kicked out again.

She'd always been fast, but in comparison to her, Barker was greased lightning. Anticipating her attacks, he kept stepping out of her range, then advancing with a new look, low and quick. Each time, she barely managed to block his strikes. Her arms and wrists were hurting just from the glancing blows.

"I'll wear you down, honey. Give it up. You're coming with me—one way or the other."

The man in the front SUV suddenly yelled. "They've got help coming from the west. Break off now. We've got the dagger."

"You're jumping the gun, Paul," Barker answered smoothly. "Give me just another thirty seconds."

The name caught Hunter's attention, distracting him. Paul Johnson? The voice sounded familiar, somehow. After avoiding a blow from the truck driver, Hunter put the front fender of the truck to his back. He tried to get a look into the SUV just ten feet in front of him, but he had no luck.

As he glanced at Lisa, he knew he had to finish Martinez off fast and go help her. Barker was toying with her, wearing Lisa down. He could already hear it in her voice—she was running out of air.

Hunter angled once again to get a look at the face of the man in the SUV. He only got a glimpse, but what he saw stunned him. Paul Johnson was really Daniel Yellowhair, the man who'd served as his *bá'óltáí*—his teacher—on the Council.

The truck driver moved in then, and Hunter took a hard kick to his midsection. He went down on one knee, gasping for air.

The truck driver stepped back, pulling a pistol, and Hunter knew he'd never reach it in time.

"No!" Martinez yelled, shoving the truck driver just as he fired. Hunter felt a tug at his left shoulder, but still managed to get to his feet.

Martinez turned on the driver, throwing him to the ground. "We need to bring them in *alive,* you idiot!"

His shoulder was on fire, but then he heard Lisa cry out his name. Barker had pinned her against the side of the pickup in a chokehold. Energized, Hunter spun around, but Martinez grabbed him in a bear hug, pinning his arms.

Hunter saw Lisa kick Barker in the groin. As he doubled over, gasping, she stepped forward, striking for the back of his neck. Barker threw his left arm up, barely deflecting the blow.

From the murderous look on Barker's face, Hunter knew he was through playing with her now. Hunter's shoulder throbbed, but the pain faded into the background as rage filled him. He yanked his arms down, breaking free of the bear hug, then struck Martinez in the jaw with his elbow. Martinez staggered back, and Hunter delivered a solid kick to his chest.

Freed, Hunter went for Barker next.

Seeing him, Barker pushed Lisa, bouncing her against the side of the pickup, then turned to face Hunter. "You and the woman...something's there, isn't it?"

"Can't you find something better to do at a street fight than gossip, Barker? You sound like my grandmother at the laundry."

Wounded, Hunter knew he was no match for Barker, but he *would* stop him from taking Lisa. He tried a knee kick. Barker eluded that, jabbing him in the shoulder.

Barker laughed. "Don't try to fight with a professional, boy. You just don't have what it takes."

"Then make your move," Hunter said, circling.

Lisa came at Barker from behind, kicking him in the small of his back. But he whirled around, delivering a glancing blow to her throat.

Lisa staggered back, choking.

In a barely controlled rage, Hunter moved in on Barker, kicking and striking blows that drove the man back. He felt no pain now. Fury pulsed through him as did the need to pound Barker's miserable face into the ground.

Barker was still blocking most of the strikes, however. "You're not going to be able to take me, and when you go down, I'm taking the woman. But don't worry. I'll eventually return her to you...though perhaps not in the same condition."

Shouting came from farther down the road, as did the sounds of vehicles and sirens.

"Break off! Break off *now!*" the voice from the SUV ordered.

That voice...Johnson? Hunter was almost sure

he'd recognized it, but it was getting hard to concentrate now. His shoulder burned and the pain was hitting him in waves.

"You and me...another time," Barker spat out, kicking at Hunter's chest. Hunter blocked the kick, but the impact sent him reeling back.

"Bring it on," he said, and managed to keep his voice strong. Hunter steadied himself, but it was too late to stop Barker from climbing into the SUV.

The truck driver waved his pistol in Hunter's direction, warning him back, then barely managed to dive in himself as the vehicle pulled away, tires squealing.

"Look out!" Lisa shouted.

Hearing a vehicle right behind him, Hunter dove onto the hood of the pickup just as the second SUV raced by.

"Lisa?" Hunter looked back anxiously, scrambling off the hood on the passenger side.

She was back by the tailgate when Hunter reached her. "Are you okay?"

She nodded, still fighting to catch her breath. "I'll live. Thought you were about to get run over."

He brushed the hair from her face tenderly. "You shouldn't have stepped in," he said. "I could have handled Barker."

"Not after getting shot. You needed me," she said, coughing.

"I do need you...in one piece," he said and drew

her close. He held her tightly, possessively, almost unaware of his shoulder wound.

"You're wounded, but you still went up against Barker," she said in a strangled voice. "I needed…to help you. But I couldn't force him away." A tear spilled down her face, but she brushed it away quickly.

"You're all right now," he said, cupping her face in his hands. "And I'll be fine, too, so stop worrying."

Lisa jumped, hearing the loud blast of a car horn. Four vehicles had pulled off the eastbound lane of the highway beside the median. Ranger was standing beside the first car—the sporty blue sedan he'd driven earlier. He was waiting, and watching them as the sirens in the distance drew closer.

Hunter shook his head. Ranger went back to his car, and the four vehicles pulled back out onto the highway and drove east.

"Your brother, and the rest of our backup?" she asked.

"Yes, but they're no longer needed."

"Yes, they are! You're bleeding."

"I've been shot before. This isn't serious."

"You're *bleeding*," she repeated.

"You're not going to faint, are you?" he asked, teasing.

She glared at him.

He chuckled softly. "We've done what we set out to do. Now let's get out of here before the police arrive. They've got some vehicles to remove from the highway, no doubt stolen earlier today." He looked at the abandoned eighteen-wheeler, then turned to point out the low-rider car.

Using his good arm, Hunter tossed her the keys. "Time to hit the road."

Chapter Twelve

Following Hunter's directions, they arrived at a forest ranger's cabin at the northern end of the Chuska Mountains, often called the Lukachukais. They were surrounded by forest except for a blue mountain lake about one hundred yards north, down a steep, grassy slope.

As Lisa pulled to a stop in front of the log building, she glanced over at Hunter for the hundredth time since they'd left the scene of his shooting. She'd bandaged him carefully, using a first aid kit that had been stowed behind the seat, but there was a lot more than needed to be done. She could see the beads of perspiration on his forehead and the way his eyes were narrowed with pain.

"I'm taking you to a hospital right now," she said flatly.

"*No.* The shot was deflected when Martinez intervened. It was a small-caliber bullet, and it's not imbedded deeply."

"But the bullet will need to be removed and the wound cleaned. You've also lost a lot of blood," she added.

Fear tugged at her, undermining her courage. To see him in pain was almost more than she could stand. She understood now how deeply she'd come to care for this man, despite all his secrets. Though he could face an opponent with fierceness, with her, he was tender and gentle. It was all that, and the combination of intangibles whispered by her heart, that told her she was falling in love. The thought left her bewildered, but there was no time to dwell on it. His words soon brought her back to the present.

"The bullet didn't hit anything major. You did a good job of bandaging the wound, and the bleeding has stopped. There'll be more first aid supplies inside, and I'll guide you through the next few steps."

Her eyes widened. "I can clean and bandage a wound with the best of them, but I'm no emergency room physician, and certainly not a surgeon." She spoke quickly, more afraid now than when she'd faced Barker. "I...care about you," she added. "That might make me hesitate at exactly the wrong moment. There's a reason why doctors don't operate on their own families, you know."

"I can talk you through it. I have EMT training. We all do."

"All the warriors of the Brotherhood?"

He pursed his lips and shook his head. "Don't ask me questions I can't answer."

"We risked our lives for one another. I've earned your trust, just as you've earned mine," Lisa said.

"There are some secrets that aren't mine to disclose. But trust, the real kind, assures you of one thing—you can depend on me," he said, then added, "Let's go inside."

She went over to his side of the pickup, placed her arm around his waist when he climbed down, then helped him into the cabin. The key had been just where he'd said. She also noted the small carving at the corner of the doorway. "Another Brotherhood of Warriors member?" she asked, not expecting an answer.

"Just know that we're being watched over."

She looked around but saw no one.

"Believe me, they're keeping watch. They know I've been injured."

Finding the bedroom just past the living and dining area, she helped him over to the bed, then eased him down onto it.

"There's a complete first aid kit beneath the bathroom sink. Get that."

When she returned, she had the first aid kit and some bottled water. She set the first aid kit down, then handed him four white pills. "Take them for the pain." Her hands were shaking so badly, she spilled some of the water when she handed him the bottle.

"You don't have to be afraid, Lisa," he said softly. "I know what I'm doing."

"That makes one of us," she answered in a shaky voice.

"Help me take off my shirt. Just unbutton it in front, then cut the rest away with the scissors. Moving my arm right now is not a hot idea."

She smiled thinly, then began to unbutton his shirt. "Under other circumstances, I think I would have enjoyed this a lot."

Even in pain, his eyes lit up with a dark fire. "I would have made it a night you'd remember."

His husky voice sent its ripples right to the center of her soul, and she found herself wishing things *were* different—for both of them.

She cut his shirt all the way up the back, through his collar, then eased it off his shoulders. The wound was an angry red with blackened edges, and had started seeping blood from the movement.

"It doesn't look good," she said quietly as he lay back.

She aimed the gooseneck lamp on the bedstand and leaned over him, her hand barely resting on the flat of his belly. "The bullet has already started to work its way out. I think I can see the back of it about a quarter inch from the surface."

"Good."

As she sat up, her hand slid low on his stomach, barely touching his skin. He drew in his breath sharply.

Lisa pulled away quickly. "Did I hurt you?"

"Hurt?" He smiled thinly. "My shoulder isn't the problem. Even now, I want you." He touched her face in a light caress, then drew a line with his fingertips from her cheek downward until he reached the area just above her breast.

She leaned over him, brushing his lips with a gentle kiss. "You're trying to distract me, to keep me from being afraid."

"And it's working," he answered with a wicked smile. "Fear's not the first thing on your mind now."

She smiled. "You think so, do you?"

"I know so. You and I are connected…it's been that way between us since the day we met," he said, his voice filled with tenderness.

Lisa started to deny it, but she couldn't even turn away from the intensity of his gaze. "We can't talk like this anymore. I need to concentrate on what I have to do. That means no more distractions." She took a deep breath and tried to steady her nerves. Hunter was depending on her now, and she wouldn't let him down.

"Do *exactly* as I tell you," he said.

HE WILLED HIMSELF NOT TO pass out, but as she dug into his muscle to remove the slug, an unbearable blast of pain shot through him. He clamped his mouth shut, determined not to make a sound. He could take this. He was a warrior—a member of the Brotherhood of Warriors. He'd been through worse

"Grab it with the forceps, then pull it out," he ordered. "And don't cry," he managed in a softer voice.

"I'm not—" Lisa said, just as tears spilled down her cheeks. "I've got it now," she said at last, placing the forceps and the copper-jacketed bullet on the paper towels beside Hunter. Then she pressed a thick compress over the wound.

"If the blood flow doesn't stop, you'll have to add a few stitches," Hunter said, his voice a whisper now. He had to hang on, but when she'd pushed the compress in place, everything had faded away for just an instant.

Forcing himself to breathe slowly and steadily, he managed to keep it together. "Now, pour on the alcohol to clean the wound."

"I can't stand hurting anyone—but it's worse with you," she said, her voice whisper-thin.

"Because you're in love with me?" A fierce sense of pride filled him, pushing back the pain for a brief second or two.

"I do…care…more than I should." She lifted the compress slightly and poured the antiseptic onto the wound.

He inhaled sharply as the alcohol spilled into him. "Stop."

Her hands were shaking as she drew back. "It's still bleeding. You're going to need stitches."

"I know, but there're things you need to know first," he managed, his voice weaker now. "I can't

guarantee that I won't pass out, not anymore, and
if anything goes wrong, you have to know how and
where to go find help. But first I need you to swear
that you'll never divulge any part of what I'm about
to tell you—not for any reason. Can you do that?"

"You have my word of honor," she answered
somberly. "And that'll bind me, for as long as I
live."

"I know," he managed. She was so close—her
scent, her touch. The darkness waited for him, but
she'd be his light and he'd work his way back to her.
"There's a man who lives about five miles back
down the road from here, and he's probably
watching the outside right now. His name is James
Charlie. If you go outside and see him, call him by
his war name—his secret name. Say, '*Naabaahii,*'"
he said, using the Navajo word for "raider," "'your
brother is down. *Hashké* needs your help,'" he instructed. "Then you must say the words *yéé' bii
niséyá,*" he said, teaching her the Council's recognition signal for a brother in trouble. In Navajo it
literally meant, "I went into danger and returned."

"What does that mean?"

"I'll tell you later," he said.

She started to write down his instructions, but he
stopped her.

"No, these are secrets that can't be written
down. Memorize what I've said."

It took her several tries, but she finally managed

to get it right. "Okay. If you pass out and I can't revive you, or if there's trouble, I'll go get him," she said, forcing herself to stay calm for his sake.

"If someone comes after us here, leave me behind," Hunter added finally.

"No way," she said flatly. "We either escape together, or not at all. Don't ask me to make you a promise I can't—won't—keep."

Hunter saw the set of her jaw and knew that any further argument was hopeless. Giving up for now, he looked down at the bandage on his shoulder and saw that the blood flow had slowed but not enough. "Let's move on to the next step—stitches. Use the surgical thread and the needle in the kit. It's just like sewing, kind of. I'll make it," he said, determined to live up to his word. He *would* take care of her. Not because of a debt owed, but because somewhere along the way, she'd become closer to him than his own heart.

As Lisa began cleaning the wound and getting ready to start on the stitches, he concentrated on the warmth of her body so close to his and the gentleness of her touch.

She worked quickly, and the pain was intense but, mercifully, short-lived. At the end, she looked into his face, reached for a cloth and wiped the perspiration from his brow.

"You stick around," she said gently, then leaned over and kissed him.

Long before he'd had enough, she pulled away. With little strength left, he lay still. "You and I…we have personal business to finish…" he said, his voice fading.

"Someday…maybe," she whispered. "For now, rest."

HUNTER WOKE UP SLOWLY. HIS shoulder had stopped burning. It felt stiff but was bandaged and clean now. Lisa had curled up on the bed, facing him, inches from his side. As he shifted, her eyes opened.

"Good morning," she said with a gentle smile.

"How long have I been sleeping?" he asked, reaching for her hand and glad she didn't pull away.

"About six hours," she answered. She placed her hand on his forehead. "No fever."

"Depends on how you measure it," he said as her hand slid down his face in a gentle caress.

"You're recovering *very* quickly," she said, laughing.

He started to get up, but she placed a hand on his arm. "No, too soon. Stay in bed for a while."

He gave her a wicked grin. "I'm weak and at your mercy in case you want to have your way with me."

She laughed. "Be good. You can't overdo anything right now. You need to rest."

"Okay. Hop on. You can do all the work. I'll barely move." He curled one hand behind her neck and hauled her to him. His kiss was fierce, devouring her, tasting her, demanding more.

Although it took everything she had, she pulled back. "*No.* Now behave yourself," she said, standing up. "Would you like something to eat? The pantry is well stocked. I can scramble some eggs and even put some canned ham into the mix."

"No, not right now," he said.

"How about more painkillers?" She reached for the bottle and a glass of water and handed them to him.

He downed the over-the-counter-pills quickly. "In the car, before everything went into high gear, you mentioned having made some progress with your father's clues...."

She nodded. "After turning that riddle around and around in my head, I got an idea. But there's something in his papers I want to check out first, before I say anything else."

Hunter nodded, then despite her protests, stood, and walked shirtless to the side of the window. Getting a pair of binoculars from the desk with his good arm, he looked outside. "No problems?"

"None." She paused, then added, "I remembered exactly what you told me to say to James Charlie, but thank goodness I didn't have to go find him."

"And your promise? You remember that, too?" he asked, turning to face her.

"Yes," she said quietly. "Can you tell me what the Navajo words meant?"

He shook his head. "I can't reveal much more than what I already have, but I'll share what I can with you. In my culture, we all have war names— secret names—that are said to have power. They're kept secret because that's how their power is preserved. My war name is *Haské*. It means 'fierce warrior,'" he said, then added, "Now you have power over me."

He went to where she sat on the edge of the bed and leaned over her, guiding her back down onto the mattress. "But you always did."

She yielded to him easily for a moment, loving the feel of his hands on her, and the way he nuzzled her neck. Then, with a sigh, she pushed him back and wriggled away.

"I thought you wanted me to work on the puzzle," she said playfully. "And you should rest!"

Before he could protest, she hurried out the bedroom door.

Time slipped by as he waited for her. Restless, Hunter went to the side of the window and studied the surrounding area. What he'd seen during the attack…it was all coming back to him now.

Anger coiled inside him. If he was right, then they'd deliberately kept him in the dark about things he'd had a right to know. The knowledge that he hadn't been trusted completely ate at him, making him question the ties he'd held dear—except one. The bond that had formed between him and Lisa was real and could be trusted. It was the one certainty he had left.

ANOTHER FOUR HOURS PASSED. He'd tried to sleep and had done so for a bit, but there was too much going on inside him now for him to be able to get any rest. The more he thought about things, the more he questioned loyalties he'd never doubted or thought could be broken.

"What's wrong?" Lisa asked him, coming back into the room and searching his eyes for an answer. "I could hear you pacing like a caged mountain lion."

How could he explain what he didn't understand himself? Hunter reached out to her and gently pulled her to him. There were no lies in their feelings for each other. He needed her…to feel her gentleness yielding to his strength. He wanted to feel whole again.

She sighed and rested her head against him. "Something's wrong. I can feel it. Talk to me."

"Something happened back there with Barker and his men. They came at us too soon. If I'm right, that means we have even fewer allies we can trust. There are people whose word I've never questioned and now I'm not so sure that wasn't a mistake."

"This is about the Brotherhood of Warriors, isn't it?"

He nodded, the strain ripping into his guts. "And of who and what I am."

"I know who you are, *Haské,*" she whispered. "I know you like no one's ever known you, despite all the secrets."

She could feel him reaching out to her, needing her. The wound on his shoulder he could handle. The cut to his heart was tearing at him, ripping him into pieces. She wanted to soothe him, to comfort him in the way her woman's soul yearned to do. He kissed her gently at first, and she didn't pull away, even when the fires and heat became intense.

"I want to make love to you, to ease my body inside yours until we're one," he whispered, leaving a string of moist kisses down the column of her neck.

She trembled and sighed. She was falling...but his arms would hold her.

He tilted her chin up and captured her gaze. "But all I have to offer you are moments neither of us will ever forget. I don't want there to be any promises between us that'll lead to regrets."

It would have been wiser and infinitely safer to say no and move away from him, but she couldn't do it. He needed her love. Everything feminine in her knew it and responded to him as a flower to the light. Her heart longed to show him how she felt—that crazy blend of gentle longings and soul-piercing fires that made her a woman.

"I can't stop what's happening between us," she

said breathlessly, "but I can still watch out for you. Lie down," she said, edging away from him.

Her words surprised him and he obeyed, curious and burning for another taste of her.

"When you got shot, I thought for one awful moment that I was going to lose you," she said, letting her clothing fall to the floor one by one. "Let's celebrate life."

Naked, she let him gaze at her for several crazy heartbeats, then moved toward him. The curtains were drawn, but the skylight bathed her in light. "No darkness, no secrets," she whispered.

He tugged off his jeans in a quick, fluid motion, then opened his arms to receive her.

"We'll stop if your shoulder—"

Before she could complete the sentence, he kissed her hungrily, then helped her settle astride him. "Make me forget it," he whispered, his mouth closing in on her breast.

Fire spiraled down her in waves of pleasure. "Let me do the work…let me love you," she whispered, using the tip of her tongue to leave a moist trail down the middle of his body.

It was agony, this sweet, exquisite torture. He'd been trained to control his body, but his need for her was great. Yet knowing that it gave her pleasure to pleasure him, he allowed it to continue.

Reaching into his mind for control, he brought himself back from the edge and concentrated on Lisa. Pulling her upward with shaking hands, he tasted her intimately and brought her to the edge, keeping her there at that point, prolonging her pleasure until her entire body quivered at that precipice.

She'd never felt the mind-rending sensations that shot through her as he tasted her in places no one ever had. Each caress was electric, leaving her aching and wanting more. She writhed wildly.

After he led her over that edge, he gently guided her down his body and, thrusting upward, entered her. He groaned as he felt her tightening around him. She was fire in his arms.

"Don't rush," he murmured, struggling for control. Yet as her heat enveloped him, and she pressed herself into him hard and fast, his control snapped.

He was hard and male, and she was all softness and female. Feral instincts drove him as he pushed upward into the moist heat of the woman above him.

Her eyes were closed in passion. "Open your eyes, Lisa. Look at me and remember…everything," he said, his voice raw.

She did as he asked and he pushed inside her hard then, driving deep into her. Her eyes widened, and with a moan, she matched his wildness, absorbing him into her and urging him to give her more.

When she shuddered and cried out, his body shook and he poured himself into her.

Sanity returned slowly, their bodies wet with perspiration, the joining still in place.

"It was too much…too soon for you. Are you all right?" she asked contritely. "I wanted it to be all gentleness, not…"

"Fire?" he answered with a low chuckle that started deep in his throat. "What happened was meant to be. And it was perfect."

She shifted and started to move away but he held her in place.

"No. Stay there, against me," he said.

"Your shoulder," she managed.

"What shoulder?"

Smiling, she lay her head against his chest and listened to the rapid beat of his heart.

LISA SAT BEFORE THE LAPTOP, her mind still on the man in other room. Nothing would be the same—for her or for him. In Hunter's arms she'd found a world she hadn't known existed—a world of fire interwoven with aching tenderness.

With a sigh, Lisa forced herself to concentrate on her work. The GPS in the dagger was out of range, but she'd expected that. Once they got out of the mountains and into the populated valley, especially moving toward Farmington, they'd get a location—an address for Barker. The evidence she needed to clear her father and prove that Barker, or one of his men, had been behind her father's death would follow.

She was sitting at the table in front of her laptop when Hunter came into the room. She hadn't heard him, she hadn't seen him, yet she'd sensed his presence without even turning her head.

"We'll stay here until tomorrow, then go on the move," he said.

As she turned and glanced at him, she could see the tension in his muscles, but it was the way he was trying to keep all emotions from his face that worried her most.

"Is it your shoulder?"

"My shoulder's mending fine. What concerns me is that I'm not sure who we can trust anymore. I've got a lot of questions that need answers."

"We've done pretty well so far just relying on each other," she said. "If we have to, we'll find the evidence I need, and the tribe's dagger on our own without help from anyone."

Hunter shook his head. "It'll take more than the two of us to accomplish that."

"Then let's go find the answers you need," she said. "Who do we go see?"

Again he shook his head. "This isn't something I can discuss."

They'd experienced a closeness that had transcended all the barriers between them. Yet now he was putting up new walls. He'd made no promises, and she'd accepted his terms. Yet the thought that she'd seen too much in what they'd shared—that, to him, it had been nothing more than a momentary distraction—gnawed at her, undermining everything she'd believed about herself and Hunter.

Chapter Thirteen

At daybreak the following day, they gathered up some supplies and their things and loaded up the truck.

"I'll drive today. There's someone I need to go see, but don't ask me any more. And when we get there, remember, no names," Hunter added.

"Will it always be like this...drawing closer only to have secrets drive a wedge between us?"

"Some aspects of my life...of my work...are part of something that I'll never be able to discuss with you—or anyone else. I can't change that."

With Hunter, the kind of togetherness that her heart yearned for, that left no room for secrets, would remain forever out of her grasp. Yet, sharing her life with him would demand everything she had to give. She prized security. She'd made her living making people's homes and offices safe havens. Yet Hunter's life would demand she accept uncertainty and never question it.

It was time for her to move on—physically and

mentally. "I've been meaning to ask you something," she said, forcing herself to match his tone and focus on business as she climbed into the cab. "I noticed that Barker had a tattoo on the inside of his arm…four letters. *B T R H.* Any idea what that means?"

"Born to raise hell," he answered, stepping up into the pickup.

"Appropriate. Someone as evil as he is should be well acquainted with that place."

They were underway moments later. Hunter said nothing, but the way he was gripping the steering wheel let her know that, one way or another, he planned to get some answers from whomever he was about to question.

"We're going back the way we came, but for how long? Will you at least tell me where we're going?"

"We're on our way to see a very respected *hataalii,* a medicine man. You may address him as 'uncle' as a sign of respect. But I'll go into the hogan alone."

"Is it safe there?"

He nodded somberly. "There's no place on earth we'll be safer."

They rode toward Shiprock, and before reaching town turned north up a narrow road. The terrain looked flat here, upland desert sloping gently toward the San Juan river valley in the distance. Miles beyond were the Four Corners, where Utah, Colorado, Arizona and New Mexico all came together. Ute Mountain, on the horizon, was in Colorado.

They'd traveled for about twenty minutes when she spotted a split-log corral, a small frame house and a large, six-sided log hogan. An old pickup was parked outside the front door of the house.

"We'll park a short distance from the house, then wait in the truck. When they invite us to approach, I'll go into the hogan. You'll be asked inside the house. The *hataalii*'s wife will be there."

"Are there any *hataaliis* that are women?"

"I've heard of a few in the past who've served that function when their husbands died, but, no, normally women don't become medicine…men. But don't make the mistake of thinking we regard our women as somehow less than men. Homes belong to our women, and the children are traditionally considered to be the property of the wife. Women serve a different function for the tribe, but many believe the real power rests with them."

Hunter parked about fifty feet from the hogan and began the wait, watching the blanket-covered entrance. Minutes ticked by, but nothing happened.

"It's so isolated here," she said, studying the area. "Are you sure we're doing the right thing? I'd hate to bring the trouble following us to these people's doorstep."

"Barker, or whoever has the phony dagger right now, is the one with the tracking device on them, not us. They don't know where we are.

And there's no cover for miles. No one can sneak up here, not even if they crawl. There's someone watching us right now, too, I'm sure. This place is *always* guarded."

She nodded. The *hataalii* was part of the Brotherhood of Warriors. She had no doubt about that now.

Noting movement out of the corner of her eye, she turned as an elderly Navajo man wearing a white sash around his forehead stepped out of the hogan. A few seconds later, an elderly woman appeared at the front door of the house. The gray-haired woman, her hair in a traditional bun, was wearing a long skirt and loose, colorful cotton blouse gathered at the waist with a concha belt.

"I'll join you as soon as I can," Hunter said, his gaze in the direction of the *hataalii*.

Lisa watched him disappear behind the blanketed entrance to the hogan as she walked toward the house where the woman waited.

HUNTER SAT ON THE SOUTH SIDE of the hogan as was the custom for men, and faced the *hataalii*. "Uncle, my loyalty has always been clear. I've been a part of the Brotherhood of Warriors and have done whatever was necessary to protect our tribe, but I've seen and heard something...."

Hunter paused for several seconds, gathering his thoughts, then continued. "I need to ask you about my *bá'óltái*, my teacher. You know that he and I were close. In many ways he was like a father to me. I was told he'd disappeared on a mission for the Council. Then, when he failed to return, I was encouraged to believe he'd died. But now I see that information was withheld from me. I expected more—from the Council…from you. As a warrior, I've proven I can be trusted."

The *hataalii* stared at the ground before him for several long moments before he spoke.

"There's a lot of your teacher in you," he said slowly. "You both like direct answers but, sometimes, truthful responses require more than either of you are prepared to hear."

"He *is* alive, isn't he? The man I heard, saw… the one known as Paul Johnson. That was my *bá'óltáí,* not some stranger. Am I right?"

The *hataalii*'s expression didn't change.

"He didn't die," Hunter said. "That's no longer an assumption. So why not speak of him? I can be trusted to protect the identity of someone working undercover."

"He follows his path, and you have your own. Harmony will be restored. Remember that."

"This is obviously a Council secret," Hunter pressed. "But why from me?"

"You have your job to do. When the time's right, you'll know more."

"I can't operate in the dark. I need to know for sure if the man who taught me to be a warrior is the same man who now calls himself Paul Johnson."

"Stay focused on *your* task. You are *not* in

charge, nor do you give the orders," he said harshly. Then the *hataalii* exhaled softly. "Things are out of balance for you now, and you need to restore your harmony so you can complete what you have to do." He went to retrieve a pollen pouch from the shelf. "I'm going to do a special pollen blessing over you."

The medicine man turned his basket over to use as a drum and handed Hunter prayer sticks to hold. "It's a powerful Sing, one that can't be used more than once a day. It compels the gods to come to your aid."

Hunter nodded absently. His request had been categorically denied, and he still couldn't understand the reason. He had a feeling that even though the Council was still protecting his teacher, Daniel Yellowhair, the man had done something to anger them. He almost smiled, thinking of how typical of Daniel that would be. He'd never been one to follow orders easily, particularly if he'd believed there was a better way of doing what needed to be done.

"In the beautiful trail…" the *hataalii* began, his Song rising up in a prayerful and haunting chant that filled the hogan with peace and power.

Hunter listened, wondering where the trail of beauty would lead him this time and if he'd find Lisa there with him at the end of the journey.

LISA SAT ON A METAL DINETTE chair with a duct-taped cushion. The handmade wood-plank kitchen table held only a small vase of wildflowers. "I'm known as *'Anádlohí*. It means 'someone who likes to laugh.'"

Lisa looked at her in surprise. "I was told not to use names," she said in confusion.

'Anádlohí smiled. "It's not a name, just a nickname. Since names have power, our people often use nicknames that describe a quality of the person. Feel free to call me *'Anádlohí*."

"Navajo is a difficult language for me," Lisa answered, knowing her chances of pronouncing it correctly were extremely slim.

"Our language is hard for Anglos—whites," she agreed. "It's all in the pronunciation, too. Even minor mistakes can lead to very funny situations. *Shichó* is an innocent word. It simply means 'my' as in 'mine'. But without the high tone on the *o*, it means…well, male genitalia," she said, laughing.

Lisa laughed. "I'll have to remember that."

'Anádlohí laughed with her. "Does that mean that you and *Diltlí* aren't getting along?"

"What's that word mean?" Lisa asked, knowing she was referring to Hunter.

"To be on fire," she answered. "That's the nickname I gave him, because that's the way he tackles everything in his life." She gave Lisa a long, thoughtful look. "And that's the problem, isn't it? You're afraid you'll be swept up into that, and there won't be anything of you left."

Lisa thought about it for a moment. "In a way,

yes. Life with him would demand everything from me, yet a part of his heart's already given, it seems."

'Anádlohí said nothing for a moment, setting down a plate of what appeared to be blue gelatin in front of her. "His allegiance, maybe, but not his heart. He won't surrender that easily, and when he does, you can expect it to be forever. But be aware of what you're getting into. A man like that can never be tamed. Danger calls to him because it's part of his own nature. You won't be able to hold on to him unless you can accept what he is."

Lisa thought about what *'Anádlohí* had said. She couldn't force Hunter to choose a life of relative security, but she wasn't sure she could accept the alternative. His secrets would eventually mean all-night vigils, lying awake wondering if he'd return in one piece—or at all.

Taking a taste of the food *'Anádlohí* had placed before her, Lisa glanced up and smiled. "This is great! Sweet, and with a remarkable flavor. I've never eaten anything like it before."

"It's *tó'shchíín,* blue corn gelatin. It has sugar when we make it as a dessert, or you can put it in mutton stew."

"Thank you for sharing some with me," she said, finishing. Hearing the men outside, Lisa stood and went to the window. "I think it's time for us to leave," she said, then with a smile, added, "I'm glad I met you."

"I'll give you one last piece of advice that comes

mainly from having lived longer than you have. Life doesn't provide us with perfect safety. No matter how much you plan, things follow their own course."

After thanking her, Lisa joined Hunter at the pickup, and they were on their way moments later. "You look even more troubled than before," she said gently.

"I didn't get the answers I was hoping to get, unfortunately."

"We're working together," she said in a quiet, but firm voice. "If something's wrong, you need to tell me. I have to know what I should be watching out for."

He nodded slowly. "It wasn't my intent to shut you out. I just needed time...to get my thoughts together."

Instead of heading back toward the main highway, Hunter continued down the same road, which led into the bosque, the wooded area that bordered the San Juan. "Let's find a place to talk."

Sitting inside the truck in a shady, cool place beneath the yellowing leaves of an old cottonwood, he shifted in his seat and faced her. "Paul Johnson, the man your father mentioned..."

It took all her willpower, but she didn't interrupt the silence as it stretched out.

"I can't be sure about this," he warned slowly. "But the man Barker called Paul, the one behind the wheel, sounded a lot like the man who taught me the values that define me, that make me who I am. There's always been a special bond between us—one of respect. He's less than a relative, more than a friend. He was my mentor and teacher."

She stared at him in shock. "And he's Paul Johnson?"

"I felt the same way," he said, reading the shocked expression on her face. Then he filled her in on the few details he had. "If it is him, he must be working for the tribe under deep cover. That means that only one or maybe two people know what his mission is. But there's even more to it than that, only I'm not sure what."

"What's your instinct tell you?" she pressed in a soft voice.

"Though he's completely loyal to our tribe, he never was good at following orders to the letter. He may have seriously ticked some people off this time."

"You mean he's a bit of a wild card?"

"Something like that."

"The problem with wild cards is that they're unpredictable and can screw up things without even being aware of it." Lisa mulled things over. "We only heard his voice from a distance, and you were looking through a window that had a lot of reflections. How sure are you it was him?"

"Not one hundred percent," he admitted grudgingly. "And that's the real problem. Paul was also wearing a cap low on his face so it was impossible for me to get a clear look."

"Could it be a trick Barker and his men came up with—arranging for someone who looked and sounded like your teacher to keep you guessing and distract you? If it was, then in their eyes, it worked. They got away with the dagger and you took a bullet."

"That's entirely possible," he said, nodding slowly. "I need a few minutes alone to sort this out in my head. I'm going to take a short walk. Will you be okay here for a while?"

"Of course."

Hunter felt her gaze on him as he walked away slowly. If Daniel Yellowhair was undercover as Paul Johnson, when it was crunch time, he'd help them. But if he was wrong...

He stopped at the river's edge and stood just a few feet above the point where the sand crumbled off into the dark, murky water. Once he was in possession of the dagger, getting it back safely to tribal leaders and keeping it safe for the tribe would require that he shroud its return in secrecy.

That meant he'd have to betray Lisa when the time came. He'd wanted to find a way to avoid that, but there were no other options left. She needed publicity to clear her father, but that would endanger her, him and, ultimately, the dagger.

He had no choice. To keep her safe from danger,

he would have to betray her and, in so doing, break her heart…and his own.

HE RETURNED A SHORT TIME LATER and found her working on the laptop in the shade of an old tree. "Have you made any progress?"

"We're still out of range of the GPS, but I'm not worried. The closer we get to Farmington, the more likely we are to pick up a signal. In the meantime, I've been working on my father's riddle.

In the brightness nothing's hidden,
Questions raised, and answers given
Born for blood, circle's bidden
In the four, power's evened.

"Have you figured out what it means?"

"Maybe. Remember Barker's tattoo?"

"The letters for Born To Raise Hell," he answered.

"Barker's spilled blood, one could say he was born for that destiny. The four could be you and me, Barker and Trujillo. But how that all ties together and points to a place…" She shrugged helplessly.

"Place…" he said thoughtfully. "Trujillo has one of his many estates in this area. The address is 400 Circle Loop. It's located between Farmington and Bloomfield. Could your father have hidden the real dagger right under the man's nose, figuring he'd never look through his own house?"

She nodded slowly. "Yeah, that sounds like something my father would do," she said, then, looking at his bandaged shoulder, added, "But you're in no condition to break in and go sneaking around."

"I don't sneak—I stalk," he answered with a grin.

"If the man you saw *is* your teacher, he'll have to protect his cover if we run into him. You may have to fight him."

"He'd be a very tough opponent," he said, "but I can hold my own."

Lisa started to say more, then closed her mouth.

"Go ahead, say it. Making a move on Trujillo's place will be putting both of our lives on the line, so I need to know what you're thinking."

"It was only a thought...I analyze things. It's what I do," she said, shaking her head.

"Go on," Hunter pressed, refusing to let it pass.

There was no turning back. "Maybe the reason the tribe is helping you—us, really—is because they feel you have an advantage no one else does. If you and your teacher are as close as you say, he'll protect you from the others, no matter what the cost."

He said nothing as he weighed things in his mind. "People do know how close we are," he said at last. "Your reasoning is sound. But there may be a limit to what he can do without getting all of us killed."

He went to the passenger's side of the cab. "You

drive. We'll head in the general direction of Farmington and Trujillo's place. In the meantime, I'll call some of my sources and get more information on Paul Johnson. Then we can decide if and when we should make a move."

She went down a road that ran past several farms close to the river, then took a well-traveled path in the direction of the highway. Meanwhile, he made several phone calls.

Fifteen minutes later, he set down the phone and focused back on her. "Paul Johnson, for all intents and purposes, doesn't exist. He's one of many in our tribe who was born in a hogan and has no record— no social security, driver's license, zip. He's untraceable," he said, then after a pause, continued. "He lived in Arizona most of his life and got on the wrong side of some people. Then he disappeared. He turned up in our area a few months ago."

"Are your sources sure it was the same man?"

"No, not at all. In fact, no one knows who Paul Johnson really is, so it's very possible *Bá'óltáí*, my teacher, took on his identity."

"What about Trujillo's place. How secure is it?"

"It's going to take some serious doing to get inside. We've got to contend with cameras, alarms, dogs and armed security guards."

"If my father really did get in, then there's a way."

"He might have gone in right under their noses, posing as a delivery or repair man. But that would require good fake IDs," he said.

"Not much chance of either of us being able to pull off something like that now that they know what we look like. But I've got another idea—that is, providing you can track down the blueprints to his place."

"Those are in the hands of the people who installed his security, and I have a contact there. What else?"

"We'll need someone who knows how to set fires." He grinned slowly. "That would be me."

Chapter Fourteen

By the following morning everything was in place. Lisa understood the need to hit during the day when they'd least expect it, but it was a bold move. And once inside, they'd be on their own.

The good news was that they'd found the replica with the GPS. It was somewhere within Trujillo's mansion, and if the blueprints she had were correct, the device, and the new replica dagger, were either inside or close by a special room.

She studied the blueprints one last time. Once she'd discovered the existence of a panic room in the mansion, an idea had formed in her mind. After designing numerous panic rooms for clients, both her father and she were well acquainted with the security systems that protected them, as well as the position of vents and other possible access points. Since their own system was highly sought after, it was even possible that Trujillo had installed one of Rio Grande Security's own designs. The real irony could be that the fake dagger had been locked away in the same location as the real one—and Trujillo, Barker and the rest of them had no idea.

Hunter kept the area below them under surveillance. From the hillside, they had a clear view of Trujillo's place. He'd assured her that it wouldn't be long now, and she was more than ready for some action. She'd played similar scenarios for their clients whenever their company had been pulled in to find weaknesses in existing security systems. But those had been games. Here, they'd be courting death.

"Are you sure you're up to this?" she asked, seeing him taking his arm out of the sling and flexing his arm slightly.

The worry in her tone reached him, but he pushed it aside. This was no time to indulge soft emotions. If he was going to accomplish what needed to be done and keep them both alive at the same time, he'd need total focus. "It's sore, but I need mobility. I'll have it this way without the sling."

"What if you start bleeding?"

"It's bandaged in a way that will minimize the possibility. But I'm more worried about you. The initial fire will spread a lot of fumes and smoke, and that could set off your asthma. Ultimately that'll hamper your mobility and may give away your position."

"I'm maxed out on asthma pills, and my daily maintenance inhaler. Believe me, I'll have more energy than you do. The meds act like a super jolt of caffeine—only more so. And I'll have my rescue inhaler in my pocket, too, to handle any possible problem."

The truth was that he didn't want her to go. He wanted to find the dagger himself, come back and then convince her that it had to go back to the Council in secret. But that was nothing more than wishful thinking, and he knew it.

"If we find the real dagger, I'll call a press conference and give out the news, showing it to the cameras and having it authenticated on live TV. After that, it's yours to take back to the tribe, the Council or whomever gets it," she said.

"Calling a press conference would be like painting a bull's-eye on your back," he snapped. "Everyone, not just Trujillo and Barker, would be after you instantly. You'd be lucky to be alive when the reporters arrived."

"So timing would be critical, and we'd have to have security ready for an attack. But I'll pull it off—one way or another," she said firmly.

He didn't argue with her. Instead, he focused on the area below, knowing that, first of all, he'd have to keep her safe during the next hour or so. "Looks like Barker is finally heading out," he said, gesturing.

Lisa saw three cars driving out through the compound gates in a mini convoy. Traditional security measures dictated that the VIP, Trujillo, would be in the middle car, and Barker either in the lead or with Trujillo. The first and last cars would hold their security. But if Trujillo was really paranoid about not becoming a target, he probably didn't follow a plan book. He could be in the last car, or maybe even still at home.

"He took his bodyguards," Hunter said, "but there's still plenty of manpower back at the compound. From here I can see two security guards. Both are wearing matching blue jackets and caps. There are others, too, patrolling the grounds."

"Those are your guys?" she said, pointing to what appeared to be four teenaged boys joking around, drinking beer and trying to start a big, heavy old pickup that had just coasted to a stop in the middle of the street a short distance from the main gate of the estate.

"That's them," he answered. "The pickup's got some extra cans of fuel in the bed, so it'll make for nice fireworks."

"This is too dangerous for kids to be involved," she said firmly.

He laughed. "The youngest among them is in his mid-twenties."

Lisa adjusted the binoculars and took another look. "They sure don't look it," she said, at last.

"That was the point."

She heard them laughing, and then the one behind the wheel got out to look at the engine compartment with the others. Suddenly the truck began to roll downhill.

The boys—or, more accurately, men—shot after the truck, laughing and yelling at each other, offering suggestions as they raced after it. One of them managed to jump up onto the tailgate, then ran over to the sliding rear window and reached inside, grabbing for the steering wheel. The truck turned slightly, now heading straight for the gates blocking the entrance to Trujillo's estate. The young man looked around, and one of the others chasing the truck yelled for him to get out.

The man in the pickup bed did just that, hitting the street and rolling down the pavement several feet. The other boys helped him to his feet.

"All part of the act?" Lisa asked.

"Necessary to adjust the aim of the truck," Hunter replied. "We couldn't try this with a remote steering rig. It would have looked too obvious. The steering has been tweaked to hold its course."

The truck continued downhill, accelerating and easily outdistancing the group of four, which had all but given up chasing it.

"Get out of the way!" they started yelling at the two guards in front of the main gates.

The blue-jacketed guards had been watching the boys all along, and now, as they moved out of the path of the oncoming pickup, one of the guards unhooked the radio at his hip.

"They're calling it in, but they don't act too worried," Lisa commented. "Those gates look like they can stop anything smaller than a tank."

"The bed of the truck is half-full of sand, really heavy, and the suspension is reinforced with massive shocks. The grill is solid steel, braced inside with two I-beams that come together like a thousand-pound two-headed arrow. We've tested this design. Even going ten miles an hour, it'll smash through walls or iron gates like a battering ram."

One of the guards pulled out his pistol, took aim, and shot the left front tire. The truck veered slightly to the left, but it was too late.

"Run-flat tires," Lisa noted softly. "Nice touch." Her father had often requested them on escort vehicles when providing security for VIPs.

The guard kept firing at the truck, but nothing could stop it, short of heavy artillery. The truck's change of direction caused it to miss striking the center of the entrance, where the two gates met. The pickup hit the left gate squarely in the center, barely slowing down. Alarms went off everywhere.

The impact of the collision snapped the gate loose at its hinges, and it bounced around toward the center of the entrance, where it was still connected. The pickup rolled farther to the left, off the main path, and, with a loud crunch, crashed into the rear end of a parked SUV.

The guard who'd been firing his pistol ran toward the pickup, his weapon still in his hand. A heartbeat later, the truck burst into flames, and the guard threw his arm up, protecting his face as he stopped dead in his tracks.

"One of my people rigged the truck to explode when it came to rest. I bet they end up blaming the guard who fired off the rounds."

The flames from the truck quickly ignited the SUV it had struck, and thick black smoke spread quickly throughout the compound.

Hunter and Lisa were already moving down the hill. "Now's our chance," Hunter said, urging her forward as he heard an emergency crew coming up the road. "The fire station probably got an automated call when the alarm went off."

Wearing dark blue jackets and caps identical to the ones worn by Barker's security team, they moved forward. They entered the compound seconds behind the fire department's first unit, blending in during the confusion. As they neared the main house, Hunter casually scattered several 'rocks"—actually disguised smoke bombs. They were electronically triggered, scheduled for later use.

"Don't pay any attention to the guards moving around the compound," he said, spotting the men who'd been guarding the gate. One was yelling at the firemen, and the other was on the radio. "It's the two assigned to the front door we've got to worry about. We'll have to take them down hard and fast."

"I've got this one," she said, seeing a blue-jacketed guard step out the door and onto the front steps.

"Who grabbed your pistol?" she asked loudly, stepping up to the guard and pointing to his waist.

He took his eyes off her as he looked down. Lisa hit him in the groin. The man collapsed. As he went down, she smashed the edge of her hand against the back of his neck.

The door opened behind her, and she turned just as Hunter grabbed the second guard by the arm and shoulder, slamming him into the door jamb head first.

The man crumbled. Hunter hauled him into the foyer, then helped Lisa drag the other, unconscious guard in as well, placing him atop the first.

"Move quickly," Hunter whispered, removing the guards' weapons as he spoke. "I'll keep anyone from coming in this door," he added, setting off one of the electronically triggered smoke bombs with a small device in his pocket.

"Good." Lisa stepped out of the foyer into some kind of generic sitting room that looked more like a hotel lobby without the front desk. There were three doorways, and she took the one in the center, running down the long, wood paneled hallway. She passed four doors, ignoring the photos hung along the wall and the impressive collection of edged weapons mounted on brackets near the end of the corridor.

She'd studied the blueprints and memorized them, and knew exactly where the panic room would be. Between the sirens and alarms going off all throughout the compound, everything was in a state of chaos. Yet, even so, she figured she'd have less than ten minutes, fifteen tops.

She entered the den, which was unoccupied, and walked to the door leading to the panic room. The entrance was disguised as one of the wall panels in the den, and if she hadn't known the spot from the blueprints, she wouldn't have even noticed it. The panel fit right into the rest of the room, and even had a painting of a desert landscape hung in place. A small plaque representing a local service club award, at just the right height, concealed a keypad.

She smiled. It was the keypad type that her father had excelled at defeating. Her father would have loved hiding the dagger here—in Trujillo's inner sanctum.

She looked down at the override codes she held in her hand, available to select professionals who installed and serviced these locks. There was one code for each series of locks manufactured, but she'd have to take the outer mechanism off with a special tool to examine the serial number. Unfortunately, that would cost her time.

Instead, she decided to play a hunch. She looked at the ten-digit keypad, 0 to 9. Codes were set by the owner, and they tended to pick numbers they could remember, such as birth dates, all 0s and so forth.

Taking a chance, she punched in the numbers 2-20-18-8, which represented the letters of the alphabet for BTRH, Born To Raise Hell. That didn't work. Then with a new burst of inspiration, she tried BTLH. Trujillo's motto would have spelled out his key position—Born To *Lead* Hell. The panic door slid open, and she hurried inside the oversized closet.

Trujillo had his weapons collection here, everything from expensive Italian shotguns to pistols and automatic weapons. There were also boxes of ammunition, business ledgers, cash boxes and even survival supplies like bottled water and MREs, military-style rations. With no time to waste, she checked the vents and looked behind the boxes and containers, working her way around the room.

The daggers simply weren't there, neither the real one nor the replica. As she started to check the ledgers, hoping to find one where the paper inside had been carved out to hold the dagger, she came across loose papers of various sizes.

Looking more closely, she realized that they were notes, sketches and other papers that had belonged to her father. Some looked as if they'd been salvaged from his trash, but others were still on the pads that he'd used in his office.

She gathered as many as she could find, sticking the papers inside her jacket, then stepped out of the panic room and closed the door behind her.

Across the den, blocking her way to the exit, stood Michael Barker. Surprised, with her back to the wall now, literally, she got ready for the fight of her life.

"I'm so glad you've decided to pay us a visit," Barker said, standing between her and the only way out.

She kept her eyes glued on him, wondering where Hunter was. She'd have to stay in one piece until he arrived. The only way they'd be able to take Barker down fast was if they combined forces. Unless they could do that, they'd never get out alive.

"So I gather you have no idea where the real dagger is, either," he laughed. "Yes, we caught on to your little con."

Careful to maintain his position between her and the open door to the hall, he took one step, then tossed something onto the desk between them. It was the GPS they'd had placed in the dagger replica.

"That phony dagger looked so real, we were fooled at first. But we couldn't figure out why your father would have taken out the diamond. Soon it became clear that it was the only part of the real dagger you couldn't fake, so you left it out on purpose. That's when we X-rayed the replica and found this little toy in the handle."

"That's only half of it, Barker. Your arrogance is going to be costly. You should have gotten rid of the GPS. We knew it would lead us to whoever was responsible for my father's death. But I found something that's going to nail you anyway. You'll never get all of Trujillo's illegal transactions—the ones in those ledgers—out of that cute hidey hole before the police arrive. I bet you don't even know the entry code." She made a point of looking down at her watch. "You'd better start trying some numbers, quick. The police are going to raid this place unless I'm back outside your gate in five minutes. If I were you, I'd run out the back way during all the confusion. Let Trujillo take the fall alone."

"Not bad fiction, Miss Garza. Believable—to a point. But even if there were cops on the way, the only ones going to jail would be you and that Indian of yours. Breaking and entering, assault and battery—those are crimes. But don't worry, you won't be arrested. You'll be dead. It's too bad that you didn't partner up with us from the beginning. You may have lived to tell the tale."

"Yeah, sure. Let me guess—honor among thieves."

"Such skepticism," he said, clicking his tongue. "You should try to be nicer. Dying can be easy and fast or slow and hard. I do know the code to that door. I could lock you in that closet for a few days— minus water and food, of course, and those inhalers you probably have in your pocket."

"But you won't do that because your boss, Trujillo, won't be quite that patient—not after the mistakes you've made. For example, bringing a tracking device that places you at the crime scene right into his own home," she countered, ignoring his references to her asthma.

"If you answer all my questions, you may get out of this without any permanent scars," he said. The deadly tone of his voice contradicted his smile, and somehow made the gesture even more menacing.

The man was a hard-core professional, and instinct told her that if she fought him, she wouldn't win. The most she could hope for was to injure him enough so that Hunter would be able to finish him. But she'd die in the process.

He knew about her asthma, too. To make matters worse, the smoke *was* getting to her. She needed her inhaler now. Yet reaching for it at the moment would have been suicide. She had to attack.

As she kicked, he countered and grabbed her leg, but she jumped up and kicked him with her free leg, sending them both tumbling to the floor. That last move had forced him away from the door. Rolling to her feet, Lisa made a run for it, but he grabbed her ankle, throwing her off balance. Barker held on, pulling her toward him.

She started to topple forward when Hunter suddenly appeared at the doorway, caught her and aimed a hard kick at Barker's neck and shoulder. The man groaned and let go of her leg. Before Barker could recover, Hunter yanked her out, and closed the door.

She turned around, grabbed a heavy broadsword from a display on the wall, then jammed it under the door as hard as she could, wedging it in place. "He'll be stuck in there for a minute," she said.

Together, they ran down the hall. When they reached the front door, they could see the fire crews in the compound, spraying the wrecked vehicles with water from their big red pumper, which was half in, half out of the ruined gates. They moved across the compound, circled around the activity and began to inch toward the compound gates.

By the time they slipped past the fire truck and were walking back up the road, Lisa could feel the incredible tightness in her lungs. What had only been a minor wheeze was now loud enough for even Hunter to hear clearly.

"You don't sound so good," he said.

"You don't look so good," she shot back with a shaky smile as she reached for the inhaler. "I overestimated the power of the medications and the trouble the smoke would create for me. And when things started to go south and I needed my inhaler, Barker was right in front of me. If I'd have reached for it, he would have had me for sure."

She took a deep puff, then held up her hand, indicating she couldn't talk for the moment. She kept still, waiting for the air sacs to open up again. Finally, after a few anxious minutes, her breathing eased. She started walking again in the direction they'd parked their pickup.

"Next time, Lisa, you might consider giving me a heads-up. You could have used that thing once we corralled Barker."

"We needed to get out of there fast. But we made it. That's all that matters now," she answered. But next time she wouldn't overestimate her capabilities.

AT A MOTEL ROOM IN DURANGO, Colorado, about forty-five miles northeast of Farmington and well off the reservation, she went through the papers she'd taken from Trujillo's panic room. Her breathing was back to normal, she thought, until Hunter came out of the shower, a towel slung slow on his hips and another in his hand.

"Anything?" he asked, drying off his hair with the smaller towel.

She turned around to look at him. He stole her breath away…in a good way…but that wasn't such a good idea right now for a variety of reasons.

He'd noticed the small hitch in her breathing, and his expression gentled with concern. "Still having problems? Are you *really* okay?"

"Sure," she said, quickly covering for the momentary lapse, her gaze still on him.

He gave her a killer smile. "You gonna stare?"

She turned around quickly and pretended to study the papers. Then she heard the towel that had covered him drop to the floor, and couldn't resist. Ducking her head slightly, she sneaked a look.

"You're not fooling anyone," he said. "If you want to look, just do it."

"I wasn't… Yeah, okay, busted," she said, her eyes back on the papers. She heard the rustle of clothing as he pulled on his jeans, then the sound of the zipper closing, but, though she was sorely tempted, she didn't turn around.

He laughed and the low throaty sound sent a shiver up her spine.

As she took a breath, she realized that in the relative silence of the room, her wheezing sounded like bagpipes gone crazy.

"Are you sure you're okay?" he asked quickly.

"Yeah, but the smoke's caused some problems that'll take a while to clear up," she said. "I'll go get some coffee from the machine down the hall."

"You sleepy?" he asked, surprised.

"No. Coffee's got chemicals that are similar to those used to treat asthma. It really helps."

He came over and rubbed the back of her neck. The feel of his strong hands made her skin prickle. She was aware of the fresh, soapy scent on his skin and was acutely aware of the warmth of his body so close behind hers.

"How can I help?" he asked.

Hating her asthma, and hating herself for allowing something as innocent as a neck rub to distract her, Lisa forced herself to focus.

"Don't worry. Once I get some coffee in me and remain inactive for a bit, I'll be fine." She'd said it for her own benefit, not his, and as she looked over at him, she realized that he'd sensed that, too.

"Let me get some for you," he said, then left the room. He came back moments later with two large cups of hot coffee and placed them on the desk before her.

She sipped the strong brew as she studied the papers she'd taken from Trujillo's secure room. "There's something interesting here. There's one image in different stylized versions that my dad drew over and over again in these pages. It's the Zia symbol…. Come to think of it, that may be what he was referring to in the riddle."

"New Mexico's state emblem," he said, nodding. "A circle with four lines at each of the four major points of the compass."

"It fits, if you think about it.

In the brightness nothing's hidden

The Zia is the symbol for the sun.

Born for blood, circle's bidden

That could be a reference to the color of dawn and the circular sun.

Inside the four, power's evened

The Zia symbolizes the circle of life—four winds, four directions, four seasons and the four sacred obligations—clear mind, pure spirit, strong body and devotion to family. That's what he tried to tell me with the compass he had made."

"But the Zia symbol is *everywhere,* even on the governor's stationery. You see it at the Albuquerque Sunport, state and local offices, even at the University of New Mexico. If that's a clue, it'll be almost impossible to pinpoint the dagger's location from it."

"The Zia symbol is common, that's true, but he drew one Zia symbol that's not like the rest."

He looked at the paper she held up. "What's in the middle of that?"

"At first I thought it was a cross, but it's not. I think it's a stylized dagger."

He nodded slowly. "You're right. There's a circle on the center of the cross. That might signify the diamond," he said, taking a closer look.

"Or we're way off the mark, and it's just a stylized crown over the cross—a religious symbol." She leaned back in her chair. "I know that my dad's office at home has many versions of the Zia symbol in art, pottery and the like. He was always fascinated by it."

"What's that at the bottom of the page?"

She leaned over the page, but even so, the writing was incredibly small and hard to read. "It looks like two letters, *C* and *I*. Maybe initials…or Roman numerals. *CI* would be 101. It may mean something, or not. Remember my father went out of his way to leave false trails."

"Is it possible your father hid the dagger in your own home, like in his office where you mentioned there are many Zia symbols around? It would have been easy for him to keep an eye on it then," he asked.

"He wouldn't have risked exposing Mom, or me for that matter, to the kind of people who are after the dagger. But to answer your question more specifically, I searched Dad's home office already," she said, then added slowly. "But then again, the Zia symbol held no particular significance to me at the time…."

She stood up abruptly. "We need to go back. Barker may have come to the same conclusion you did, which means my mother and a very dear friend are in the line of fire." She closed the laptop and gathered up the papers. "Let's go."

Chapter Fifteen

It was close to 6:00 p.m. by the time they arrived at Lisa's home in Albuquerque's north valley. Her mother, Elena, met them at the door and brought them inside. Elena's dark brown eyes contrasted with her short, simply styled hair, and the combination added to the easy elegance she'd always exuded.

"It's so good to have you home safely, Lisa. I fixed plenty of dinner, so I hope you haven't eaten." Elena glanced at Hunter and smiled. "And you've brought a friend!"

Lisa introduced them. Elena, who'd always been the perfect hostess, never offered to shake hands, obviously familiar with Navajo customs.

"I was worried about you, Mom," Lisa said quickly and hugged her.

"Me? Why? Your friend Bruce has been taking really good care of me. He's outside somewhere right now, standing guard. I've tried to get him to come in, there's a storm brewing and the winds are starting up, but he refuses."

"He needs to be out there to do his job, and spot any potential intruders before they can get close to the house," Lisa answered. "Speaking of that, has anything unusual happened around here?"

"Except for last night, it's been quiet," Elena said.

"What happened last night?" Lisa asked quickly.

"I heard a noise near your father's study window. Before I could even yell for Bruce, he was there. He said we'd surprised a burglar."

"Did he make an arrest?" Hunter asked.

"No, whoever it was ran away just as Bruce came around the side of the house. But at least he never broke in."

"You said you *heard* a burglar. But what about the alarm? You have been turning it on, right?" Lisa asked.

"Yes, of course. Bruce and I talked about it, and we think that whoever it was figured out our code number and shut it off."

"That isn't an easy thing to do," she said, shooting Hunter a quick look. "Mom, we need to go into Dad's study for a while and maybe look through some of his stuff. Is everything still the way he left it?"

She nodded, and dabbed at the corner of her eye with a tissue. "I haven't been able to go in there. Everything—even the scent in the office—reminds me…" She paused and shook her head.

"It's okay, Mom," Lisa assured quickly. "We'll work in there for a bit and then join you."

"And have dinner with me?" she asked, becoming the mom Lisa had always known.

"Yes. We'll meet you in the kitchen once we're done."

Lisa led Hunter to her father's study, bracing herself for another onslaught of memories. This had been her father's domain, and, as she walked in, she felt his absence keenly.

As she glanced back at Hunter she noticed that he held himself ramrod straight. Although he was looking around, he also appeared to be taking extra care not to come into contact with anything.

"Would you like to wait outside? A Navajo officer friend told me once that your tribe is uncomfortable around the possessions of someone who has died."

"It's a part of Navajo teachings that everyone has good and evil inside them. At death, the good in that person goes on to another place, but the other part, unable to leave this plane, remains here. To touch the possessions of the deceased is considered dangerous because the *chindi,* the part that remains earthbound, is attached to them. But I'm not a traditionalist, though sometimes the beliefs we were raised with come back to mind," he answered. "That's why I carry a flint point. It was given to me by a *hataalii,* and it's said to protect the bearer."

"Okay, then. Let's get started."

Lisa searched the pottery vases and inside books

and whatever she could find that had the Zia symbol incorporated into the design or layout.

Hunter searched through the file cabinet, looking for files marked with the Zia symbol, but there was nothing there. "We may have been wrong," he said after forty minutes.

Lisa sat on her father's chair and looked around. "About it being here, yes. I never thought it was, to be honest. I was more worried about others who might think it was. But I'm right about the Zia symbol. I can feel it in my bones."

Lisa met her mother in the kitchen after their search. Elena served them platters of enchiladas, delicious as always.

As Hunter ate, Lisa could tell from his expression that his mind was elsewhere. As hungry as she was, she enjoyed every bite, but her thoughts, too, were drifting. Someone had guessed the code on their burglar alarm system, and that bothered her a great deal. No doubt Bruce had reprogrammed it, but the fact was that finding the right numbers couldn't have been accidental. It would have required an extensive knowledge of their family background.

The code numbers, set by her father, represented the day, month and year that they'd moved into this home—a palace compared to the two-bedroom apartment in the city where Lisa had spent her grade school years. Moving in had been a special day for the three of them, a moment that would not have been shared with anyone outside the family. Whoever had guessed their simple code was a genius on family trivia, or a skilled thief.

"So tell me, Mom, what else has been happening?" Lisa asked, gathering more information.

"The university called. They need to close down your father's campus office. Happeth offered to go over there and pack up everything, but for legal reasons they'll only let you or me do that. They wouldn't give her access."

"I'll handle it," Lisa said.

"I don't know if you've been down there since they relocated his office. Your father mentioned it to me about a week before.... Well, anyway, it's still in the Anthro building." She looked at a notepad beside the phone. "Used to be 104, now its room 101."

Lisa glanced at Hunter, who said nothing, but the look on his face made it clear he, too, remembered that number.

There was a knock at the door just then. "That must be Bruce. I took him his dinner earlier," Elena said.

As Elena opened the door, Bruce handed her his empty plate, then he glanced over and gave Lisa and Hunter a nod.

Hunter recognized the police officer instantly. Bruce Atcitty wasn't a member of the Council—he'd chosen a different path—but his grandfather was their *hataalii*.

Lisa greeted Bruce warmly, then, gesturing for Hunter to accompany them, stepped into the next room with both men while her mother answered a phone call.

Once they were alone, Bruce gave them a full report.

"I couldn't catch whomever tried to break in, but there's something else you should know. I never corrected your mother's assumption because I felt it would scare her. But the window they were trying to open wasn't the one to your father's study—it was her own."

Lisa froze, sudden fear undermining her confidence. Her inability to break her father's code and find the dagger had led to this new threat. The danger that had been circling for the past week was now sweeping down on her and her family. She had to find answers fast.

The feeling that she'd failed her father—and ultimately herself—brought back all the insecurities and doubts she'd harbored as a girl. She'd been the gimp back then, the one no one wanted on their team, the person who was always last.

Lisa pushed the thought firmly out of her mind. She wasn't that girl anymore. She'd used her brains and talent, not her physical endurance, and had become a professional. She'd fought hard for her place in the world and was the best at what she did. One way or another, she'd see to it that Barker and Trujillo paid dearly for messing with her family.

"Someone's been working against my father— and me—all along. It's got to be someone who knew a lot about him, about our family. Someone he trusted."

"Your father didn't trust many people…" Bruce said.

"He trusted my mother and me…and Happeth," she said, at last.

Bruce nodded slowly. "She's been working for your father for several months, is that right?"

She thought back, trying to remember. "She began working for him in late winter, maybe March, just before I stopped freelance consulting and became his partner. But that was way before the tribe hired my father to protect the dagger."

Hunter shook his head. "No, that decision was made back in January, though I'm not sure when your father was actually approached."

"It was May, I remember. But Happeth really admired my father. I can't imagine her not being loyal to him," Lisa said slowly.

"I'm not saying she isn't—wasn't. I'm just suggesting a possibility," Bruce said. "Someone may have extracted information from her—whether she was willing or not."

"Between your connections and mine, we should be able to get a lot more information on this woman very quickly," Hunter said, looking at Bruce.

Bruce nodded. "I was ordered by *Hastiin Sání*

to cooperate with you, and I'll do my best to honor that."

Lisa looked at Bruce, then back at Hunter. Was it possible that her old friend was also a member of the Brotherhood of Warriors? Before she could say anything, Bruce continued.

"I just want to be clear here. My allegiance to your family and our tribe means I'll help you," he said to Lisa, then looked at Hunter. "But I'm also part of a different brotherhood. I'm a police officer, and that brings its own set of responsibilities."

"Understood," Hunter answered, then glanced back at Lisa. "While he and I consult with our own resources, you might consider speaking to your mother about this. She may know more than she thinks she does."

Lisa somehow doubted that—her mother had deliberately not shown any interest in her dad's work. But she'd check anyway. "All right."

As Hunter and Bruce left, heading to Bruce's unmarked car, Lisa went to find her mother. She was in her sewing room, piecing together a quilt. As she walked in, Elena smiled.

"I'm really glad you're back home," Elena said as Lisa took a seat across from where she was working. "It got lonely here without you around."

"Mom, I need to have a serious talk with you."

"Does this have to do with the gentleman you brought with you?" she asked hopefully.

Lisa chuckled softly. "No, Mom. He and I are

just working together. There's nothing more to it than that."

"If you say so," she said with a tiny smile.

Dropping the subject for now, Lisa focused on the investigation. "I'd like to talk to you about Happeth."

Elena's amused expression vanished in an instant. "I've never liked that woman, if you must know. Your father trusted her, and I understand she was very knowledgeable about the security business, but there's something not right about her."

"Dad was a good judge of character," Lisa said slowly, "and when I was in the office, I didn't pick up any negative vibes."

Elena scoffed at the idea. "Your father, like most men, responded to flattery. Happeth *excels* at that," she said, then with a shrug added, "It doesn't hurt that she's beautiful, too."

"When I joined Dad as a partner he'd already hired Happeth. How much did he really know about her? Do you have any idea?"

Elena hesitated. "I didn't pay that much attention to your father's work, so I can't tell you much. I do know that your father initially hired her because she was willing to work for minimum, with bonuses whenever the company had a case. Your father loved what he did, but he didn't have a good head for money. The company's had many ups and downs over the years. You coming in as partner, adding your financial resources, helped put him back into the black. I just wish you two would have become partners sooner. You'd have had more time together."

"I wanted to get more experience in the business before joining Dad. I love security work," she said, then added, "But to tell you the truth, Mom, I honestly don't know how you got through the days. Your life was spent waiting for Dad to finish whatever case he was working on, and praying he'd come home in one piece."

"Your father had an adventurous soul but, at the end of the day, he needed 'mooring,' as he called it. I made sure our home was a haven he could always depend on. We each brought something different into our relationship and that's what made it work."

"But the uncertainty...of his business, or his work," Lisa commented softly. "That couldn't have been easy to cope with."

"You always had a more difficult time with that than I did. I accepted it as a part of John, but you worried about your dad constantly," Elena said with a nod. "You craved certainties just as much as your dad loved danger. That's why you went into the technical side of security work. Your work, and your goals in life, have been geared toward assuring a certain future for your clients and for yourself. But life doesn't come with guarantees. You have to take things one day at a time and do the best you can with the time that's given you. Even the best-laid plans can go wrong."

"I know," she said somberly, thinking of her father's death. As sure as she knew that he hadn't committed suicide, she also knew that death had taken him by surprise.

"Love's a daily choice. I don't regret mine. Your father and I completed each other," Elena said softly, then after a pause added, "But I guess I don't understand you anymore. I can see you're in love with Hunter, though you're fighting it as hard as you can. I know you've never let fear stop you from doing anything. Yet now you're hesitating and I'm just not sure why."

"It's complicated, Mom. Hunter has another life on the reservation…and loyalties and obligations to his tribe that exclude me from the picture," Lisa said at last.

"And you're afraid you'll get left behind, that you'll drift apart because of his other responsibilities." Not waiting for an answer, she continued. "But things like that can bring you even closer, if you'll let it. You may spend some nights—maybe most nights—worried about him. Togetherness of spirit doesn't always mean inseparability. But a little separation can strengthen the ties between you and make them even stronger. Respecting your own natures and allowing each other the freedom to be, gives love room to grow."

Before she could ponder her mother's words further, Hunter came into the room. "I need to talk to you for a few moments," he said, looking at Lisa and giving Elena a respectful nod.

As they stepped out into the hall, Lisa glanced around. "Where's Bruce?"

"Back on guard outside," he answered.

Lisa nodded. "He's a good man, and a great friend," she said. "Did you find out anything about Happeth?"

"That's what I came to talk to you about. All we could get—despite our considerable resources— is that Happeth has no police record. She grew up in southern Arizona and moved here to attend college. Before she came to work for your father, she'd been employed in various museums, setting up exhibits and such."

"Let's go talk to her tonight and get a fix on her friends and associates. But first I want to go to my father's downtown office. That's where Happeth works, and we can search her desk and check through her things at our leisure since she won't be around."

They arrived less than twenty minutes later. Hunter went through Happeth's desk, even searching below and behind the drawers.

She searched her father's office again. There was a Zia symbol on the wall behind her father's desk, a plaque from the Zuni tribe for a security job he'd done at their tribal offices a year ago. She searched behind it and around it, then moved on.

After she looked everywhere, she sat down in her father's chair, trying to put herself in his mindset. Though her father had preferred sitting close to his desk, ramrod straight, she did her clearest thinking when she was leaning back comfortably. Lisa tried to roll her chair back, away from the desk, but the caster jammed and refused to turn. Muttering a curse, she got down on the floor and tugged at the caster, trying to figure out what was wrong. A moment later, the wheeled swivel unit came off in her hand.

There was something white inside the hollow chair leg. It was a small, rolled-up piece of notepaper. She unrolled the tiny scroll and studied it. It was a drawing depicting several buildings all connected by a line. The Zia symbol was drawn on the edge of the paper.

This was similar to the drawing she'd found in the panic room except this one had the connecting line.

Hunter came into the room. "I found a memo your father wrote to Happeth about his office at the university. It was in the trash. Your father was asked to switch offices at the university with someone else on staff about a month ago, and he made it clear he didn't need her help with the transfer. I also found a letter dated two days after his death. Happeth received a notification that his office there would be closed. She responded by asking for access to remove anything pertaining to company business. Her request was denied," Hunter said, then, after a brief silence, added, "It's clear that your father wanted to keep her away from there. I don't think it was coincidence, especially because of that number 101 connection. We should check out that office."

"I saw his old campus office a few times. It was hot and cramped, right next to some steam pipes, and he hated it. I recall him being thrilled when they offered him a larger one."

Hunter seemed a million miles away, staring at Happeth's reception area. Lisa wondered if he'd even heard her. "What's on your mind?" she asked at last.

"Look at that woman's desk. People normally keep photos of kids or family on their desks, but there's nothing even close to personal in that office."

"Happeth is a single woman. I don't think—"

"No boyfriend, no dog, no cat, not even a plant. Look at it. It's as if Happeth doesn't exist outside this office," he insisted.

He had a point, though it was scarcely conclusive evidence. "I don't know what to tell you, I don't know very much about her. Most of my work for the company was done out of the office."

Originally she'd thought Happeth inordinately loyal to have stayed on even when the business had, for all intents and purposes, shut down. But now Lisa began to wonder if there was far more to it than she'd realized.

"Do you know where Happeth lives?" he asked her.

"Not offhand, but the address is in her file, inside my dad's file cabinet," she said, then retrieved it. "Since it's more or less on our way, and not far from here, let's go there first."

They locked up and drove to Happeth's apartment, just a few blocks east of downtown in a new building not far from the main university campus. Upstairs, on the third floor, they found the apartment number and knocked.

Happeth, wearing jeans and a long silk blouse, came to the door. She looked at Lisa then at Hunter, surprised. "Hey, boss. I didn't know you were back in the city. Is everything all right?"

"I have some questions for you," Lisa said, then introduced Hunter, who'd remained a few steps behind her, watching down the hall toward the stairwell.

Just as Lisa heard the sound of a door closing inside the apartment, Happeth came out into the hall instead of asking them inside. "I'll be back at my desk at eight tomorrow—and I'll continue to be there for as long as I can. Is it necessary to do this now? I've got company."

"This won't take long," Lisa said. "Did Dad write down the code for our home's security system anywhere that you know of? On a calendar, under the desk pad, somewhere like that?"

She looked at Lisa and shrugged. "I doubt it.

That doesn't sound like him. You know how careful he was about things like that."

"Did you and he ever discuss any of the codes for the security devices he was responsible for, at his offices or on behalf of any of our clients?"

"No. I did try to help your mother by cleaning out your father's office over at the university, but I didn't know the code so I couldn't get in."

"That's very considerate of you, trying to help out. But wasn't the university concerned that you're not the next-of-kin?" Lisa countered, trying not to show any signs of disapproval.

"Someone did come to check on me—but by then I'd given up guessing which numbers to punch in."

Hunter cleared his throat and stepped closer to the door. "Would you mind if I came in and used your restroom for a moment?"

Happeth gave him an apologetic smile. "Normally, no, I wouldn't mind, but I have a plumbing problem tonight. Actually, my company is the building manager's son, and he's in there trying to unclog the pipes. But there's a gas station just a block down Central Avenue. Now, if you'll excuse me, I'm checking out several job openings online."

Before either of them could protest, she stepped back and closed the door.

"Warm, isn't she?" Lisa muttered.

Hunter led her away from the door and didn't speak until they were outside again. "She looked familiar to me and, at first, I couldn't figure out why. Then I remembered seeing a photo in the hallway of Trujillo's home. You might remember the collection of photos on the wall right before the display of edged weapons. One of those photos showed Barker with his arm around a tall redhead who looked a lot like Happeth, but her hairstyle was different back then."

"So you think Barker planted Happeth in Rio Grande Securities," she commented, considering the possibility. "But if she's still sticking with the company, trying to figure out what my dad did with the dagger…

"Then Barker and his people still have no clue where it is. Maybe the person we heard in the other room at Happeth's apartment was Barker."

"That's the real reason I wanted in."

"Just in case your hunch is right, let's move fast and try to stay a step ahead of them," she said as they reached the pickup. "Let's see if we can get security on campus to give us access to my father's office tonight. I know the security code, but they'll have to unlock the building for us and convincing them to do that might be tricky."

"That's where Bruce's credentials as a cop may come in handy. I suggest we take him with us."

"What about Mom?" Lisa asked.

"Maybe Bruce can find someone to replace him. If we can make sure she's protected, then we can go ahead."

"All right." She'd been driving, so she pulled over to the curb and gave Bruce a call. When she hung up, she looked at Hunter. "He's setting it up."

Hunter had hoped Bruce would have more of a problem. He would have preferred to have had Lisa at home and well out of the line of fire. His gut tightened at the thought of what lay ahead and what he'd have to do. By betraying her, he'd lose Lisa, the woman who'd come to mean more to him than life itself. As she spoke, he forced himself to stop brooding and focus.

"I wonder if my father began to doubt Happeth's loyalty toward the end and that's why he hadn't wanted her at his university office," she said in a thoughtful voice. "No, never mind. If he'd believed that she couldn't be trusted, he would have fired her."

"Not necessarily. Remember the old adage— keep your friends close and your enemies even closer. But that might explain why your father wanted to keep Happeth away from his office on campus. Barker may be in town to help Happeth find a way to get in there once and for all, without having to do a black bag job."

"That's why we have to get in there *tonight*," she said. "We've got good connections, and I know his access code, so now all we need is a bit of luck."

Chapter Sixteen

Lisa and Hunter arrived at her father's campus office twenty minutes later. Some areas, especially in departments where research was going on, never really shut down, and there was student housing on-site. Most of the buildings, however, were locked up, and those coming and going after hours had keys.

Bruce met them at a campus security office as agreed. Once Lisa had shown her identification and business card, they were escorted to the Anthropology building and handed over to another security guard, who let them in.

They were instructed to make certain the door was shut tight and locked when they finished their business, then the guard left.

Circling around the main corridor, Lisa led them down a stairwell to the floor where her father's office was located. "I don't think they would have extended me this courtesy if it hadn't been for you, Bruce, so thanks."

"I don't think it was me," he answered seriously. "I'm surprised they didn't tell you to come back tomorrow. In my experience, the security guards don't have the authority to let anyone in without double-checking. It was almost too easy."

"Or maybe palms were greased to make it easy on us. I can think of several people who want us to find the dagger so they can step in," Hunter said.

Signs on the walls led them to the small door still bearing a sign with her father's name. Above the door was a second sign, Room 101.

Lisa unlocked the door and pushed it open. Inside, the ten-by-fifteen cream-colored room was pure chaos. There were nine cardboard boxes stacked against one wall, books piled in front of empty bookcases and file folders in a dozen stacks atop a heavy metal table in the center. In addition, there were four file cabinets, a table against the wall covered with wooden packing crates containing various security hardware and a heavy metal desk with four drawers.

"If the dagger's here, it'll take a while to find it," Bruce said.

Lisa stared at the room. Her father's office had never been tidy *before* Happeth had come to work for him, but this office was worse than she'd imagined. "Mom did say that he'd moved his stuff here recently, so maybe that's why nothing's unpacked."

"Or maybe he left it this way, to purposely discourage anyone from making a quick search," Hunter said.

"Even so, how hard could it be to find a twelve-inch dagger?" Bruce countered. "I'll start on the west side of the room and work clockwise, bottom to top."

"My father left clues. The key to the location of the dagger lies in finding the right Zia symbol," she said.

Bruce glanced around the room. "What Zia symbol? There were several on the wall murals in the main lobby and side corridors, and on the New Mexico flag at the front, but you can't stash a solid object in any of those places. Not unless he was just signaling which room it's in," he added.

"I think the Zia symbol we're looking for will be in a more private place, somewhere he could have hidden the dagger in secrecy. Let's get started and see what turns up," she said. "Maybe all we'll find is another clue leading us elsewhere."

They worked for two hours, but searching through books, files and notebooks for cutout areas where a dagger could have been stashed was time-consuming. And moving furniture, after it had been searched inside and out, to look behind it required repositioning other objects, which took even more time.

"Maybe your father never intended for the dagger to be found," Bruce said at long last. "Hiding it under riddles and clues that led in an endless circle may have been his way of making sure the dagger disappeared for good. It may have been his way of keeping it safe."

Lisa shook her head. "No. That wasn't his style. I think he wanted the search to be difficult in case an outsider got hold of his clues, but he left a trail meant for *me* to follow. It's been that way from the beginning."

Lisa sat down on the floor and started to drag a computer paper box toward her, but it refused to budge. The weight of the box took her by surprise. It was much too heavy to be just paper. She rose to her knees, lifted the lid, and peered inside at what appeared to be a large collection of cast metal door stops in a variety of shapes and sizes.

"Wait a second," she said. "This doesn't make sense. He didn't collect stuff like this."

Hunter was instantly beside her. "Those are solid, and made of iron," he said, studying the top few. "So forget about looking for something inside them. And if the dagger was at the bottom, it would have had to have been in a sturdy box to keep from getting broken by the weight. This thing must weigh close to a hundred pounds. I'm surprised the box hasn't fallen apart."

"There's logic in this, we just have to find it," she said and paused to think about it. "The only reason I can think of for him to put heavy objects in this box is to make sure it stayed put." She glanced at Hunter and Bruce, and working together, they slid the box away from its place in the corner.

While the men proceeded to search the box, bringing out the heavy door stops a few at a time, she looked where the box had been and studied the area behind it.

Something small, carved into the cement floor caught her attention. "We've got a Zia," she said. "But this makes even less sense," she added after a second. "It's on the floor, but there's nothing below us. We're already in the basement."

"True, but there are still spaces under and around us," Bruce said. "There's an extensive network of below-ground utility tunnels that join all the major buildings and connect with the university power plant. I did a paper on the network once."

Lisa remembered the odd drawing she'd seen with all the buildings connected by a series of lines. "This is starting to make sense. Maybe he was telling me to follow the trail of Zia signs. But I have no clue how to get down to those tunnels."

"I do. I went through a few as part of my research. But you'll need me to run interference for you. The gates and doors are kept locked, and the entry points are on the security schedules. One of their satellite stations is next to the tunnel junction running from this building, and they have a guard there this time of night. But I know the guy, he's a retired cop and a buddy of mine. I can keep him busy by asking him about my chances of getting to moonlight here. But the tunnels themselves are subject to random patrols, so it'll be up to you two to keep away from those guards."

"What about the locks on the gates and doors? Are they keyed alike?" Lisa asked.

"They were when I wrote the paper. It's necessary to keep the maintenance people from going nuts trying to find the right key. How good are you at picking locks?" he asked, looking at Lisa.

"Very good," Lisa and Hunter said almost at the same time.

"Too much information." Bruce smiled, shaking his head. "Forget I asked."

Hunter shrugged, then looked at Lisa. "Tunnels are often traps for odors and strong scents because of poor ventilation. Are you up to this?"

He didn't have to say it. Stealth and wheezing didn't go together well. In a tense situation, there was no telling what her lungs would do. But she was betting that she'd feel the tightness in her chest long before she actually began wheezing. To get this close to the goal then quit…she'd never forgive herself if she didn't try. "I can hold my own," she said. "And if I can't, I'll bail."

"Then let's go," Hunter said.

BRUCE APPROACHED THE GUARD, who sat behind a desk in a small room that contained monitors for security cameras at the Anthropology Museum.

Across the hall from the security office was a

big metal gate leading down a concrete-lined tunnel. Bruce, according to their prearranged plan, greeted the security guard, then led him to a soda machine down the hall. Hunter and Lisa slipped by the security room and tackled the lock on the steel gate.

Lisa, who'd learned a lot about locks in her profession, quickly picked the padlock while Hunter kept watch. As they entered the tunnel, which looked very much like the basement hallways, except for the oversized utility pipes and conduits slung from the ceiling, Lisa took a deep, slow breath. The air was stuffy, but not unbearably so.

"I'm okay," she said, feeling Hunter's gaze. "We'll have to lock up behind us," Lisa whispered, turning and reaching through the narrow bars on the gate to refasten the padlock. "We can't afford to have the guard notice."

Hunter nodded. "Better hope we don't have to come back this way. That lock will be hard to pick, reaching through the gate."

They walked quietly down the dusty tunnel. The cheap fluorescent bulbs overhead cast a dim yellow glow that made the long corridor dark and spookier than she imagined it would be. Fortunately, they had flashlights that enabled them to check the dark corners and along the concrete floor.

"See any Zia signs?" he whispered, aware of how sound carried.

She aimed the beam of her flashlight down, expecting any more Zia symbols to be low and inconspicuous, rather than at eye level. "Not yet. Judging from what we saw in his office, they'll be small and easy to miss," Lisa said.

Once they'd reached what she believed to be the halfway point to the administration building, they discovered an intersection that split into three tunnel branches.

"Which way now?" Hunter whispered.

Lisa studied the bottom section of the wall and noticed a minuscule, incomplete Zia sign down near the corner. Instead of four sets of rays, it held only one, pointing to the more southerly-bound tunnel. "This way—southeast, if my sense of direction hasn't abandoned me completely."

They made steady progress, approaching another side tunnel on their right. Leaving the search to her, Hunter went ahead, keeping watch and scouting for trouble. She continued to look for the small Zia signs, trying to ignore the fact that the deeper they went into the tunnels, the stuffier the air became.

Lisa's breathing soon grew labored. She paused before they reached a fork in the tunnel, used her inhaler and noted a trace of a wheeze as she inhaled. Wheezing meant that there was at least enough air flow going through her lungs to make the sound. It was even more dangerous when her labored breathing made no sound at all. Taking heart, they continued.

Lisa located another small, scratched-out Zia symbol. Just beyond, they discovered a wide section of tunnel that led into a locked storage area. While Hunter kept watch, she picked the padlock, and they both hurried inside, closing the gate. Lisa put the lock in her pocket this time. If the dagger wasn't hidden in this section, they'd want to move on in a hurry. The air here was stale and dusty, and her breathing was getting worse.

Lisa aimed her flashlight along the base of the wall. There was another Zia symbol, this time beside a small vent.

"Here," Lisa whispered, then started coughing. She stood up, brought out her inhaler and took a puff. Still in distress, she took a second puff, then waited, hoping for some fast relief.

Hunter placed a concerned hand on her shoulder and gave her a gentle squeeze. She managed to give him an encouraging smile, though she knew she was running out of time. Lisa reached into her pocket and brought out a combination knife that had a screwdriver head. She bent down to unscrew the vent cover, but just then they both heard footsteps from deeper in the tunnel.

Hunter leaned over and whispered in her ear. "There's only one person. My guess is that it's the guard. I'll head him off by going back in the other direction."

"No. I'll go." The words tore at her soul. She'd wanted to see this through and now that she was this close... But her wheezing would give them away for sure. She had to trust Hunter now—there was no halfway. Yet he'd never made a secret of the fact that his priority was to get the dagger back to the tribe. It had been his mission for the Diné since day one.

The tribe would gain nothing by making its return public. In fact, it would be in their interest to keep it quiet. But she needed the publicity to restore her family's honor, and to substantiate the chain of evidence that would establish her father hadn't committed suicide.

Though words of love had never been spoken by either of them, she knew the feelings between them were real. What bound them went beyond skin tone and sworn loyalties. She'd have to trust in that now to see them both through.

"Stealth is no longer an option for me. I'll go to the gate leading into the administration building and pretend to be locked in." She handed him her pocket knife, the one with the screwdriver head. "Will you meet me back at the truck with the dagger?"

"You can trust me to do what's right," he said softly, brushing a gentle, quick kiss on her lips.

Lisa nodded, knowing she was doing what had to be done—and terrified that she'd find that, to Hunter, some loyalties superceded what they'd shared.

"Good luck," she whispered. "I'll put the lock

back on, then make sure the guard doesn't come back this way."

Wishing more than anything she could have seen things through together with him, she hurried down the hall. This time she made no attempt to mute her wheezing.

She reached the gate leading into the basement hall of the administration building then started rattling the gate. "Hey, anyone. Let me out, I'm trapped in here."

It wasn't long before the guard came up from behind her.

HUNTER WATCHED LISA HURRY AWAY. He was worried about her. After the death of his wife, he'd sworn never to fall in love again. Yet he'd have to be crazy to deny how he felt about Lisa. Although he would honor the oath he'd taken as a member of the Brotherhood of Warriors, he'd have to find a way to do that without betraying the woman he loved.

Hunter worked quickly, removing the vent cover. About twelve inches inside the interior he found a tan, padded envelope duct-taped to the top of the vent shaft. He worked it loose and pulled the envelope out.

Hunter slit open the package and, inside, found the obsidian dagger, diamond and all, encased in a sturdy, black leather case with a metal clip. He attached it to his waistband, then, looking down the tunnel toward the administration building, noted that Lisa and the guard she'd alerted were already gone.

As he hurried down the hall, Hunter heard a rush of footsteps right behind him. Then a hand suddenly grabbed him by the shoulder.

In a lightning move, Hunter tore free of the grip that held him and spun to face his assailant. Martinez, clad in black slacks and muscle shirt, stood five feet away, arms out in an offensive posture.

Martinez grinned. "I'll be taking that dagger now," he said, delivering a punch straight at Hunter's face.

"Dream on," Hunter responded, dodging. The blow missed him completely, and he countered with an uppercut that caught Martinez on the cheek, a glancing blow at best.

Hunter stood his ground as Martinez stepped back, shaking off the hit. Noticing the radio at the man's belt, he realized that his assailant had other allies within range. He had to end this fast.

"There are guards down here, and if we get caught neither of us wins," Hunter warned, sending out a body punch that Martinez managed to divert.

"Your woman took care of the only guard in this part of the system. They went upstairs together. With her making so much noise just to get his attention, we figured she was trying to buy you some time. So I backtracked to here."

Martinez faked a punch, then kicked out. Hunter blocked the attack, moving to his left.

Martinez continued his taunts. "And if you think your buddy upstairs can come to your rescue…well, let's just say he's out of commission at the moment. It's you and me."

"Then let's see whatcha got." Hunter feigned a jab, then kicked out hard and fast, catching Martinez in the stomach. As Martinez wobbled, Hunter moved in and delivered a blow to the side of his neck with the edge of his palm. Martinez slid down beside the wall, unconscious.

The radio on Martinez's belt was crackling with voices now. Hunter knew that the others were probably only seconds away.

He couldn't risk meeting Lisa by the truck now, not without leading the others straight to her. It was time for a new plan. As long as he had the dagger, they'd be on his trail, not hers.

Chapter Seventeen

Lisa's breathing improved steadily out in the fresh air in the building's main lobby, and they questioned her for a half hour. She stuck to her story about getting turned around in the basement of her father's office, and entering the tunnel by mistake. Since no one could prove differently, and she'd entered the building with permission originally, she was finally released.

A campus police officer, not connected with the security guard firm, was called, and he escorted her back to the pickup. Then a patrol car followed her until she drove off the campus.

No one had ever mentioned either Bruce or Hunter so it was possible they'd made it out undetected. But experience told her that Barker and the others would be waiting the second Hunter came out of the building.

Lisa tried to go back. Hunter was counting on her to be there. She went in from the northeast end of campus, but seeing a security patrol vehicle, was forced to continue south. Extra security patrols were now combing the campus, possibly looking for her two companions. When she saw some Albuquerque Police Department vehicles parked across the street from the main Central Avenue entrance, she knew going back was out of the question.

Lisa drove home, taking a circuitous route at first to throw off anyone who might have been following her, though, at this late hour, most traffic was off the streets.

Praying that Hunter had managed to elude their enemies, she pulled up in the driveway of her home a half hour later. The porch light was on, and everything seemed normal, including the presence of her mother's car and the vehicle belonging to the person guarding her.

As she reached the front door she found it unlocked, and that was unexpected. The stillness inside was also a surprise. Her mother loved to watch late-night TV, but all she could hear was the dishwasher in the kitchen. Lisa called out, but no one answered.

A cold chill ran up her spine, and she waited in the entryway for a moment, her back pressed to the wall. Where was her mother and the person guarding her? Maybe they were on the back patio. It was a warm evening for October.

Not really believing that explanation, Lisa grabbed the big umbrella from the coat closet, then moved forward quietly, makeshift weapon in hand, her heart pounding. That's when she saw James Spencer, a security guard who'd frequently worked for her father, sprawled out in the hall. Lisa rushed over to where he lay. He must have heard her, because he jerked his head around and tried to sit up. "Oh, it's you."

"What happened?" she asked him quickly, helping him to his feet.

"A man came up to the door dressed in one of those delivery uniforms. When he showed me the package and asked if he was at the right address, I looked down. That's when I got tasered." He glanced around. "Mrs. Garza?"

"I don't know," she said, fear creeping into her voice.

They went through the house, room by room. The kitchen was a mess, showing signs of a struggle. A bottle of bleach was open on the cupboard, and the scent on the floor suggested it had been spilled or scattered. A pink stain around the perimeter of the spill suggested blood.

"Blood cleaned up with bleach. Mom must have managed to cut somebody," Lisa said in a whisper, "and the creep used bleach so we couldn't identify him." She looked at the kitchen table and found a note.

The dagger for your mother's life.
You'll be contacted. No police.

The words left her brain spinning. Somehow they *knew* Hunter had the dagger, and they were using the only card they had left to try and get it—her mother. That meant Hunter had slipped right through their fingers, and that gave her momentary comfort.

"Your mother has been kidnapped. We need to call the police," James said, reaching for the phone. The cord had been cut. "Do you have a cell phone on you? They took mine," he said, searching his pockets.

"We can't call the police yet. Go outside and keep watch. A Navajo man named Hunter should be coming soon," Lisa said, praying she was right. "I need to talk to him first."

"You sure, Lisa?"

She nodded. "Just don't touch anything else in case we end up needing to get the police involved."

He nodded, then left the room.

She sat down and looked at the note again. Hunter still wasn't here...so where had he gone? Anything could have happened. But maybe he'd just been delayed. Without a vehicle he would have had to find another. But what if he'd decided to take the dagger directly to the Brotherhood of Warriors instead? If that was the case, then he might not ever return.

Fear undermined her courage, and she began to tremble. She'd never felt more alone in her entire life.

Hearing someone coming down the hall, she

walked quickly across the kitchen, hoping against hope that it was Hunter. As Bruce came into view, she forced a thin smile.

"Are you okay?" he asked quickly. "James told me your Mom had been taken, and there was a note. What happened?"

She gave him the details, then added, "When they call, I'm going to lie and tell them I've got the dagger and set up a meet. It's the only chance my mother has now."

"Bad idea. What if they saw Hunter leaving with it? Wait for him to make contact, then work something out with him."

"Hunter may be on his way back to the reservation for all I know. I still haven't heard from him, and the kidnappers are going to be calling soon. With Hunter gone—"

"I am *not* gone," came a familiar voice from the doorway.

Lisa gasped as she saw Hunter standing at the kitchen door. Heart racing, she started to throw herself into his arms, but stopped short as she saw the deep bruise on his jaw and the dried cut over his eye.

"Are you all right?" she whispered, reaching out with a tentative hand.

He took it in both of his and pressed her hand to his heart. "I had a minor disagreement with some of Trujillo's people, that's all," he said, his eyes locked on hers. "What's going on here?"

The story came out in a tumble of words. "My mother's life is hanging by a thread," she finished. "I know that it goes against everything you set out to do for the Council, but I need you to turn the dagger over to me. Trujillo plays for keeps and he'll kill my mom unless I accept his terms."

He took a deep breath, then let it out slowly. "To hand the dagger over to the tribe's enemies goes against everything I am," he said, then after a pause continued. "But the dagger's claimed enough lives. I'll help you." He slipped the sheath off his belt and handed it to her.

The fact that he'd handed it to her freely told her far more than words ever could, and for a moment, she couldn't speak.

"You *knew* I'd help you, didn't you?" he said, pulling her back into his arms and signaling for Bruce to give them a moment alone.

"I wasn't sure..." she said, trembling with emotions.

"Remember what I told you before. You can *always* count on me."

The deep timber of his voice reverberated through her, filling her with courage and hope.

Before she could find the words to tell him what was in her heart, he took her mouth in a deep, searing kiss that practically made her knees buckle.

Heartbeats later, he eased his hold and, looking down at her, held her gaze. "You've risked your life repeatedly to clear your father's name. No one has the right to take that away from you now. But your emotions are clouding your thinking. You can't lead with your heart when you're going up against people like Trujillo and Barker. If you give them the dagger, don't count on any promises they make. They'll kill you and your mom anyway because you know too much about them."

"I realize that what we do—or don't do—will determine whether my mother lives or dies. We need a plan—"

The phone rang suddenly and Lisa picked it up immediately. Hunter stayed close by, intending on listening to the caller.

"Lisa?" It was her mother's terrified voice.

Before she could answer, a man with a slight Spanish accent got on the line. "We get the dagger or she dies."

"Where do we meet?" she clipped, recognizing Evan Martinez's voice.

"You have one hour to deliver the dagger. Come back to the university campus, alone this time. There's an outside access panel in the sidewalk just south of the Anthropology building, main entrance. Lift up the plate—it'll be unlocked—then climb down into the tunnel and go north. Someone will meet you."

"I give you the dagger and you free my mother? How can I be sure you won't kill us both?"

"If you don't comply, we'll send your mother back to you one piece at a time until you cooperate."

"I'll cooperate," she said flatly. "But I need more time. The tunnels…" The caller hung up.

Lisa placed the phone down, remaining silent for a long moment. "You were right," she said to Hunter at last. "They have no intention of letting me or my mother go once they have the dagger. I could hear it in his voice. The way I see it, we only have one chance—go back into the tunnels, meet them and pretend to cooperate, then grab my mom and fight our way back out."

Bruce, who'd been standing near the doorway, glanced from Lisa to Hunter, and added, "I'm in."

"You sure? There'll be twice as many of them as there are of us," Lisa warned.

"I'm in," he repeated firmly. "Down in that section of the tunnels they'll be less able to take advantage of their superior numbers, too. It's pretty narrow there. Their own maneuvers will be limited."

Lisa looked at Hunter, who nodded. "The tunnels…we need a clearer picture of the layout in there if we're going to come up with a plan and the right tactics," he said.

"I can give you the plans," Bruce said. "I wrote my report last year and I've still got the blueprints."

"Get them," Hunter said, then turned his attention to Lisa. "I'm worried about you going down there. You had problems before."

"Yeah, I did, and I can't guarantee that I won't have them again, but what choice do I have? I'll take stronger pills—I've got them—and I'll use my long-acting inhaler right before I go. The rescue one will stay in my pocket, close by. Either way, I've got to see this through."

"We're in for a hard fight, and our own options are limited. We might not make it out alive," he said quietly.

"If anyone has to die, let it be them, not us," Lisa said, struggling not to give in to fear. She grew silent, then added, "I wish it…could have gone down differently."

"Me, too," he whispered, his palm brushing her cheek. "Just remember one thing. No matter what happens, I've got your back."

"And I'll have yours," she answered.

IT WAS HALF PAST THREE IN THE morning, fifty-five minutes later, when Lisa climbed down a vertical shaft into the tunnel. The dagger was clipped to her belt near the small of her back. She'd also devised a plan—something that would guarantee she'd come out with the evidence to nail her father's killers. There hadn't been time to tell Hunter, but she knew she'd made the right move.

As she stepped off the ladder onto the concrete floor at the bottom, fear pounded through her with every beat of her heart. But she was ready. Hunter would be following, then Bruce, down another entrance a hundred yards away, around another corner. Their first priority was Lisa's mother. They'd already decided that she'd refuse to hand over the artifact unless Elena was freed.

Once that happened, they'd all fight to get the dagger back. Neither Martinez, Barker nor any of their men would leave with it while she still had breath in her body.

She walked down the tunnel, then turned the corner. Ahead, the tunnel network split in three directions. That would be a likely meeting spot.

Ignoring the orders her mother's kidnappers had given her, Lisa had purposely left the vertical access shaft open at the top and was now rewarded with a slight breeze. She'd have fresh air one way or another tonight. When she reached the junction, Lisa saw Happeth standing there, waiting.

"You're two minutes late," the tall redhead said with a mirthless smile. "Do you have the dagger?" she asked, looking Lisa up and down carefully.

Lisa patted her jacket, pretending the dagger was beneath it. "Do you have my mother?" she countered.

Happeth nodded. "Show me the dagger."

"Show me my mom first."

"Just as I predicted, stubborn witch. Follow me."

They continued at a brisk pace, changing directions several times. Then Happeth stopped and whistled low, and soon Michael Barker appeared, coming out of an unlit section into the light. At least three other figures remained farther back, barely visible in the shadows. Happeth took a position behind Lisa, who was now trapped between them.

"Lisa!" Elena cried out, stepping forward.

One of the other figures quickly clamped a hand over her mouth and pulled her back into the darkness.

"The dagger?" Barked snapped, holding out his hand.

"Release my mother first."

He shook his head. "Not until I've got the dagger. And let me remind you that you have no choice."

"Neither do you. I'm the only one who can show you where the dagger is."

Barker looked across at Happeth, who shrugged. "You might order her to take off her jacket," she suggested. "My guess is that she's hidden it beneath her clothes."

Barker's gaze sliced through Lisa. "If you're trying to pull something, woman, I promise it'll cost you. And your mother will be the first to pay."

"Let my mother come join me. Then I'll give you the dagger. You can check it over before we leave."

Barker turned around. "Mr. Trujillo, it's your call," he said.

Trujillo came forward into the light, then turned and nodded to someone still in shadows behind him.

A moment later, Elena stumbled up next to Lisa, and gave her a hug. "You shouldn't have come."

She started to reply, but Barker cut her off. "The dagger, ladies. I'm out of patience. And, for both your sakes, I hope you brought the real thing."

Lisa unclipped the dagger from the back of her belt, then tossed it casually over to Barker. Surprised by her move, he almost dropped it. Trujillo cursed.

Barker stared angrily at her for a second, then took his gun out of his shoulder holster and handed it to Happeth. "If they move, kill them."

"Gladly," she said. "I'm sick of having to suck up to these whiney losers," she added.

Happeth's eyes turned cold and the change in her voice made Lisa shudder. She had no doubt that Happeth would shoot them without giving it a second thought.

"Once they confirm that the dagger is the real thing, nobody will need you two anymore," Happeth said, smiling at Lisa. "You *do* realize that, right?"

Lisa stepped in front of her mother, placing herself a little closer to Happeth. "My father always treated you with respect. Why have you turned against us?"

"Idiot, I was never on *your* side. I never gave a damn about any of you or that cut-rate security company. Your father was a piece of work. He never even saw it coming. He was on his way home when I lured him to the side of the road. It was easy making it look like suicide. I knew where he kept his pistol at work, and John was such a sucker. He was still reading the phony letter I'd just handed him when I stuck the pistol right in his face. He would probably be alive today if he'd have just had the common sense to deal with Mr. Trujillo."

"*You* killed my father?" Lisa whispered.

She shrugged. "Hey, I caught him trying to hack into my computer system. A few more tries and he would have discovered who I really work for. It was his own fault for prying into my e-mails like that."

Rage tore through Lisa and her tears came naturally, but she held her ground and waited for an opening to strike. Revenge was best served cold. All she needed was for them to lower their defenses for just a second or two.

Happeth turned her head slightly toward Barker, then looked at Trujillo. "We're going to do this here, right?"

"Happeth, dear, a ricochet could kill us all. Can't you at least wait until we get to the van?" A familiar voice called from the shadows.

To Lisa, it had sounded just like Paul Johnson. "Looks like the whole gang is here tonight," she said, giving the signal.

A baseball sized object came bouncing around the corner and Lisa moved in an instant, kicking the gun out of Happeth's hand.

Then she closed her eyes tightly. A flash of light

that rivaled the sun was accompanied by an ear-shattering bang that almost knocked her down. The flash-bang grenade was intended to momentarily blind and disorient.

Barker recovered quickly, striking out with a roundhouse kick, but Lisa had already moved, yanking her mother along with her, and the poorly aimed move struck air.

Hunter came around the corner just then, ducking Happeth's blind lunge as he passed by.

Half-blinded but still deadly, Barker whirled, grabbed a knife from his belt and swept out with the blade. Hunter slipped past him, kicking Barker in the side.

Lisa placed herself between Happeth and her mother. Happeth had taken a slender throwing knife from her boot, and was jabbing and striking, trying to keep everyone at bay until she could recover.

With Hunter in front of Lisa, to the left, nobody else could join the fight. The tunnel was too narrow, just as Bruce had predicted.

Bruce came up behind her then, having circled around the tunnel system, and quickly helped Elena to her feet. Happeth reacted instantly, shouting an obscenity and throwing her knife. Bruce blocked the attack with his arm, and the blade struck him in the left forearm.

Bruce grunted, but still managed to haul Elena around, staying in front of her.

"Get Mom out of here," Lisa yelled, moving in on Happeth.

Hunter, ahead and to her left, was facing off with Barker. Both were exchanging blows, having knocked away each other's knives, but with most of their martial arts attacks blocked by equally skilled defensive moves, neither was gaining the upper hand.

"Lisa, go! I'll keep them back," Hunter called out, blocking a kill blow to his chest.

Barker laughed. "You can barely take care of yourself." The words had barely left his mouth when he was upended by a short kick to the back of his knee.

Lisa kept the pressure on Happeth, sliding under a high kick and catching the redhead in the chest. Happeth fell into Trujillo, who'd come forward to protect Barker, who was down, and under Hunter's pressing assault.

Out of the corner of her eye, Lisa saw Johnson grab Trujillo's arm and hold him back.

To assure herself that Johnson was really going to help Hunter, Lisa took her eyes off Happeth. In that fraction of a second, a roundhouse kick caught Lisa on the shoulder, and spun her into the tunnel wall to the right. Her head hit the wall, and she staggered back, dazed.

Hunter dove sideways, springing to his feet in front of Lisa. With catlike precision, he turned and forced Happeth back.

Barker had followed Hunter's change of direction, and moved in from behind him and secured him in a choke hold. Hunter slumped for a second instead of resisting, then pushed off the wall. The two went flying backward together, and Hunter landed on top. He rolled free instantly and turned to face his enemy.

Barker sprung up, and with a roar, launched a flurry of kicks that drove Hunter back. Behind the two, Johnson and Trujillo were locked in combat, rolling around on the floor, grappling.

Just then Lisa spotted the fire alarm on the wall behind Happeth. If she could set it off, Barker and the others would have to make a run for it or risk running into dozens of anxious firemen.

As if reading her mind, Happeth jumped and her kick caught Lisa in the ribs. Pain shot through her in blinding waves that choked the air from her lungs. Asthma wouldn't be far behind. Lisa knew she was almost out of time.

Happeth smiled. "Liking the smell of blood and fighting for the love of it is a skill. You haven't got it in you, no more than your old man did. Your father could have tried to grab the pistol away, but he just stared at me in surprise as I pulled the trigger."

Pain and anger rushed through her. Lisa tried to strike Happeth in the mouth with a straight jab, but she moved, avoiding the blow.

"Come and get me," Happeth said, moving her arms away from her body.

Happeth had been expecting a kill blow to the throat but, instead, Lisa crouched, and put everything she had into a kick directed at Happeth's kneecap. The woman, who'd moved to block a higher blow, howled with pain and fell back.

Lisa dove for the fire alarm, and set it off just as another blinding wave of pain engulfed her rib cage. Barely able to take a full breath now, she reached for her inhaler.

Lisa sat on the floor, her back to the wall, fighting for air. Trujillo came at her, but Johnson grabbed him in a choke hold before he could get close. Lisa heard a sickening crunch, and Trujillo fell lifeless to the ground.

Happeth was crawling away on her side, but her cries of pain were almost lost in the din of the fire alarm. This wasn't a bell, it was an electronic screech, and the light on the device was flashing.

Barker and Hunter, still locked in battle, were oblivious to the racket. Barker knocked Hunter back with a blow to the chest, then hurled himself at Hunter, who was on his knees. Hunter didn't meet the charge. Instead, he lurched forward, putting all his strength and motion into the heel of his hand and caught Barker right in the nose. The man shook, then fell to the floor.

Paul Johnson came forward then and quickly slipped Hunter the dagger. Then, in an apparent turnaround, Johnson hurried to where Happeth lay, crying and holding her injured leg. Lifting her up, he carried her down one of the tunnels and disappeared.

Wiping blood from a cut on his brow, Hunter switched off the fire alarm, then came over to where Lisa was sitting. Crouching before her, he brushed the hair from her eyes. "You okay?"

"Yeah, except for the hot steel poker in my ribs."

"That'll heal. But you're wheezing."

"Guilty," she said. "But it's not bad. I can still talk."

Remembering, Lisa reached into her front pocket and brought out the small audio recorder she'd turned on when she climbed back into the tunnel. It was still recording, so she turned it off. Happeth had sealed her own fate, no matter where she went now.

"Smart lady," Hunter said.

"Paul Johnson…he left with Happeth," she managed between breaths.

"He was there for me, and for you. That's all I need to know for now."

Lisa looked at the dagger safely tucked in Hunter's belt. "I asked you to let me use the dagger to get my mother back and you did. The next step is up to you. Do you want to take it back to the tribe immediately, or will you let me make its return public?"

"The Council is made up of honorable men," he said after a pause. "Once they know that the threat to the dagger is past, there'll be no reason to keep

you from publicizing its return so you can clear
your father's reputation. With Happeth's confession on tape, things should go smoother all the way
around." He tilted her head upward and held her
gaze. "You've wanted to know about me—who
and what I am. Come with me to return the dagger
and share what we've learned."

His invitation touched her deeply. This was the
ultimate sign of trust and of the depth of his
feelings for her. Somewhere in their journey to hell
and back, the bond between them had become un-
breakable.

Before she could answer, the tunnel was filled
with uniformed police officers and several firemen
carrying extinguishers. Bruce, his arm loosely
bandaged, was in the midst of them.

Chapter Eighteen

The drive to see the Brotherhood of Warriors was tense for both of them. Although he knew that they'd been watched from the second they'd entered the reservation, neither of them had actually spotted anyone. His fellow warriors were like shadows created by the setting sun.

"What if they don't like the fact that you've brought company?" she asked, excited, curious and just a bit apprehensive.

"You've sworn that you'll never reveal what you see here and my trust in you is enough for them. But it *is* very rare for anyone outside the Council to be allowed to come this far." He paused for several long moments. "After the dagger is in the right hands, there are things…that have to be said…that I need to say to you…" he said at last, then shook his head in exasperation.

She'd never known him to show any uncertainty or hesitation. "What are you trying to tell me?"

He ran a hand through his hair and gave her a

befuddled look. "It's…complicated, woman." Lisa would return to her own world soon, but his place was here. He wasn't sure how to work out a future for them—or even if such a thing was possible. No promises had been made, so no promises could be broken, but he couldn't—wouldn't—lose her now.

He pulled to a stop and glanced over at her. "We're here."

"Here where?" she asked confused. "The only thing for miles around is that old house and that sturdy-looking barn," she said, then added, "You know I've never seen a barn that big in my entire life. What's it house, elephants?"

"That's where we train—where we gain our skills and confidence." He stepped out of the truck, then came around and took her hand as she stepped down from the cab. "This is my world."

LISA STOOD ALONE NOT FAR FROM the front entrance inside the barnlike building. Inside, in the middle of the arena where the ground was soft, nearly twenty men were engaged in martial arts training. All were stripped to the waist, chests glistening with perspiration, as they practiced attack and defensive moves. Shouts, grunts and the dull thud of blows filled the air.

Hunter came out of one of the rooms at the side and joined her. "Window shopping? Be careful. I might get jealous, then I'd have to do something to make you remember why you chose me."

"Bring it on," she whispered, not surprised that her heart had skipped a beat. He was so male, so strong, everything female in her responded.

Before he could reply, the *hataalii* she'd met once before appeared at the door of the room Hunter had just left and invited them to enter. The tape recorder she'd given Hunter was on the table before them.

"I can count on one hand the number of non-Navajos who've ever seen what you just have," the *hataalii* said, closing the door behind them.

"You've honored me," she answered simply.

He nodded, approving of her answer, and returned Happeth's taped confession to her. "Thank you for allowing us to hear that."

Hunter unclipped the dagger from his belt, and gave it to Lisa. She, in turn, handed it to the *hataalii*.

The gesture was clearly understood. "On behalf of the tribe, we thank you both," the medicine man said, looking at Lisa, then Hunter.

Hearing the door behind them open, they turned around and the man Lisa had known as Paul Johnson stepped into the room.

Hunter laughed and grasped his hand in a warrior's greeting. "You took your sweet time," he said, looking at Daniel Yellowhair. Then glancing at the *hataalii,* he added, "But it would have helped if I'd known what was going on from the beginning."

"It was for your protection and his that we handled it the way we did," the *hataalii* explained. "You two were close. It was important that you believed he was dead. If your reactions hadn't been genuine, it might have aroused suspicion. At the time we had no way of knowing how good their sources were."

"What happened to the woman who killed my father? I have her recorded confession, but if she's escaped, then my hope for justice vanished with her," Lisa said, her voice taut.

"You'll have justice," Yellowhair said. "I convinced her to lead me to where the other stolen artifacts were hidden. Once I had that, the FBI moved in. The woman's in the hospital now, guarded by Bureau agents. It was a smart move making that recording. Once it's played to the police, it'll be the finishing touch. All the remaining members of Trujillo's gang have been identified and are under arrest or on the run."

The *hataalii* looked at Hunter. "You won't be working undercover anymore. Your face will become too well known after all the reporters are notified. You'll be entering a new phase with us— as an instructor. You'll work with *bá'óltáí.*"

Yellowhair stood by the door looking at the open area in the center of the building. "They think that once they know how to fight, their training is complete. But the few that make it to the next phase still have a lot to learn."

Hunter nodded to the *hataalii,* then glanced at Daniel and added, "We'll meet later."

Hunter took Lisa outside into the gathering twilight. "We've done what we set out to do, but I love you too much to let you go," he whispered, taking her into his arms.

"I've wanted so much to hear you say those words," she said, nuzzling his neck. "I've loved you for such a long time."

He tilted her chin up and gazed into her eyes. "Words mean that much to you? But I've *shown* you—"

She placed a hand over his lips. "Sometimes a woman needs to hear the words, too," she said, leaning into him and resting her head on his shoulder.

"You're mine and I'm yours," he said, tightening his hold. "The rest is just…"

"Possibilities."

"I like that. To possibilities," he whispered, covering her mouth with his own.

* * * * *

Look for the second book in Aimée Thurlo's
Brotherhood of Warriors *series*
in September 2007.
RESTLESS WIND
Available wherever Harlequin Books are sold.

MEDITERRANEAN NIGHTS

Join the guests and crew of Alexandra's Dream,
*the newest luxury ship to set sail
on the romantic Mediterranean, as they
experience the glamorous world of cruising.*

*A new Harlequin continuity series
begins in June 2007 with
FROM RUSSIA, WITH LOVE
by Ingrid Weaver*

*Marina Artamova books a cabin on the
luxurious cruise ship* Alexandra's Dream,
*when she finds out that her orphaned nephew
and his adoptive father are aboard. She's
determined to be reunited with the boy...but
the romantic ambience of the ship and her
undeniable attraction to a man she considers
her enemy are about to interfere with her quest!*

Turn the page for a sneak preview!

Piraeus, Greece

"THERE SHE IS, Stefan. *Alexandra's Dream.*" David Anderson squatted beside his new son and pointed at the dark blue hull that towered above the pier. The cruise ship was a majestic sight, twelve decks high and as long as a city block. A circle of silver and gold stars, the logo of the Liberty Cruise Line, gleamed from the swept-back smokestack. Like some legendary sea creature born for the water, the ship emanated power from every sleek curve— even at rest it held the promise of motion. "That's going to be our home for the next ten days."

The child beside him remained silent, his cheeks working in and out as he sucked furiously on his thumb. Hair so blond it appeared white ruffled against his forehead in the harbor breeze. The baby-sweet scent unique to the very young mingled with the tang of the sea.

"Ship," David said. "Uh, *parakhod.*"

From beneath his bangs, Stefan looked at the *Alexandra's Dream.* Although he didn't release his thumb, the corners of his mouth tightened with the beginning of a smile.

David grinned. That was Stefan's first smile this afternoon, one of only two since they had left the orphanage yesterday. It was probably because of the boat—according to the orphanage staff, the boy loved boats, which was the main reason David had decided to book this cruise. Then again, there was a strong possibility the smile could have been a reaction to David's attempt at pocket-dictionary Russian. Whatever the cause, it was a good start.

The liaison from the adoption agency had claimed that Stefan had been taught some English, but David had yet to see evidence of it. David continued to speak, positive his son would understand his tone even if he couldn't grasp the words. "This is her maiden voyage. Her first trip, just like this is our first trip, and that makes it special." He motioned toward the stage that had been set up on the pier beneath the ship's bow. "That's why everyone's celebrating."

The ship's official christening ceremony had been held the day before and had been a closed affair, with only the cruise-line executives and VIP guests invited, but the stage hadn't yet been disassembled. Banners bearing the blue and white of the Greek flag of the ship's owner, as well as the Liberty circle of stars logo, draped the edges of the platform. In the center, a group of musicians and a dance troupe dressed in traditional white folk costumes performed for the benefit of the

Alexandra's Dream's first passengers. Their audience was in a festive mood, snapping their fingers in time to the music while the dancers twirled and wove through their steps.

David bobbed his head to the rhythm of the mandolins. They were playing a folk tune that seemed vaguely familiar, possibly from a movie he'd seen. He hummed a few notes. "Catchy melody, isn't it?"

Stefan turned his gaze on David. His eyes were a striking shade of blue, as cool and pale as a winter horizon and far too solemn for a child not yet five. Still, the smile that hovered at the corners of his mouth persisted. He moved his head with the music, mirroring David's motion.

David gave a silent cheer at the interaction. Hopefully, this cruise would provide countless opportunities for more. "Hey, good for you," he said. "Do you like the music?"

The child's eyes sparked. He withdrew his thumb with a pop. *"Moozika!"*

"Music. Right!" David held out his hand. "Come on, let's go closer so we can watch the dancers."

Stefan grasped David's hand quickly, as if he feared it would be withdrawn. In an instant his budding smile was replaced by a look close to panic.

Did he remember the car accident that had killed his parents? It would be a mercy if he didn't. As far as David knew, Stefan had never spoken of it to anyone. Whatever he had seen had made him run so far from the crash that the police hadn't found him until the next day. The event had traumatized him to the extent that he hadn't uttered a word until his fifth week at the orphanage. Even now he seldom talked.

David sat back on his heels and brushed the hair from Stefan's forehead. That solemn, too-old gaze locked with his, and for an instant, David felt as if he looked back in time at an image of himself thirty years ago.

He didn't need to speak the same language to understand exactly how this boy felt. He knew what it meant to be alone and powerless among strangers, trying to be brave and tough but wishing with every fiber of his being for a place to belong, to be safe, and most of all for someone to love him....

He knew in his heart he would be a good parent to Stefan. It was why he had never considered halting the adoption process after Ellie had left him. He hadn't balked when he'd learned of the recent claim by Stefan's spinster aunt, either; the absentee relative had shown up too late for her case to be considered. The adoption was meant to be. He and this child already shared a bond that went deeper than paperwork or legalities.

A seagull screeched overhead, making Stefan start and press closer to David.

"That's my boy," David murmured. He swallowed

hard, struck by the simple truth of what he had just said.

That's my *boy*.

"I can't be patient, Rudolph. I'm not going to stand by and watch my nephew get ripped from his country and his roots to live on the other side of the world."

Rudolph hissed out a slow breath. "Marina, I don't like the sound of that. What are you planning?"

"I'm going to talk some sense into this American kidnapper."

"No. Absolutely not. No offence, but diplomacy is not your strong suit."

"Diplomacy be damned. Their ship's due to sail at five o'clock."

"Then you wouldn't have an opportunity to speak with him even if his lawyer agreed to a meeting."

"I'll have ten days of opportunities, Rudolph, since I plan to be on board that ship."

* * * * *

*Follow Marina and David as they join forces
to uncover the reason behind little Stefan's
unusual silence, and the secret behind
the death of his parents....*

*Look for
FROM RUSSIA, WITH LOVE
by Ingrid Weaver in stores June 2007.*

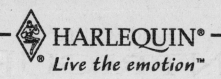

HARLEQUIN®
INTRIGUE®

BREATHTAKING ROMANTIC SUSPENSE

Shared dangers and passions lead to electrifying
romance and heart-stopping suspense!

Every month, you'll meet six new heroes
who are guaranteed to make your spine tingle
and your pulse pound. With them you'll enter
into the exciting world of Harlequin Intrigue—
where your life is on the line
and so is your heart!

THAT'S INTRIGUE—
ROMANTIC SUSPENSE
AT ITS BEST!

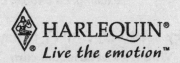

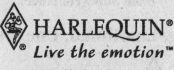

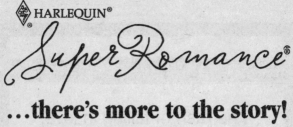

HARLEQUIN®

Super Romance®

...there's more to the story!

Superromance.
A *big* satisfying read about unforgettable
characters. Each month we offer *six* very different
stories that range from family drama to adventure
and mystery, from highly emotional stories to
romantic comedies—and much more! Stories
about people you'll believe in and care about.
Stories too compelling to put down....

Our authors are among today's *best* romance
writers. You'll find familiar names and talented
newcomers. Many of them are award winners—
and you'll see why!

If you want the biggest and best
in romance fiction, you'll get it
from Superromance!

Exciting, Emotional, Unexpected...

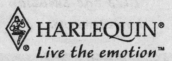

HARLEQUIN®
Live the emotion™

Harlequin® Historical
Historical Romantic Adventure!

*Imagine a time of chivalrous
knights and unconventional ladies,
roguish rakes and impetuous
heiresses, rugged cowboys
and spirited frontierswomen—
these rich and vivid tales will
capture your imagination!*

*Harlequin Historical . . .
they're too good to miss!*

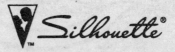

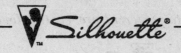

Emotional, compelling stories that capture the intensity of living, loving and creating a family in today's world.

Modern, passionate reads that are powerful and provocative.

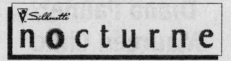

Dramatic and sensual tales of paranormal romance.

Romances that are sparked by danger and fueled by passion.

passionate powerful provocative love stories

Silhouette Desire delivers strong heroes, spirited heroines and compelling love stories.

Desire features your favorite authors, including

Annette Broadrick, Diana Palmer, Maureen Child and Brenda Jackson.

Passionate, powerful and provocative romances *guaranteed!*

For superlative authors, sensual stories and sexy heroes, choose Silhouette Desire.

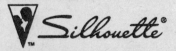

passionate powerful provocative love stories